MW00390317

Copyright ©2019 by Velada Allard McElroy

Dedicated to my beautiful mama!

MY MOTHER'S EYES

My mother had the most beautiful deep brown eyes

My father, oh how lucky was he

To be the first one of us to see

Just how loved and blessed by her,

We all would be.

Born....us kids were to her.

She, ever so gentle, loving and kind

Whose eyes us kids would seek out,

When life overwhelmed our adolescent minds

It was our mother we needed without a doubt.

Our lives, one early January day, changed so fast.

All in the shortest blink of an eye

Without a warning, chance or even a prayer

We, all of us, were forced to say goodbye,

A loss, a pain, oh so heavy to bear.

Even through all of our grief, she made sure we saw

The gift she gave, we're all still in awe.

You see! She donated herself upon her passing

So another could have the gift of sight everlasting.

Velada Allard McElroy

Acknowledgment

My gratitude goes to you, reader, for allowing me to share this novel with you as it is very dear to my heart. I was extremely fortunate to have been able to draw upon my mother's memory while the novel took shape. I will forever cherish those long talks and stories she loved to share about her grandparents as well as her childhood. I learned so much about her during those visits and keep those memories close to my heart.

I am indebted to Linda Garton for her knowledgeable editing skills and helping me polish the final draft. Thank you for all your hard work. You are truly a gift to me.

My extended family, friends, co-workers and boss deserve a special thanks. I was constantly amazed at how supportive you have been through this journey.

To my children, Patrick, Leila, and Lexis: you gave me encouragement on the days I needed it the most. Always allowing me to work on the novel even when you knew it would take time away from you and did so without a hint of resentment. You all have such sweet, generous souls it makes me so proud to be your mom.

Thank you to my sister and personal cheerleader, Rochelle Orme, who was there for me building me up every step of the way. To my brother, John Allard, who always believed in me making me feel valued.

And last but not least by any means my husband, high school sweetheart, and best friend, Neil. You have been there every step of the way, riding the low waves as much as the high ones with me, always making sure I knew I wasn't alone. You are an amazing partner and without you, I wouldn't have had the courage to continue on when my mother passed away. Thank you for always holding me up and being my constant rock.

Table Of Contents

Chapter One

F rank looked out over the dry desert landscape surrounding him and wiped his sweaty brow with the back of his wrist as colorful wildflowers waved in the light breeze outside Silver Lake's only livery stable. The prepossessing nineteen-year-old was deep in thought when he heard his grandfather's boots shuffle through the hay. Frank had been working hard since early sunrise that morning. Spot wagged his tail and followed close behind Grandfather, hoping for a friendly pat.

Birds chattered up in the rafters, snug in their nests. Frank grabbed his slouch cowboy hat off the wood counter, waiting to hear what his grandfather was going to say, and pulled off his dingy mustard yellow work gloves that smelled like horsehair, grain, and leather. He watched patiently as his grandfather inspected the job.

"Lad, if yur gonna make dat broodmare's shoe fit right, ye've ter nail it down so it's tighter," Grandfather spit out while puffing on his ancient tobacco pipe and finished up walking around the horse, mumbling. Spot, the black and white Border Collie, gave up and got nestled on his blanket as he watched little barn mice dash in and out of holes. His ears perked up as Grandfather continued, getting louder. "Me hell! 'Tis 'otter in 'ere than a whorehouse on nickel noight!" George swiped at the flies with his hat before running his hand through his long dark gray hair.

Frank chuckled lightly trying not to encourage his granddad. "You know old man, Grandma would give you hell if she were to hear you." Grandfather Duncan waved off his comment, smiling, and was back to hitching up a carriage for some new customers coming through town when he stopped and looked over to where Spot was sitting.

The dog's ears perked up, and soon he was crouched down, warning them with a low growl which was immediately followed by a loud vicious bark that startled Frank. With a stiff neck and strained muscles, Frank glanced at his grandfather, then followed the dog's eyes outside where Thunder Cloud sat stone cold on his beautiful Chestnut horse in a grove of Oregon White Oak trees. It was all too familiar. Frank instinctively lowered his hand to the Colt Navy .36 he kept at his hip and cleared his throat.

Before George Duncan knew it, he was locking eyes with Frank, telling him put his gun away, Thunder Cloud would never do anything to hurt either one of them. Sure as the sun was scorching hot he knew his word to be true. George Duncan trusted that the leader would never harm either him or his grandson; however, he wasn't too sure he could say the same about the others. It was the two brothers that followed behind their older brother that worried him. Before the men could blink or say any more, Thunder Cloud was already gone.

"How long you spec't they'd been there watching?" Frank asked his grandfather, removing his hat and wiping his forehead again.

"Oi not long son. Dis 'ere is thyr land though. Thy alwus do show up whaen ye ain't watchin." His spunky old Irish grandfather walked over to the well where he pulled up some cool water and splashed it on his warm face and neck. George took out his blue bandana and dried himself off then shoved it back in his pocket. "I speck it's 'is way o' saying 'ello to us." He smiled and went back to work, remembering what an honest, hard worker Thunder Cloud was after the Modoc war years ago when he offered him work on his farm. It was the least George could do for the poor lad. He was just a kid then, when the war took everything he loved away from him and his family.

George never forgot that beautiful horse Thunder Cloud still rode. He remembered the spring when she was born. It was the day before the trial started for Thunder Cloud's cousin, Captain Jack. Yes, George would know that horse anywhere, with her unique white lightning bolt down her nose and beautiful shiny auburn coat that was a striking reddish-brown in the sun.

Finally done with his mare's shoe, Frank pulled out his pocket watch, flipping open the silver-plated cover. It was time to hitch up the wagon and head to town for supplies. His lungs tightened with excitement flooding the very veins that ran to his heart when he thought about the chance of seeing *her* today.

Bending to pick up the grain sacks, Granddad yelled out, "Be back before we's is s'pected fur dinner, yer 'ear?" trying to insult Frank, knowing he would take his time if that darling new gal that just moved to town was milling around Silver Lake. "I'll finish up 'ere an git de 'orses ready for de morning's customers, aye?"

Frank pulled the ladle off the hook and took a drink letting water run down his chin wetting his shirt before he nodded to his granddad that he heard him.

Frank had always possessed a natural charm and pleasant personality. It showed in his easy-going behavior, always enjoying the good things in life by showing respect for everyone around him. Being over six feet tall, he had a lean muscular frame and natural wavy brown hair that was parted on the right side. Sparkling happy blue eyes showed the soul of a tender, caring person inside.

Frank whistled sharp and loud so the old sheep herding dog could hear him. "Come on boy." He helped Spot jump up into the old beat-up wagon. The dog's ears perked up, excited, ready for a ride into town.

Duncan & Sons Livery Stable was just a half a mile from town, but George Duncan, who was known by everyone in Silver Lake as Uncle George, knew that his favorite grandson was going to take more time than he should in town. Frank had been distracted all week; he suspected he knew why, but would eventually find out for sure soon enough. He was also pretty sure he knew how Frank's week would end up. He was a lad himself once upon a time, and that new gal who just moved in town from the Willamette Valley was not just a looker but the sweetest little gal he'd ever come across. Frank's grandfather looked up in time to see the horse set off in a slow gallop, jerking the wagon forward and kicking up dust. He swatted at the flies following him around all morning and took a puff on his pipe again.

George Duncan sure did admire and love that grandson of his. He didn't feel that way about all of his grandsons, however. There hadn't been anything but problems with Frank's younger brother, Otto. They were as opposite as night and day. Frank had always been the one Grandpa Duncan compared himself to when he was a lad—jovial, smart, a looker, and witty as hell.

The reins relaxed in Frank's hands, and as the horse strolled along he scanned the horizon. The late June morning sun was quickly heating up the day and adding degrees by the minute. Frank was a few minutes away from arriving at the McFarling's Mercantile in the middle of town, across from the old pioneer cemetery where Canadian Geese hovered watching over the deceased. He got a little nervous thinking about the girl who'd moved to Silver Lake with her family a few weeks before. He wondered where she was this morning, and if he'd get the chance to run into her and say hello. Just to look at her was a gift he was grateful for.

The wagon jumped up and down, creaking at every dirt clod and rock along the way. Spot sat straight up as the two of them pulled up to the front of the hitching post, and the spoiled old dog panted, knowing a treat was waiting for him. "Whoa" Frank called out to his horse, Juniper, who stopped abruptly at his firm, deep, and commanding voice. Pulling the wagon brake back, he stepped down after tying off the reins to the hitching post where the gelding stood patiently waiting.

Two young, dirty little boys in raggedy worn out overalls were throwing a dark leather ball back and forth while waiting for their mother, who was in the store shopping. "Down boy, you know you can't get out." Frank patted the top of Spot's head, calming him. Spot's eyes, one blue and the other a dark watery brown, eagerly watched the ball bounce over his head.

Frank's side kick stayed put, but wasn't too happy about it. He obeyed Frank's command and laid his head on the light wood seat and whined.

"Mornin, Mrs. Syers," Frank called out to his elderly neighbor, tipping his hat to her. The old woman looked up under her white flowery hat to see Frank through thick spectacles. "Franky dear," she croaked, missing a step off the mercantile front porch steps. Old Mrs. Syers just smiled gingerly, showing her four teeth, as he caught her frail body.

He thought to himself how she felt as light as a feather. Mrs. Syers didn't seem to even notice she'd almost fallen and just kept smiling at Frank and continued walking. He smiled and shook his head. 'Some things never change,' he thought to himself when movement in the store caught his attention.

"You boys run along, goes somewheres else to play with that ball," came the yell from the gruff old storekeeper down the street, Mr. Chrissman, who owned Chrissman Bros. He was out on this hot morning sweeping the boardwalk in front of his store. "Shoo, come on now...git outta here," swiping the broom at the boys, running them off, his face red and puffy from getting his dander up.

Frank watched as they took off like bats out of hell, running for their lives. Reaching for the door he saw a hand-painted poster that was tacked up. It read:

A patriotic march

Columbus Glory Grand Celebration At Silver Lake

July 4th

The people of Silver Lake and vicinity will

celebrate the nation's 118th birthday.

The mayor and his wife will lead the parade

with the Pledge of Allegiance

Frank saw people moving around inside the store again, and when he realized who they were his heart danced with a thousand butterflies in the pit of his stomach. Several women were standing around looking at new bolts of cloth in back of the store. Frank felt his face get hot, he was getting embarrassed staring through the window like a schoolboy, so he moved quickly before they saw him and opened the heavy door and stepped inside. Forcing the lump in his throat down so he could breathe, he couldn't help but be excited when he saw she was there and just as perfect as the first time he'd laid eyes on her. Each time he looked at her now he was overcome and dumbfounded at her ability to knock the wind out of him better than an enraged bull bucking him off at rodeo time. Pearl, her younger sister, and their mother were busy looking at the new materials Pearl's aunt just brought over. The women noisily prattled like little girls at a tea party in the back of the Mercantile.

The velvety smooth feeling of this imported material was quickly forgotten when they saw the handsome cowboy. Pearl was also taken by surprise, but it was because of her own reaction, not the one he was causing. She had no idea anyone could conjure up excitement in her like that. He was walking towards her now.

Frank smiled when he saw she noticed him. Those curious oval caramel eyes of hers peered right into his soul and melted it.

Pearl's mother was a wise woman and knew she was witnessing something exclusive before her. She was secretly thrilled watching this interaction because her daughter had not wanted to move to Silver Lake. Leaving her life and friends behind in Eugene City frustrated the eighteen-year-old. So this was a wonderful gift, and besides he was a handsome young man that seemed to have a kind, gentle innocence about him.

The women continued to chat among themselves and fumble through all the fun new patterns while Frank pretended to be interested in the books the McFarling's fifteen-year-old daughter was putting on the shelves. Abbie Jean was doing what she could to get Frank's attention, but Frank had already put the book back and was walking away from her towards Pearl when there was a loud crash on the floor. Once everyone gathered their nerves off the hardwood floor, Frank turned to see what had caused it.

"Oh my! Now look what I have done!" Abbie Jean ingenuously exclaimed while gazing at the shards of light pink glass all around her. Though her head was down her eyes were burning into Pearl's soul. Annoyed at the attention Pearl was getting screamed hatred all over the young girl's envious face. Maeve clicked her Irish tongue at her daughter while her husband's face turned a shade of crimson red. Abbie Jean was a spoiled, controlling, and sometimes immature young woman who had been infatuated with Frank and his younger brother, Otto, for as long as she could remember.

Abbie Jean knew by the way Frank looked at Pearl she would have to fight for the attention she'd always craved from him. Pearl was beautiful, Abbie Jean had to admit to herself. But wasn't she told she was a beauty herself? Everyone said they loved her thick black curls that accentuated her clear, pretty, ocean blue eyes. But she was young. Too young for Frank to take any notice of.

Pearl tried to get back to shopping with her sister, giggling to herself as she watched Abbie Jean out of the corner of her eye. She was on to her, knew her little game. Pearl even played it once or twice herself when she was younger. Frank helped clean up the broken glass and gave Abbie Jean a quick hug, telling her she needed to be more careful.

"Oh, why, yes Frankie. I just don't know what got into me. I appreciate your help," she flirtatiously replied.

Young Abbie Jean was a great actress. Years of being the only child in a wealthy home gave her plenty of time to perfect the art of deception.

Abbie Jean's father, Liam McFarling, was watching the actions of his daughter, annoyed because she caused them to lose money on that lamp.

Frank tipped his hat to her and then to her father, whom he was always friendly with and liked, before moving towards the back of the store. The old chime hanging on the main entrance door clinked against the glass door window as new customers came into the store. He greeted them, but Frank didn't take notice. His attention was all wrapped up with Pearl, who he was trying to build up enough courage to approach.

Pearl's curious eyes were fixed on Frank. She couldn't look away and didn't even care. Forcing herself to stop. She saw he was smiling at her before he turned to finish up his shopping. Lost in his kind smile, she carefully reached up and touched her hair, making sure the bun was knotted tight on the top of her head. Hearing the chatter at the other end of the store and movement outside, she stood there lost in thought.

'Thank goodness I spent the morning, with Aunt Elizabeth's help, styling my hair in tightly curled French twists.' Not realizing how beautiful she was and how the curls framed her round face perfectly. She was just happy she looked halfway decent, thanks to her favorite aunt, who knew these things were important to a girl of courting age.

Frank put the supplies on his grandfather's credit, said his goodbyes to Liam and Maeve McFarling, and then tipped his hat and nodded to Pearl and the women surrounding her as he exited the store. Jumping down off the south side of the porch, anxious to get out of there, he heard "Oh Frankie!" Running to catch up was Abbie Jean, who confidently swayed her hips as she hurried down the steps towards him. She boldly slipped her hand through his arm he was resting on the hitching post as his other hand pet Spot who was busy scratching fleas. "Frankie," she started, twirling her hair while digging her boot into the dirt below, "You are goin' to the picnic and Fourth of July celebration?"

Frank looked through the buckled glass window to see if Pearl could see him talking before turning his attention back to her. Answering with a red face he replied "You betchya, I'll see you there, Abbie Jean." Loose dirt twirled around in a small dirt devil where they stood, dry heat scorching everything in its path. He reached out and gave her chin a brotherly squeeze with the gentle tips of his fingers then finished untying the leather reins from the hitching post, the whole time thinking about Pearl and those beautiful happy eyes that sent shivers up his spine. He led Juniper, pulling the empty wagon to the side of the mercantile where they would load up his supplies for Grandfather Duncan before heading back to the stable.

Chapter Two

A small but cozy old weathered farmhouse sat on several acres belonging to Jesse and Sarah Emmaline Bunyard. The couple's two sons, Frank and Otto, were born and raised in the old house that was beginning to fall apart, but with a little tender loving care, the family managed to keep it upright year after year. Several cows, some goats, and a beautiful herd of horses grazed in a fenced pasture next to the new barn, where bright yellow sunflowers proudly stood greeting anyone who entered. It was just a few years ago the old barn caught fire and, as always in times past, the town of Silver Lake came to help. The town hosted a 'barn raising' party, and the Bunyard's never forgot how hard the community worked getting the barn up in just a few days. Whole families came out to help. Wives and daughters brought casseroles, homemade pies, peach cobblers and farm fresh fruits and vegetables with them to feed the hard workers. The kids made homemade ice cream for the barn dance and celebration the night after the barn was completed, which was remembered years later with great fondness.

Frank woke up more relaxed than he had been in a long time. It was already early mid-morning on the fourth of July. Rubbing the sleep out of his eyes, allowing himself a little extra time to enjoy a second cup of a strong black coffee, he waited for his favorite breakfast his mom fixed him on special occasions like this, the breakfast she was famous for. It was just what the hot and sticky July day demanded. Thick bacon, scrambled eggs, and mouthwatering hoecakes sizzled on the frying pan, filling the warm morning air.

It was days like this Sarah Emmaline couldn't get enough of. Especially now that her sons were raised. She missed having little ones around, and hoped for grandkids someday soon to fill that void she felt with great intensity these days. While she cooked and visited with Frank, she could hear clucks coming from one of the runaway hens who were approaching the kitchen's open door. "Shoo," Sarah Emmaline gently pushed the hen away with her foot. "*Shoo*," she insisted again, with firmness this time.

"Cluck cluck cluck"

Frank and Sarah Emmaline laughed at her favorite hen, Dolly, and how she was trying to bully them into extra crumbs from his father's left-over breakfast. She didn't like getting scooched out of the doorway and was chewing out mother and son the whole way back to her hen house, looking for scraps along the way. "She always waddles herself over here, especially when she smells me cooking with the door open."

Frank leaned back in his chair straightening his long legs out in front of him and crossed his arms, chortling as he watched the steam from coffee his mother just poured and savored the fresh aroma. "Land sakes Ma! Dolly knows you're going to give her the leftovers first before the others get'em any."

Frank's father was already dressed, had his breakfast and three cups of coffee, all before anyone else made a move to get out of bed. Jesse wasn't much for sitting down, relaxing, taking a break, or for 'mindless chatter' as he called it. There were always chores to be done on the small ranch, and the harder he worked the happier he seemed to be.

Frank released a heavy sigh, deep in thought, taking in the succulent breakfast smells and thinking what he would say to Pearl when he had the chance to see her again. He couldn't get those fiery brown eyes and her beautiful oval face out of his mind since he ran in to her at the McFarling's Mercantile.

His mother glanced back at him from where she was standing at the well-used blackened cook stove. Spatula in hand, she asked him what he was working up in that overzealous head of his. Frank just gave her a sly halfcocked smile and jumped up to grab some more kindling. He'd always been skilled at distracting her and dodging her loving, but intrusive, questions.

It was obvious to her something was going on he was excited about. But she was a little confused; if that was excitement, then why was he fighting so many other emotions? It was like there was an internal battle being played out in his head. A nervous anxiety, pleasure, uneasiness, and something else she couldn't quite put her finger on were all afflicting her son, but he did look content with whatever emotion was winning at that moment. "Hmmm….." She just sighed to herself and turned back to what she was doing.

After enjoying every morsel of food on his plate and his coffee, Frank rose and stretched, "AAAHHHH," letting his arms relax before he pushed his chair in. Before Sarah Emmaline knew it, he was hovering over her, wrapping his arms around her, and asking, "How am I ever going to find a strong woman like you momma?" Frank bent over and kissed the top her red head-wrap.

Jerry, the orange and black tom cat, came running in and dropped a garter snake he had caught at their feet. "Shoo, get that thing out of my kitchen." Sarah Emmaline didn't mind snakes, but not in her holy kitchen. Before he let the cat play with it again, Frank grabbed the dead snake and tossed it outside for Dolly. "Frankie!" Oh how she adored her son. She grabbed his strong freshly shaven chin, "You are a good boy!" Her droopy soft brown eyes tightened, full of love. "Alright, now git on with you." She beamed with love and appreciation only a mother could, and tightened her starched white apron strings around her thick middle before getting back to pumping water to boil for dishes.

Spot came in from outside, growling. The Border Collie had been watching everything unfold by the back door, relaxed and licking his paws, when his mood suddenly changed. He caught the scent of something he didn't like. Sarah Emmaline turned to say something about the picnic they were getting ready for when she was cut off by the dog's loud bark, causing her to jump. As usual, her youngest son was determined to make a loud and obnoxious appearance.

Hearing Otto's voice at the same time, after shushing Spot, Frank and his mother had the same annoyed look on their faces when their eyes met. Spot cowered down with his tail between his legs, shaking. He'd been kicked too many times by Otto and trembled anytime he heard, felt, or saw Frank's younger brother around. Stumbling into the kitchen, ruining the once peaceful morning, Otto stood with that stupid drunk smile he always came home with.

15

Sweaty odor smells overpowered and suffocated the once happy smells in the kitchen. It was obvious Otto had been out several nights and he reeked of pungent, rotten hooch and stale tobacco. It was apparent he hadn't bathed or groomed himself in several days by the nasty stench smothering him. He was an unshaven, unsightly mess. His once white shirt, which Sarah Emmaline had made, was torn and hanging off his sunburned shoulder, and his trousers were smeared with grime, cow manure, grass stains, and torn in bizarre spots his mother noticed after looking him over.

Annoyed and exasperated, Sarah Emmaline wrinkled her nose and turned away, retreating once again into her anger. Otto was so brutal at times that it made even his own family despise his behavior. They had all tried to help him because they knew there was a good guy under the angry mask. He made it so difficult for people to care about him most of the time, but a mother's love has no end and she always took him back and loved him just the same. "Otto, you know I'll always love you, you're my son, but we'se expect more from you." His mother would say time and time again "Your father and I didn't raise no drunks." He wouldn't listen though and broke his mother's heart every time he left in a huff, mad at the world but always taking it out on those who loved him most.

His father was another story, however. Jesse didn't put up with an ounce of bad behavior from either one of his sons. He taught his boys better than the behavior Otto displayed, and Jesse ruled with an iron fist. He tolerated very little of Otto's rebellious attitude when he was around, which usually meant he sent his youngest son packing just a few hours after arriving.

16

"Otto, go clean up and drink some coffee, you reek to high heaven and mom don't need you in here making a mess for her!" Frank chided his younger brother as quietly as possible, so their father didn't hear. Frank noticed his mom's mood shift when Otto came home hungover like this.

"Oh…..go on….worrying bout yoouuouuurself Frankkkiee," still drunk, Otto foolishly stuttered, spitting words at Frank while he stood there swaying, trying not to fall. Everything was moving fast around him. He was dizzy and felt woozy again.

Frank stood quickly and forcefully grabbed his arm, pushing him outside. "Come on! Like I don't have anything better to do today then baby sit a lazy crook head like you." Frank grabbed the clean pressed clothes their mother had laid out for him in hopes he would be home for the family picnic. Frank pulled out a new bar of lye soap their ma just made, and the two boys headed down to the North Shore Lake that inched up against their property.

After washing up with some cool lake water, an hour of sleep, and drowning himself with some strong coffee, Otto finally came out of his incompetent state. He softened up and wasn't so distressed when he sat down to eat some left-over breakfast. Frank sat down next to him at the large round oak table after bringing in more firewood and kindling he just split. He threw the kindling into the basket by the cook stove and opened his mouth, hoping to share that he and Grandfather had a visit from the Modoc warriors.

But their father walked into the kitchen demanding structure and obedience. The old Collie stayed in his basket when Otto was home, feeling the tension in the room. Jesse's dark black hair sparkled with silvery specks of gray and he had a finely combed mustache which emphasized the high cheekbones on their father's stern face. Jesse turned his head quickly, squelching his surprise to see his youngest son had returned home. He quickly nodded a greeting to Otto who, he thought to himself, wasn't looking half as bad as he had seen upon previous returns. "Son," he greeted nodding his head, mouth straight and serious, as always.

Otto shifted uncomfortably. Disappointment set in when Otto nervously coughed and looked up into his father's piercing serious black eyes. Otto was desperately trying to focus and not screw this up. He thought it best not to speak. He still wasn't sure if he was sober enough to try a conversation with a guy who had no problems tossing him out anytime he was displeased. He knew the man in front of him could tell when he'd been out on a drinking binge, even though he had help from his brother and was clean and presentable.

Otto had always felt that uneasy disappointment his father never hesitated to display. The boys started to quickly finish what little chores they had and get the wagon and horses hitched for the ride to town when Jesse came out asking to have a word with his youngest son.

Otto stood silently on the parched ground and glanced over at Frank for a reassuring look from his older brother. Otto then turned slowly and walked with great hesitation; carrying that burden on his back was taxing.

Jesse's expression was fierce and serious. "I don't want any trouble today, you understand?" The mid-morning sun was burning into their eyes, heating things up. "Your mother's been preparing for this all year and excited about it for weeks now." He spit dark brown tobacco juice before finishing, "It's time for family and enjoying ourselves." His voice deepened with a frightening calmness. "Ya hear? Not time for foolish nonsense," he finished with contempt.

Watching his tight jaw muscles and clenched stained teeth, Otto knew his father was serious. "Yes Sir," was all he got out when Jesse turned to walk away, cutting Otto's soul in two. Otto put his head down, displaying that sullen sad look that always made Frank feel remorseful. He put his anger and frustrations aside when he knew his brother must feel like everyone gave up on him. Otto was still his little brother and he felt, and always would, a moral obligation to help him.

Drawing in the smell of fresh-cut hay mixed with the smell of ripe pears, Frank helped his mother into the wagon, and then he and Otto jumped up on the back next to the picnic basket and folded Modoc Indian blankets. He took one last look around the battered yard and pasture where the cows and sheep grazed openly. His father gave the command to the horses and they were off.

Chapter Three

S arah Emmaline's heart soared with excitement. She sat as straight as humanly possible on the rough wagon bench watching all the dull yellow sulfur flowers drift by and smiled, tickled pink with excitement. Both of her boys made it after all, and looked dashing.

Her parents would be sitting with the family today. It wasn't often they had the chance to all spend a day like this together. They lived a humble western frontier life, too busy to lavish in this luxury all day except a couple holidays a year. Even then, the animals all needed watered and fed while the cows needed milked, eggs brought in, and the garden watered, and produce picked. It wasn't like you could just put it aside for another day, but at least on these holidays, the amount of work was limited, and they only did what absolutely had to be done.

Sarah Emmaline's older sister, Sarilda, her niece, Lucinda, and her three and half year-old energetic great nephew, Easton, would be waiting to see their loving great auntie today. Her great nephew reminded her of Frank and Otto when they were that age. Because she wasn't blessed with any grandkids to pamper just yet, she and her sister shared spoiling little Easton, who of course had no objections and thought he was lucky to have so many grannies.

The band was set up near the community center and playing some of the old American favorites. When Jesse, Sarah Emmaline, and their two sons finally reached town, 'Little Annie Rooney' was being performed, which instantly put the family in a light festive mood and helped make everyone forget about the morning's contention. Children ran around in circles playing and singing the Silver Lake jingle just as they did every year. It was a song granddaddy taught the kids years before and it stuck and became a favorite with new generations.

When I went down to Silver Lake,

I met a little rattlesnake,

He ate so much Jelly cake,

It made his little belly ache

"I loved you boys singing that song with your cousins," Sarah Emmaline chimed in when she saw the kids holding hands in a circle singing it. "Do you remember?" She looked back at her sons who were caught rolling their eyes.

They simultaneously answered, "Yes, Mama," and everyone laughed. Otto and Frank thought they even heard their father chuckle and gave each other a shared look of surprise.

With her family close behind her, Sarah Emmaline found her parents waiting, saving them seats. Her parents, Louisa and George, had saved a spot in the shade along the boardwalk outside the bank on First Street, where the parade was beginning. The large group, made up of several small families, sat together and watched the Mayor greet people when Sarah Emmaline and Sarilda saw Elizabeth and Will, old family friends. Pearl and her family were close behind her aunt and uncle, frantically looking for a place to sit as the parade got started. Frank glanced back to see what Otto was doing after he saw Pearl's family heading his way, being waved over by his mom and aunt. He wanted to make sure Otto hadn't noticed Pearl, but it seemed to Frank that Otto hadn't noticed much of anything, except a splitting headache. 'Serves him right,' thought Frank.

"Plenty of room over here," Sarah Emmaline said as she waved the Hardisty's over. Frank's collar seemed to tighten and beads of sweat formed around his forehead.

"Mornin," Frank said to Pearl, tipping his hat as she sat down by him.

"Afternoon," she replied as her eyes radiated beauty on the hot day. Pearl, Laura, and their mom smiled and nodded, looking around at Frank's family, as Aunt Elizabeth introduced everyone. The rest of the group had known each other for years and were longtime friends. When the band started again it got everyone's attention by playing the national anthem. The families who were sitting together along with the whole town rose to their feet as the mayor, with his wife by his side, walked hand-in-hand down Main Street and the kids waved their flags that had been handed out. Their young grandson followed close behind, proudly holding the United States flag that consisted of forty four stars. The parade was ready to begin, as was the love affair that would connect these two families together for generations.

Chapter Four

The hot parched eastern Oregon day was quickly changing into a cool nippy evening. Silver Lake was known to put on a fantastic firework display that people from all surrounding areas like Fort Rock, Christmas Valley, Paisley, Plush, Adele, Summer Lake, and even as far as Valley Falls came to enjoy.

The fireworks dust settled, taking thick gun powder and black smoke with it. It was a comforting relief after the days of scorching July heat. The hired band had taken a break, and almost everyone went to get ready for the dance, except the old farmers who retired to their homes for the night.

Pearl had been with Frank most of the day, where they had been enjoying one another's company, and they found it easy to speak freely. There was an informal comfortableness between them that was kind and friendly.

The dance began late in the evening after the orange sun relaxed behind Tabletop Mountain. Abbie Jean was already at the barn dance, leaning up against the wall in the back, when Frank and Pearl showed up together. Her immaturity hid nothing. Jealous icy blue hateful eyes watched every move they made. She moved over to where her friends were sitting on the haystacks, gossiping, sharing stories, telling secrets and she plopped down next to them on large bales of hay decorated with red, white, and blue ribbons. Still observing Otto and the way he drooled over Pearl, Abbie Jean pretended to talk among her peers, the whole time

24

seething and wishing the Hardisty's had never moved to Silver Lake. It was all too obvious to Abbie Jean that everyone was drawn to Pearl's kind and gentle personality. Every muscle in Abbie Jean's jaw tightened and her body shifted. She daringly decided to make a bold move and started over to where Otto was standing all alone.

She flipped her shiny long black hair over her shoulders with a brisk confidence the group of girlfriends she left behind only dreamed of. She had what seemed the perfect life. Her peers admired and envied the wealth and greed her family possessed, knowing she received anything she asked for. Abbie Jean knew this and used it to her advantage often.

Otto had a small flask of his favorite harsh whiskey and would sneak a sip of it when he thought no one was looking. He didn't care if someone saw him drinking; he just didn't want anyone to think he was already drunk. It would ruin his plans. Abbie Jean, who'd always been wise beyond her years, caught on to what he was doing, and she wanted to be a part of it. Whatever it took to break Pearl down and force Frank and her apart, she was ready for it.

"Otto, what ya doin?" she asked, twisting her finger around her bouncy, shiny hair, tilting her head. She was trying hard to turn his interest towards her when she lost him. Pearl caught his attention again. It was as if Abbie Jean wasn't even standing there talking to him. He was trying to keep Pearl in view and didn't have time to be bothered.

Guarding his space, Otto took a deep breath and finally turned to see what she needed. He was a bit exasperated over being interrupted when he was trying to focus so hard on his next move, alcohol swishing around making it hard to concentrate. He knew she was beside him the whole time, talking, but he'd been so annoyed with her interruptions he thought being rude and standoffish towards her would do the trick. No, not Abbie Jean, he should have known. She was a fighter, having a strong spirit even when she was a little kid, one he'd never forgotten. Playing with her at lunch, even though they were a couple years apart, he remembered her headstrong attitude about playing baseball with the boys and how he and Frank were surprised at how good she was. Remembering it now, standing there at the dance in the barn on this Fourth of July evening, he learned one more thing about her, once he turned to tell her to buzz off.

He stopped and stumbled in his tracks. Abbie Jean was gorgeous! She had grown up and was a real beauty, and he couldn't take his eyes off her now. Surprising even himself, looking her up and down, he took another deep breath, giving some thought to what he wanted to say to her while she waited. She was a little too young for him and her parents would never approve, but he could have some fun, and she could be used to get what he really wanted: Pearl.

He raised an eyebrow and his eyes sparkled; the alcohol was feeling really good right now. "Abbie Jean, I ain't doin' a damn thing, how' bout yous an me goes-n-dance?"

She was elated and got what she wanted.

Otto led Abbie Jean on to the dance floor and then grabbed her arm, a little more forceful than he should have, but she was willing to ignore it and walked with great aplomb, hoping others noticed he had asked her to dance. Everyone was swinging to 'Old Glory', plucked by just one member of the band on his banjo. Abbie Jean quivered, too excited to think straight. They got to the dance floor just in time. Another member soon joined in on the harmonica which was followed by hoots and hollers from all those who followed them out to the dance floor. Besides Otto being Otto, she was having a great time. 'Hopefully Pearl and all my girlfriends are watching,' she thought, twirling around.

On the other side of the barn Frank and Pearl stopped dancing for a few minutes so he could take a break. 'She is just the finest girl I have ever met,' he was thinking to himself, head in the clouds, all smiles as he walked away, hating to leave her, even if only for a quick privy break.

Pearl waited for him, watching the other couples dance, lost in thought about all the great events of the day and the fun time she was having with Frank; one of the best in her life. Leaning up against the refreshment table she tapped her toe to the rhythm of the music. She hadn't stopped thinking about him since that hot and humid June day when she saw him at the McFarling's Mercantile.

Pearl loved standing aside, observing all the people coming out for the dance. She had come to know many of her parents' friends, but now it was her turn to befriend those closer to her own age.

Pearl finished her drink and put the cup on the table when she saw Otto pull Abbie Jean onto the dance floor. He was being so mean and harsh she was shocked over his behavior, and it made her sick watching the way he was holding onto Abbie Jean's arm as he pulled her around the dance floor like a rag doll.

"Why is he doing that?" she whispered under her breath, biting her pinky nail, a habit she had when worried. He was being so reckless and the skin on Abbie Jean's arm was turning dark red from the strength of his tight grip. Pearl was surprised she wasn't trying to get away, especially with the stunned look on her face. Her arm looked so painful but maybe she was scared of what he would do if she tried. Pearl canvased the area looking for Frank again when her eyes met Otto's. Fierce daggers shot across the room at one another, neither willing to look away first. Pearl wasn't about to pretend she didn't see what he was doing to the young girl he'd just asked to dance.

Her hands were getting sweaty and she felt shaky. It wasn't any of her business what other people did, but she did not want Abbie Jean to be hurt by Frank's younger brother, who'd acted shifty all day, following her and Frank around when he thought they didn't notice him. Scanning the area once again, in hopes she would find someone who could help, Pearl turned her full attention back to Abbie Jean and Otto. There was no Frank in sight and no one else seemed to notice what was going on. She nervously kept watch, trying to see if she could tell what Otto was doing or why he was trying to hurt her.

'What was taking Frank so long?' she wondered. Just then Otto spit his tart tobacco juice when he stepped away from Abbie Jean, letting the dark thick juice hit the hard plank wood floors where it splattered up on her beautiful canary skirt. Pearl felt Otto's small beady eyes across the room still fixed on her. His angry glare spelled violence. 'He's disrespectful and nasty!' Pearl was fuming. He was an awful kind of mean and didn't even have enough respect to say a proper thanks for the dance, just left Abbie Jean standing there looking foolish and feeling a deep humiliation. She looked Pearl's way and sent feisty daggers like it was all her fault. Rolling her eyes, she crossed her arms over her chest and turned away, still huffy. Pearl could see it. It was written all over her body and facial expressions. Her body tensed as she awkwardly rubbed at the back of her neck, still looking around for Frank.

Giving in to mixed feelings of fear and dread, Abbie Jean turned and ran out the back door, her canary skirt flying behind her. She knew her so-called friends were intently scrutinizing her situation and would secretly enjoy snickering behind her back to each other. She prized herself watching other people's imperfections, and had a terrible habit of running those innocent and sometimes unfortunate people into the ground so she could feel superior. She got played, and the worst part about it, she got played in front of everyone she wanted so desperately to impress.

Otto was on his way to Pearl, dismissing Abbie Jean's reaction with a wave while he staggered around swaying back and forth like he was standing in a small boat fighting tall angry waves in a storm. Feeling sly as a fox, he was sure he'd make a move on Pearl and get under that fancy petticoat of hers sooner or later. Glowing in her iridescent pink dress with her honey golden hair and flawless porcelain-like doll face.

"Pearl? Right?" Otto asked trying his jovial charm on her. Hoping to impress her as much as he did Abbie Jean, he let the alcohol do the talking. He didn't even have to try with Abbie Jean, she was so easy. But Pearl, he wasn't so sure about her, especially when he saw the look she was giving him.

"Yes, it is," she replied firm and poised, "And you're Otto, Frank's younger brother," she said, staying calm and trying to sound decorous and kind at the same time, but she really wanted to slap that drunk smirk right off his insolent face.

Frank had warned her about Otto and his annoying, deceitful ways. She knew what Otto was up to, having dealt with a few like him in Eugene City.

'Finally!' Exhaling breath Pearl didn't even realize she'd been holding, she relaxed a little when she saw Frank walking towards them. Dropping her shoulders, she sighed. However warm and comfortable he made her feel, her happiness was short lived. 'Oh no.' A fingernail found its way to her mouth again. Chewing on it she took a small step backwards. Frank's face reddened. His large neck veins thickened and throbbed when he saw Otto's reckless drunken sneer. He'd been watching Otto trying to cozy up with Pearl from a distance and couldn't get to him fast enough.

Pearl held her breath and moved further back out of the way. After all he had told her about Otto, she couldn't really blame him for being angry at his brother's foolishness, feeling he was destined to a life of damage control.

This foolishness was frustrating Frank even more. He didn't care for the way he saw his brother's eyes address the best thing that ever walked into Silver Lake and into his life. Previous experience told Frank he needed to deal with Otto straight on and be forward with him. So, he sucked in a big deep breath and tried to remain in control.

"The night's young, Otto. Why don't you go find yourself someone to dance with?" Frank insisted. There was no way he was backing down now. He walked closer to his brother, showing who was in charge, at almost half a head taller, and started to open his mouth to chide Otto when he smelled the reason for Otto's behavior permeating his breath. Overwhelmed and aggravated, it took everything he possessed to govern his anger. 'My hell!' he thought. 'How dare he get drunk tonight. Pearl's not going to like this, she has more class than putting up with drunken fools.' Frank debated over what to say to Otto, not wanting to set him off into one of his foul moods he knew Otto would take to the next level.

"You don't have to be a horse's ass, Frank. Pearl and me's here was just talking, ain't nuttun' wrong with that," he stammered.

Frank apologetically glanced over to Pearl. "Come on! Otto! There's a lady in front of you." His pulse quickened. "No need to use that language and be rude," he hissed.

Pearl sensed the twisted heaviness that lived in Otto; her chest tightened, not sure what she should expect out of him. She was frozen with fear, sensing she was going to witness something bad and dreaded what may come next. Frank noticed Pearl's concern and the worried look on her face and nervous expression, eyeballing the brothers back and forth. He didn't want to spoil their fun and ruin the whole night, so he tried to calm himself and his brother down, but it was too late for Otto.

He was fuming now, feeling cornered like a caged animal. The look he gave Frank said he wasn't going to back down, and then made a bold move and reached over, forcefully grabbing Pearl's arm. He knew this infuriated his older bossy brother.

Pearl was shocked and tried pulling away from him. "Stop this!" she quietly cried out, worried about drawing attention which was usually followed by gossip. His grip tightened. Her throat constricted. Frank had no other choice than to take charge and stop his brother's lawless behavior.

Pearl tried, but couldn't pull loose from him, for he had a surprisingly tight grip. People were starting to stare and she was getting uncomfortable and embarrassed. Otto backed up out of reach when Frank lunged at him, then finally let go of Pearl right as she was pulling away, causing her to fall backwards. She quickly corrected herself but Otto overcompensated and carelessly stumbled, knocking over a large table filled with refreshments. A loud clatter and crash interrupted the dance and stopped the band from playing. The punch bowl shattered leaving tiny pieces of red glass and fruit juice soaking into Frank's trousers. Otto had it all over him, along with fragments of food. Part of the table that flipped over was lying on top, pinning him down. Frank reached over, lifted the heavy wood table off his brother, and helped Otto to his feet. Frank was filled with an unjust fury. Anger and resentment raged within him for ruining everyone's fun.

Otto planted his legs far apart to help him balance. His face was as red as the fruit juice dripping off his clothes. He squared his shoulders and looked at Frank with such raw hatred it sucked his breath away. Humiliated, he blurted out "Thanks a lot Frank. Thankkkks a lot, you stupid ninny," then stumbled backwards away from the dance, vanishing into the cool desert night where ugly talk followed him like fleas on a mangy dog.

Chapter Five

Frank was left standing in his brother's toxic air, disappointed that the dance ended the way it did, especially after the amazing day he'd enjoyed with Pearl. He hated when Otto fought with him, and detested it worse when it was happening in front of other people. It was humiliation he knew his parents despised too, and didn't deserve. He tried hard so many times to forgive Otto and give him the help he really needed. He just didn't know how to change him, and Otto wasn't ready for change. Trying to always prove something, his younger brother carried some deep anger and hatred that, for some reason, was always directed at Frank.

Even though that's not exactly how Otto thought or felt about his older brother, he was just an easy target because he knew Frank didn't stay mad for long and always went to bat for him, helping at times no one else would, no matter the price. He forgot how acrimonious his brother was until his drinking got the upper hand leaving an ugly heaviness to fill the empty air.

Pearl reached out a gentle hand touching Frank's arm, bringing him back to reality. They looked down at the mess together then back into each other's empathetic eyes. "Frank, I'm really sorry," Pearl whispered. "Do you mind escorting me home, like you assured my father you would?" She didn't want to be associated with this type of arguing and behavior, like Abbie Jean seemed to enjoy, but she also knew it wasn't Frank's fault. She could see the problem his family had with Otto and felt nothing but compassion for them. It made her grateful for her sweet little sister. They were close and took care of one another.

"I'd be happy to Pearl, if you wouldn't mind waiting a moment? I need to clean this mess up. I can't just leave it," he said, looking around thinking about how the mess resembled his brother's life. It was always the same. Frank was left to pick up the pieces, after a scene was made and embarrassment was left for him to deal with while Otto took off and did whatever he did that made him feel better about being a jerk.

She saw what a good, honest person Frank was, and her heart melted. She wanted to help. She knew he was somebody she wanted to share more time with. Pearl saw the love Frank felt for his brother, but at the same time pitied his rebellious behavior and choices. She realized this must be a struggle and a painful feeling for Frank to always deal with.

"Here, let me help, Frank," she said as kindness filled her face and gentle brown eyes. She went to locate a broom and started sweeping up the tiny pieces of glass after Frank picked up the big ones. Once they had the whole mess cleaned up and people were back to having fun and dancing again, they began walking to the wagon. "Oh, shucks I forgot my shawl," she said and turned to run back in.

He stood there thinking about the miserable night's ending. When she came back to where he pulled up the horses, she could see disappointment fill his demeanor as he waited for her. He walked around to help her put the sweater up over her shoulders when she did something that surprised them both. A cold hand wrapped around his strong arm, and then she sympathetically leaned her head against him. "I'm so sorry, Frank."

Frank stopped walking and looked down at her. There he held her gaze for what seemed like a lifetime as the universe stopped moving. Overwhelmed by her tenderness his heart was aching for her. For more. Forgetting about the frustrations his brother caused and the ruined dance he took a deep breath, drawing in the cool night air and slowly whispered, "I appreciate that Pearl," an affectionate moment shared between them. Her, loving the way he said her name.

They visited comfortably the whole ride to her Aunt Elizabeth's and Uncle Will's home as lightening flashed far off in the desert's darkness. Once they arrived at the home where her family had been staying, he helped her down out of the wagon as scents of wildflowers and lavender teased his nose. While he was enjoying the new smells she was watching him, and couldn't help but notice his clean grooming, especially for being a rancher and working at his grandfather's stable. He was a man who cared about his appearance, but wasn't arrogant about it.

The horses shifted their weight, giving gentle nudges and flicks of their tails. Frank reached over and grabbed some dried greens for them to munch on while Pearl and he stood in the moonlight and talked a bit longer.

"Well, momma will get worried if I don't go in soon," Pearl shared, hating to leave him. Her heart fluttered every time she thought about their brief encounter earlier in the evening when she held on to his arm, or the way they danced together and the stories they shared when walking down streets full of food and vendors. It was a fun and magical Fourth of July. She didn't know what the future held for them, but for now she knew that treasuring the magic they'd shared today her life would never be the same. Pearl turned to wave him goodbye. When their eyes met, their hearts spoke, saying everything they wouldn't be able to until their next encounter.

Chapter Six

It was half past eleven when Pearl entered through the front door where her mother left the Queen Ann oil lantern burning for her. She was in such deep thought about the night's events as she walked towards the back of the house that she didn't hear a door open, or the creaky sound following it.

"How did you do tonight, Pearl?" Electa Caroline asked, causing her daughter to jump. Pearl was so engrossed in her thoughts about Frank—remembering his smell, his wavy brown hair, his thick muscular arms and the way he protected her as well as worried over his brother—that she didn't hear or see her mother until it was too late. Pearl recoiled so hard she spilled some oil from the lamp on to the floor.

"Oh, heaven's mother. I never even saw you!" Pearl exclaimed as her mother worked quickly to get the mess cleaned up and the rag thrown outside so the oil could evaporate into the cool night air.

Electa Caroline giggled when she came back through the living room and hugged her daughter who was still a bit jumpy and lost in thought. "I don't think I've ever seen you this way." A smile crossed her mom's face, amused by what she was witnessing. Soothingly, in her soft gentle way, she turned her daughter around by the shoulders so they were facing one another and she asked, "Are you alright?" still smiling only half joking.

Pearl gave her mother a dismissive wave. Electa Caroline jokingly reminded her daughter that she could see the whites of her eyes when she told a fib. It was a joke Electa Caroline learned from her mother who learned it from her mother. The two women shared a laugh whenever Electa Caroline tried that line on Pearl over the years. When she was just a little girl, Pearl used to fall for it, until she realized everyone had white in their eyes.

Pearl's cheeks reddened some. "Oh, I am quite fine, mother," she answered, knowing she wouldn't be able to withhold information from her. After all, she was her best friend. Electa Caroline and Pearl were close, more like sisters than mother and daughter.

"You were with the Bunyard boy all afternoon," Electa Caroline affirmed, grinning at her daughter and trying to whisper so she didn't wake anyone. It was a statement, not a question. Pearl's large brown eyes sparkled when she watched her mother continue. "Aunt Elizabeth said he's a real nice boy."

Sitting Pearl down at the kitchen table while she went to the ice box and got them some milk to warm up, she continued, "Your Uncle Will says he comes from good stock, and is a real hard worker, too."

Pearl was ready to explode. Keeping it all in was ailing her. "Oh mother!" Pearl gushed. "I just don't know where to begin." Electa Caroline started a fire in the blackened stove, all ears. "He's honestly wonderful!" Pearl prattled on gazing into her cup, circling the rim with her finger.

Electa Caroline's long, wavy light brown hair with natural highlights drizzled down her back. Pearl's mother was a beautiful, elegant woman who loved everything about life, always having a positive attitude and loved to laugh and have fun with her girls. She always had a good story to share, and would put work aside to live life beside those she cared about most on this earth.

Wrapping her thin red cotton robe around her waist she sat down next to Pearl, who was blowing her milk mixed with a touch of vanilla, waiting for her mother to settle in so she could tell her everything that happened. Well, everything that is, save those extra special looks and touches between herself and Frank. Those were keepsakes just for her.

Chapter Seven

I t wasn't even mid-morning yet and the angry sun was throwing scorching hot rays over the Silver Lake basin as Charles and Pearl threw in their fishing lines from the creek's edge. Enjoying the day together, Pearl removed her brown leather laced up boots and socks she'd just repaired the night before and dipped her hot feet in the creek's cool water.

"Awww...." she sighed and leaned back. The calm creek felt amazingly refreshing. Pearl relaxed and leaned back, allowing the huge oak tree above to shade her and her father, who was copying her. He had just finished giving the horses a drink before hobbling them to a group of Amur Maples close by. She watched her father's brow relax under the cool shade, and hoped it was the right time to bring up Frank.

Charles watched as his daughter's cheeks turned a shade of red and he wondered if the heat was getting to her or she had something up her sleeve. He'd never seen nervousness in her like this.

Struggling, not knowing where to begin, she stared at Midnight's silky black coat next to her father's chestnut brown gelding and thought about how to approach this question feeling her father's eyes on her. 'Now or never,' she thought, before timidly starting, "Papa? What do you think of Frank?" She found a dirt clod against the creek's edge and let it distract her. Nervous, she rolled it around with her toe waiting for his response.

41

Charles thought a moment. Pearl couldn't stand the anticipation and kicked the clod into the water, which she knew would chase away the trout they were trying to catch, but she didn't care. Any distraction was better than the silence. Frogs croaked, answering one another as a smile worked its way around Charles's thin lips hiding under his thick handlebar mustache.

"I think Frank's a fine young man, lamb. He also comes from a good hard-working family that takes pride in their livestock, family, and..." Charles studied his daughter. "And," not sure how to continue, "why do you ask?"

Charles was impressed and touched that she would ask him what he thought of a man she was falling in love with.

"Well, Papa," answering with her head down, hiding from him best she could, "If he came calling on me, would it be alright with you and Momma if I went with him?"

It was a hard question for his daughter to ask. He could tell by the stress in her voice. "I trust your intuition. If you feel he's a respectful man, and one you want to share your time with, then your mother and myself would honor that." To his surprise she jumped up and hugged him. "You have our blessing," he said squeezing her back, and finally she relaxed.

"You're the best, Papa, thank you."

He laughed out loud, smiling ear to ear.

'Dear old Papa. Never has denied me a thing in my life!' Pearl thought to herself. She was overjoyed by his reaction.

Her father knew the day was coming that she would be Frank's pride and joy. He and Frank had had some good talks, unbeknown to Pearl. "We better get going before we scorch ourselves out here in this heat."

It was afternoon by the time they were back to setting traps and marking them. After sharing a lunch of cold biscuits, ham and cool well water from their canteen, they were on their way home. Both were quietly thinking, lost in their own thoughts, enjoying the peace of each other's company, both always on watch for Indians.

Trotting down the long dirt road towards the small cabin they shared with her Aunt and Uncle, Pearl saw unrecognizable figures out in front. Charles looked at Pearl and watched her reaction as she slid her leg over Midnight. Getting closer, once on the ground, her father asked, "Who's that talking with mother?" There was a man on the porch, but Pearl and Charles couldn't see who it was in the approaching dim evening.

Frank was in the middle of a sentence, visiting with Electa Caroline and Pearl's Uncle Will, when they heard riders approach the house. Smiles broadened on everyone's faces when they recognized one another. Pearl waved to her mother and Uncle Will, then took both horses and walked them to the barn behind the house after saying a special, "Hello," to Frank. Frank quickly followed in Pearl's direction after he handed over the freshly-baked bread and huckleberry jam his mother made to Electa Caroline and Charles. who were left wide-eyed staring at each other.

Electa Caroline watched the two of them walk away, then looked back at her husband. Charles, feeling much of the same way as his wife, put his arm around her waist and squeezed her close to his dusty, tired body. She laid her head on her husband's burly shoulder, glad Pearl and her husband were home safe. He bent down and gave his wife of almost two decades a gentle loving kiss before heading inside.

Frank hurried up to Pearl and spit out his words before he lost his nerve. Crickets sung as the sun lowered. He shuddered a little before asking if she would like to join him next Sunday for a picnic. It was easier to get it out if she wasn't directly looking at him, so he rushed the words between his lips before he could rethink his question, while she was unbuckling and removing the saddle off Midnight's back.

Taking his hat off, he bashfully lowered his head. "I bit the bullet and asked your father already. I hope that's proper." The sun was setting, and evening was calming down, leaving a swarm of mosquitoes behind.

"Oh, is that so?" she smirked, giving him an evil eye.

"Well, yes, and permission was granted," he smiled brightly, giving it right back to her.

"And what did Papa say?" she was toying with him as she continued brushing Midnight, enjoying every minute of it.

"He said he wanted you home before dark." Kicking at the dirt with the tip of his boot he added, "And to take good care of his little lamb." Then Frank moved his stare from the ground under him and met her dark beautiful eyes, which were staring at him with enthusiastic passion. Low soft hoots were heard in the distance from an owl looking for his first meal of the night.

Frank's anxiety melted away when Pearl declared, "Oh, I would love to!" She didn't give her words time to spin around in her mouth; she was excited and ready to jump out of her skin. "I mean, yes, I would be delighted to enjoy a picnic with you. Would you like me to have a picnic ready?"

Politely repositioning the words, they both smiled, pretending not to see the other one's eagerness. "Sounds nice. Alright. Well then..." he stumbled, trying to spit the words out he'd been chewing on. "I'll see you later then Pearl." Frank's huge smile warmed her insides.

He turned to go before he got caught gushing in front of her. But before he could get too far, he wanted to look at her just one more time. She was so perfect. He loved watching how graceful and caring she was with her horse. Talking to Midnight, she bent down to grab a handful of fresh grain. Pearl sensed Frank was still nearby. He had a hard time walking away from her. A little embarrassed getting caught, he quickly covered by saying, "Midnight was the best choice for you, she's a great horse. You will really enjoy her," and ducked from a bat swooping down trying to catch a mosquito.

She tenderly responded, "I already am, thanks," and brushed her face up next to Midnight's soft, silky head. Midnight nudged Pearl, returning the love. "Hey, Frank," Pearl yelled out before he walked too far away, "By the way, when did you ask my father?" Pearl knew he had followed her too quickly to the barn, so there was little time to question her father when they came home, and she was curious.

"Sunday last," Frank admitted, adding, "After church." He smiled that kind, fun spirited smile again that always made her insides turn to mush.

Fitting his hat back onto his head, Frank winked at Pearl and backed away slowly after bowing to her, as a large gray barn cat rolled around in the dirt where Frank was just standing. She giggled like a little schoolgirl, stroking Midnight's side, and finished up with the horses then headed to the house to clean up and get ready to help with dinner. Crickets continued getting louder as nightfall approached, and the scent of horses, leather, and farm filled the air, relaxing the July night.

"Oh fiddlesticks! A whole week," she complained to herself removing her riding boots outside the house. Containing her excitement until next Sunday was absolutely going to kill her. She was sure of it.

Chapter Eight

Sunday finally arrived after the longest week of Pearl's life. The midafternoon light was impossibly bright with a burning yellow sun shining down. Pearl was ready to go, picnic in hand, when she saw Frank ride Juniper up to the house after church service. They rode their horses through the Western Junipers and Ponderosa Pines out to one of Frank's favorite quiet spots in the country. It was perfect for their picnic.

They both tried to conceal their feelings and eagerness that they were given the chance to go alone. This was a chance to get to know each other on a more personal level that was nearly impossible around other people. It wasn't a normal practice for unmarried, courting couples to be alone without escorts or siblings, and Pearl's little sister Laura would have relished the chance to tag along, but to Pearl's delight she was sick at home with a tummy ache. Besides, Charles wasn't concerned. He had a great amount of respect for Frank, as well as Frank's family.

Once they arrived at his favorite picnic spot a few miles out of the town, Frank started towards his favorite tree that he had spent many exhausted days under, relaxing after a hard day's work. Even as a young boy in Silver Lake, Frank took solace knowing he could get away from life in town and harsh work in the country and come out to this place he loved, escaping for a couple of hours.

No one was around for miles, just the two of them. They rode unhurried at their own peaceful pace, enjoying one another along the way.

"This is a great view, Frank." Despite the growing heat, she was struck by the pastoral beauty of the setting he chose, and took a minute to look around at the stunning desert landscape that surrounded them and listen to all the different kinds of birds chirping, with the quiet relaxing breeze brushing up against her warm skin. The desert was so different from the Willamette Valley where she was raised. To her, it felt open, relaxed, and like a person could breathe in all the fresh clean air they wanted, whereas the valley felt claustrophobic at times with all the trees and mountains that surrounded the town. A soul could lose themselves in this beauty with a clear sky for miles and miles.

Pearl swung her leg over the saddle and started to slide off her horse when Frank saw and hurried over to help, and she allowed him to wrap his large hands around her waist, helping her down. She was soaking up all the attention from Frank she could get. After stretching and searching the area for rattlesnakes, removing pine cones and little tiny brownish lizards that seemed to be everywhere on the hottest part of the day, Frank helped Pearl spread out the picnic cloth. Soon she was setting up the food while Frank tied the two horses to a nearby tree, after removing their saddles and feeding them some apples and grain he'd brought. She scanned the area again, taking a deep breath, calming her nerves.

She could feel his eyes on her, lost in thought. "So, tell me why your mom and dad named you Pearl?"

She was intrigued by his question. No one had ever asked her that before. Opening the wrapped cornbread lathered in homemade whipped honey-butter, she answered, "Well, I'm their first born, father gave mother a pearl on their first anniversary after moving to Eugene, so I suppose that is why. They both liked the name, I guess." Pearl continued to lay out the picnic and a few minutes passed, neither saying anything.

Then, "The name fits you." He raised an eyebrow and his deep blueish-gray eyes sparkled.

"Well, thank you." Pearl's face turned a thousand shades of red at the genuine compliment. Taking their time eating their lunch spread out before them, they found it easy to share stories of their childhood and families. Just like the Fourth of July when they spent the day together, today felt much the same.

Pearl started sharing a little about her life when he opened that conversation with her name. "Your mother and father are nice folks." Frank was relaxed, enjoying the cold chicken she'd fried up before church and leaned back.

"Thanks. I'm lucky to have them," she replied. Pearl bit her thumb nail, a bad habit, one she never could control. "Mama was always my best pal when I was little, before Laura and the boys came along and took up more of her time." She stopped biting and sat back. "I remember once when we were living right outside Eugene City in the country, before we moved into town, I was about 5 years old and wanted to see my best little girl friend who had been sick and lived on a ranch next to ours. My mother was friends with her mother and wanted to make it a special outing for us.

49

So, Mama bundled us up. I grabbed my doll, and with my other hand I held tightly to my mother's dress as she carried a basket of fresh-baked bread and fluffy butter she'd just churned for the family. She asked me what I thought if we took a short cut through the neighbor's ranch instead of going around the long way. I was excited to go on an 'adventure' so, of course, jumped up and down with excitement. Mama looked down at me and laughed.

"We were walking up a hill and came to a large muddy pasture where a huge black bull of theirs, named Prince, was grazing. Mama didn't know Prince had been let out of the fence or she wouldn't have put us in danger like that. I remember she looked down at me and yelled, 'run!' About halfway through the pasture we looked up to see Prince bellowing, getting ready to come for us." Pearl used her hanky to dab her forehead under her sunbonnet, for the afternoon sun was shining directly on them, causing beads of sweat to form. Frank was rapt with attention as she continued, "I dropped my dolly and cried. Oh, I cried!" Pearl giggled at the memory again. "Mama grabbed it and me as quickly as she could. We made it to the fence and on the other side by the time Prince got to us."

Smiling, she continued, "I'd never been so scared in my whole life. I can still remember how mean he looked as he stomped, slobbering and pawing up the earth right in front of us."

Franks eyes got huge as Pearl was telling the story. "I bet your mom always stayed on the main road after that, huh?" He tittered.

"Yeah, I haven't seen Mama take a 'short cut' since that day." They were enjoying the afternoon together and sharing stories just like they'd known one another their whole lives. "What about you? You've lived here all your life, right? You like to ranch and work with your grandfather at the stable?" Pearl asked with wide eyes and a look of affection for Frank as she spoke.

"I love Silver Lake. It's beautiful country and the open range is my life. I don't know anything else. I don't want to know anything else," he said with ease. "I hope to buy my own ranch someday, and my Grandfather said the Livery Stable will be signed over to me someday down the road." Frank picked at the poky burs stuck to his pants. "And I love ranching; it's hard work but very rewarding," he admitted, smiling at her. "Everything I know is in Silver Lake. I plan on staying here, finding the right gal and raising my family here." Surprising himself he looked over at Pearl and couldn't avoid her sweet interested eyes. Worried he'd said too much he tried to correct it, "I mean, when I find that gal."

She chuckled, and because she fully understood what he meant, she nodded her head in agreement. Then he relaxed.

Something frightened Pearl a little, and then it dawned on her they were really all by themselves. To her, it kind of felt like her and Frank were being watched. She was sure it was just because there were red tail hawks kept circling overhead, but still she wanted to ask him. "Frank, do you have problems with hostile Indians around here?"

The hot, heavy wind rustled through her wavy hair, leaving wisps of curls to hang loosely around her concerned face. It had always been a question in the back of her mind since moving there, but she'd never been alone with anyone except her father when trapping, unless her whole family was together, so she never really had reason to be concerned.

Frank showed no apprehension or uncertainty, only a calm resolve when answering, wanting to be truthful without causing alarm. "I wouldn't really say problems, but sometimes they meander around town." Frank could tell Pearl was fearful of Indians. Rightfully so, with all the stories about the Pine Ridge ghost dancers that were perceived as savagely violent and frightening to those who read newspapers that were still circulating the country. Wounded Knee was fresh in everyone's mind, and it wasn't all that long ago that the Modoc war, which was closer to home, had happened.

He tried to quickly comfort her with his words as he tried distracting her. "When I was a little boy, Otto and me would sit on Gradfather's lap and listen for what felt like hours to his stories about the Modoc and Klamath tribes, who were in disagreement with one another about twenty-five years ago." Branches from the Atlas Cedar tree above them rubbed together. The hawks had move on and the insect chatter started again. "Grandad had a great respect for the Modocs and wanted what was right for their people."

Pearl looked around before taking a piece of meat off the chicken bone in her hand. She studied him carefully, and then wiped cold grease from the chicken on an old cloth. Frank went on to explain, "Well bad things were happening to the settlers because they were on the Modoc's land. Their legacy of who they were, their culture, their way of life— Grandfather wanted that to be known. There are a lot of hardnosed people out there who don't care or want to think differently. Maybe it's because he knew the Modoc tribe and worked with them some that he cared about them." The distant sounds of birds calling out to one another in the blazing sun set off a calm aura around the two of them. The slight wind brushed up against their warm faces. Frank felt the Modoc spirits surrounding him. Sitting there, sharing with Pearl, was the same feeling he experienced when he was sitting on his strong and loving Grandfather's lap. "Those are some of the best memories I have from being a child.

"I loved when Grandfather would get all excited, riling up the boys. He was the best story teller, making the war whoops seem magical and the battles real. My stomach would tense with fear as he told us every story."

Frank helped Pearl up so they could move the picnic cloth to the shade. Time was quickly passing, and the sun seemed to move rapidly. Once they fed, watered, and moved the horses to fresh shade and grass, they settled back down in a cooler, covered spot and Frank continued, "I couldn't wait for the next story, and always hated when my Mama pulled us boys away from him to get to bed."

Pearl laughed when the picture went through her mind of the two little boys whining because they didn't want to go to bed, giving their mother a hard time. 'He must have been such a darling little boy,' Pearl thought to herself as she watched Frank talk with such charismatic grace. He sure was something to watch, something special. "Will you tell me some of the stories? I'd really like to hear about them." Pearl shifted positions gracefully on the blanket they laid out, sitting sideways and ladylike, removing the pins that held her hair together in a bun at the base of her neck to get comfortable.

Franks heart got caught in his throat watching her settle in. He knew she would soon be hooked and learn to love the Modoc stories the same way he did.

Chapter Nine

Wintoka's buckskin short dress hung on her small spirited frame while her silky raven hip-length hair waved in the soft wind against her dark, butterscotch skin. The bright morning sun was out generously spreading warm rays on the sixteen summers old girl, who was busy scraping her second deer hide this week that her cousin, Red Eagle, killed, thinking about what she planned to do when she could sneak away. She was terrified at the thought of her father, Hunting Bear, finding out her secret. She would be dishonoring him and their tribe to know she was even around the Modoc's, much less in love with one of the young braves. News like this would cause a horrible disgrace to her family, and they would immediately be outcasts from their band.

The Tribal Elders would never approve of this match, something Wintoka didn't care about. She was fiercely angry that her friends, who she had known her whole life, were being mistreated.

Her mother would never be able to control her rebellious daughter's behavior. She was unlike any of her four other daughters. She was powerfully strong-willed and went against everything they said, causing an uprising every day and everywhere they went. It was always a struggle. Her mother and father came from the prosperous Link River Klamath tribe's richest. They owned slaves, which they traded several times a year with the Yainax, Paiutes, and Yreka bands. Klamath were known as the more fortunate Indians in this area. The land was theirs, or so they thought.

More than once Captain Jack's band was denied blankets, beef, and flour at the Klamath reservation, so they went against the Treaty of 1864 and left the reservation. Since that time both tribes fought bitterly.

Hunting Bear was a brave Klamath War Chief with a large white scar across his cheek leading down to his throat from a bear attack years before Wintoka was born. He was honored for being a respected fighter among the tribe and one who stood up to the whites without fear.

His oldest daughter, Wintoka, knew her father was prideful among her people, and despised him for hating the boy she loved. It's what fed her rebellion. She knew this from the time she was a little girl and found it intriguing to go against her father for this very reason. She felt she was born to prove them wrong. Wrong about the family she would someday be a part of, with the boy she loved and cared so much about. She knew her free spirit showed a unique bravery that most girls her age would shy away from.

After she was done with scraping the deer hide she made up a lie that she was going to pick berries. It was just an excuse to get off the Klamath reservation. She was supposed to be watching her younger sisters while her mother was gone assisting her aunt give birth. One of Wintoka's cousins said she would watch over the girls along with her own children, and to go ahead, clueless she was excusing Wintoka to go with Thunder Cloud.

The beautiful, tall, young Klamath woman reached Lost River four miles later. She was surreptitiously hunched over in the tall grass where she quietly slithered over the ground around the sulfur flowers and sagebrush. "Caaawww caaawww." The youthful girl tried to be discreet so Thunder Cloud's younger brothers wouldn't see her. The beads at the bottom of her dress clinked together, making a swishing sound she worried might make them look over, so she tried to move slower. Thunder Cloud spotted her near his family's wickiup and looked back in his brother's direction to see if anyone else had. The girl who lit up his life and gave it meaning was at his home hiding like a skunk waiting to wreak havoc with its spray.

Pony, who was only two years younger than Thunder Cloud, was pulling camas roots up as fast as he could, trying to get done so he could climb and explore before night settled in. His idea of fun was not digging cattail or camas roots for his mother but swimming and trapping the beavers in Lost Lake or Tule Lake and exploring every inch of their land. Sometimes he would spy on a ranch and watch those strange white people plow with weird looking long thick pieces of wood hooked up to bulky animals. Pony kept these secret outings to himself, though. He didn't think there was a need to share with others about these odd and peculiar white people who just kept coming and taking over and fencing off all their land.

Pony's root basket that was made from mule leaves was full and ready to explode with root tips poking through. Pony's mother said his cattail basket must be full before he could escape into the wilderness he enjoyed exploring. He argued that picking roots was woman's work, but his mother slapped him upside his head and handed him the basket with that look that meant 'do it now'.

A strange noise came from behind him just as he was finishing up. Something made Pony jump so he yelled out to Thunder Cloud, telling him that he saw something move in the grass. "Brother! I go, get my rocks, we sling and kill that Kolichiyaw." He started for his soft deer bladder bag full of polished rocks and was going to prove that he was a good strong hunter like his older brother, who he looked up to and tried to impress, when Thunder Cloud pulled Pony down, grabbing him by the neck, making him understand.

"Look little brother! There could be danger lurking in that tall grass you see. You mustn't disturb. What if more of them are to come. We cannot do it alone. Go get La'as to help."

Pony slouched shoulders and shrugged his brother's hand off forcefully. "Get off me, Cloud. I can do it. I don't need your help. Or little brother's help."

Thunder Cloud knew what he said to Pony was foolishness. Desperation meant grabbing at anything he could imagine quick enough. Amazed but frustrated that Wintoka would jeopardize their companionship and love by doing such crazy things in the middle of the daylight, Thunder Cloud thought harder for something to get his brother to leave so he could go be with her. He knew their relationship was a death sentence, but controlling her when she made up her mind was impossible, and he knew that it was no use to try.

Pony was determined to go look in the tall grass. Puffing up his chest, ready to show off, he headed towards Wintoka. "Pony!" their father called for him. He needed his help. His annoying little brother was called by their

58

father just in time. Thunder Cloud shared a quick small prayer to the lava rock god before running to Wintoka's hiding spot. He laughed to himself, thinking of Pony and La'as coming back ready to pounce. Nothing would be there, not even their older brother. Thunder Cloud would pay hell for this later. But for now, Wintoka was bruising his heart and nothing else under the scorching sun mattered. Getting a few hours away with her was the only thing that would help heal it.

She laid motionless, suppressing laughter after what she just witnessed. Getting close enough, he tried scolding her, "Wintoka, why?" His hand brushed over her long hair, putting it behind her ear and running his long fingers across her thin lips, wanting more than ever to taste them. Taking a risk of getting caught he leaned in to kiss them. "Q'ay noos? aywakta?" It was a question he knew the answer to but needed to ask every time she did this to him.

Wintoka had a wild, carefree, daring spirit and was just a plain crazy Link Klamath girl. He cherished her most for that, and loved every inch of that girl who would someday share his life with him.

"Come Cloud," she said, rising once they were out of view and far enough away from his village and brothers.

Thunder Cloud glanced around one last time before he followed her to Tule Lake, escaping from the fear that held them back from showing their love publicly. Their tribes. Their lineage. That's who they were and where they came from. It was also the biggest hurdle they would have to jump someday, but for now they would enjoy each other and escape from their own history and culture that dictated separate lives, even if it was only for a few hours at a time.

"I have often imagined Wintoka's spirit still living, wandering this land," Frank said. He looked over at Pearl for a reaction as he remembered the faint smell of his granddad's Durham's smoking tobacco.

Confused, Pearl probed "Why would they have to hide their love?" She had heard stories of Captain Jack's stronghold in 1873, but still didn't understand why Wintoka and Thunder Cloud couldn't be together if they loved one another.

"There was a lot of fighting between the settlers and Modoc's. A large group of men surprised Captain Jack's father, who was the chief, killing him as he was just leaving his wickiup to get water while Captain Jack hid and watched. That was in the early fifties. It was before granddad came over on the Oregon Train with Grandma Louisa and her Rinehart family. Granddad told us the story of Ben Wright's massacre that ambushed Captain Jack's clan early in the morning, taking as many lives as they could just to show off the scalps when they got to Yreka. I remember Otto and me bein' scarr'd out of our minds and played like Ben Wright's ghost was coming after us long into the night when we should have been sleeping. If Mama ever caught us, father would have beat us good and give us whippings for days."

Frank laughed out loud, remembering all the fun he and Otto had. "Then when Thunder Cloud's clan was moved to the Klamath reservation, they weren't treated right by the Klamath Indians either. Having nowhere to go forced them into fighting for what was theirs in the first place. It's not just that, though. Grandfather said it was like the Modoc gods were mad at them or something. As if they didn't go through enough, the government lied to Captain Jack and his warriors and assured that their people would be treated fairly and that all the Modoc's would soon have their own reservation close to their ancestral lands. It was out-and-out deceit, and soon after that Captain Jack pulled his band into the lava beds and the stronghold began."

Pearl shook her head, deeply saddened by what she was hearing. Frank was a composed and methodical storyteller. She was thoroughly enjoying herself.

Little by little she was starting to understand who Wintoka and Thunder Cloud were, and why they couldn't be together.

"Too much hatred and bitterness lived within their people's hearts to forgive the past," he went on and she enjoyed studying his profile as he shared his childhood memories. She let the moment carry her away as she thought about everything he was telling her. She opened her heart and mind to these people using her clever and thoughtful imagination as he continued.

It was as if nature had created a romantic setting just for them. Wintoka and Thunder Cloud hit the water running when they reached Tule Lake and stripped off most of what little clothes they were wearing and played naked like the kids that still lived in their hearts. Their youthful dark bodies splashed and playfully teased one another in the cool water under the sweltering sun.

Wintoka's lean body bent and went limp as she let herself fall backwards, looking up at the cloudless blue sky above. Thunder Cloud swam over to her and massaged her back. His strong hands tenderly caressed her smooth skin, desiring everything they touched. He could feel the cool water rush around his body as he gently kicked and fluttered, staying afloat. How he loved her. Loved how she risked everything to see him. She was crazy and wild and knew how to enjoy life. He loved looking at her body, and desired her more than ever now as the sun glistened off her firm golden skin as he watched her glide over the lake's cool water.

Laying his head sideways in the water to look at her, he reached out, touching her first on the chin, guiding her closer to him, then her cheek, ending at her lips when she surprised him by slowly licking his finger before putting it in her warm mouth. Giving her a lustful look, he turned her around and softly moved up behind her. Pulling her long black hair out of the way, he kissed the nape of her neck. She felt his hard body press up against her, pushing tightly, making her melt into him. She relaxed completely, letting go, overwhelmed with affection for him. Wintoka let him take over while loving every minute of it as they became one together.

Time stood still as cattails and lily pads floated by. Canada Geese flew overhead in a 'V' formation, squawking to one another. Short-nose sucker fish swam around them, nipping at their toes. It was a perfect day Wintoka and Thunder Cloud were sharing until they noticed the bird's endless chatter. Concerned and alerted, Thunder Cloud put his finger to his mouth to quiet any words Wintoka might be thinking to say. They could feel the ground shaking before they saw the dust cloud following Indian ponies racing towards them.

Sure they were undetected, they moved stealthy with Indian grace to the side of the lake where the brush and shrubbery covered their bodies. "Our clothes?" She whispered, giving him a questioning look. He shrugged. They could only hope no one noticed anything.

The riders were in a hurry. This could be a tragedy if they were found out. Their bodies close together, they took long deep breaths to still the water and not be heard, quietly only speaking to each other through the movements of their dark eyes.

The ponies came to a stop, dust settling around them. The young men, dressed in old torn Levi's and calico button-up shirts with bandanas tied around their short greasy hair, jumped down off their ponies. Thunder Cloud's eyes moved restlessly. Counting, he could see there were about eight of them. It was obvious to him right away they were part of the Link Klamath tribe. Wintoka's tribe and some of her cousins were a part of this rebellious gang. He recognized a few of them from when he and his family were forced to live with them on the reservation, the reminder before him of why they were hidden camouflaged in cool water, unable to move.

Red Eagle, Wintoka's reckless cousin, was the ringleader of these crude young men who thought the world was made to revolve around their bravery. He was the first to issue orders to his younger brother, Black Bear, who listened close and sprang into action at every order given. "Take him to that tree, tie him up." Red Eagle barked orders as if he had dictated himself the next Klamath War Chief. Black Bear and one of the other boys grabbed a mentally slow Modoc boy half Thunder Cloud's age.

Little Horn was crying, terrified at what they were going to do to him. Snot dripped down his nose, hitting his chin before it fell on to his tight shirt that accentuated his large tummy. Slowly, he looked around for help, knowing it was useless. That much was at least clear to him. There were too many of the Klamath boys to outrun—he'd already tried that, and this is where it led him. Little Horn wasn't only part of the Modoc clan, but was Thunder Cloud's cousin's son.

Wintoka and Thunder Cloud could only watch, knowing exactly what the other was feeling. Breaking their hearts, they watched Little Horn's torture begin. Red Eagle pushed his tall black hat up out of his eyes becoming more animated. "Why you on our land?" he yelled, spitting into Little Horn's face. "You no good."

He began circling around Little Horn, who was tightly bound against the scratchy bark pine tree scraping and stabbing his back. The others pursued, following Red Eagle's fearless lead, poking, whipping and stabbing at the distressed little boy. One by one they spat in his face, hawking up nasty phlegm. Distraught, Little Horn cried out, louder than before. He was known to be slow by the Klamath kids and often targeted because of it. Over and over the simple-minded boy was taught by his elders how to be brave and endure pain, but Little Horn didn't understand and was too feeble minded to try.

Thunder Cloud's blood was boiling to see his cousin be torn down by them. He vowed to get revenge and make them pay. Breaking the boy's spirit, satisfied with the damage they'd done, the young gang was ready to leave, but not before Red Eagle took it a step farther and lashed out at the boy one more time before calling it quits. He picked a large rock out of his tote and rode up to Little Horn, threw the rock towards his head, leaving a huge gash in the back of the boy's greasy shoulder-length hair.

Red Eagle kicked his brown and white spotted pony in the sides, making him rear back, scattering rusty red dirt up behind him, then took off racing the pony back to the reservation. Black Bear followed behind his brother, leading the others, all the way back to the reservation, yipping an unnerving warrior cry that could be heard for miles as they rode away.

"Be strong, Little Horn, until I can get to you," Thunder Cloud kept whispering to himself. Wintoka's soft brown eyes said a harrowing good-bye to Thunder Cloud as she quietly slipped out of the water and grabbed her somewhat hidden clothes.

Drawing in a big breath, composing himself, Thunder Cloud surreptitiously climbed out of the water, hearing distraught, hysterical, panicky cries as he dressed quickly and ran to his cousin.

"Listen to me, Little Horn, I will help you." He took the bindings off his hands and used his cloth to wipe the blood and spit off his scratched up injured face. Blood was still tricking down the back of his head where there was a huge gash that was starting to clot. Little Horn looked at Thunder Cloud, completely confused why he was there. Not wanting to baby his cousin, angry he was crying, he sternly told Little Horn, "Come. We go home. 'Balaq Hak' tell nobody." Feeling sorry for him, he added, "Hurry up, brave man-child!"

As the sun dipped behind the sparse trees, Frank leaned back on his elbows and flicked a cricket off his shirt as he chewed on a piece of dry grass. He was happy and energized in Pearl's company. She squinted into the sun and dabbed at her sweat-beaded forehead with a purple hanky again. Pearl looked beautiful, sitting there enjoying herself even if the afternoon sun was suffocating them.

She hung onto every word Frank shared. He leaned back, all the way lying flat on the blanket, turned on his side, raising his right hand under his head and looked up into the still orange hue of the late afternoon sun and watched every detail of her face. Each time she spoke it sent a chill through his spine like he'd never known. "Well, I'd better get you back before your father sets out some of those traps for me." They shared a laugh, getting caught looking into each other's eyes again.

She agreed, knowing they had a long ride back. "You saw all the fox and cougar hides nailed to Uncle Will's barn, huh?" she teased. Frank reached out and touched Pearl's hand. She let him.

A slow burning heat of desire and sparks that felt like tiny bolts were attacking her while she held his hand. She was in love. No doubt about it, and before she gave it another thought he asked, "Will you be my girl, Pearly?"

It was the first of many times he would call her this in their years shared together. She melted under the trance of those rich cobalt eyes. "I will," was all Pearl's lips would let escape before Frank tenderly took her other hand and squeezed it, and she giggled like a schoolgirl.

He hopped up, raising his arms out to the side and stretched before brushing off the pine needles and debris that collected on his clothes then, like the gentleman Frank was, he reached down and helped Pearl up when she gave him her hand. They cleaned up the rest of the food and picnic blanket, packing everything up on their horses before giving them a drink of water for the journey home.

Riding away from a forever memorable afternoon, Frank turned back to their picnic spot that wouldn't be his alone anymore. Thinking about the struggles and war Wintoka and Thunder Cloud suffered made Frank think about what love meant. He could only imagine what they experienced, and prayed he would never have to go through the same struggles and broken heart Thunder Cloud had to with this woman riding beside him.

Chapter Ten

O tto had stayed far away from his family ever since he and Frank fought the night of the Fourth of July. He lost all interest being at home where he angered his father, broke his mother's heart, disappointed his older brother, and had the constant reminder he wasn't good enough for a real beauty like Pearl.

The Bunyard's black sheep spent most of his days now in Lakeview, where he worked wherever he could for a day or two until they got tired of his drinking and the fights he caused. He'd move on to the next ranch until he got fired at that one and spent the rest of the night losing at cards until they turned him out for belligerently fighting and cheating.

While Otto was wallowing in his misery, Frank was the happiest he'd ever been in his life. He was relieved Otto kept his distance. He didn't want his brother's sadness to tarnish his happiness.

It was late in September, on a Saturday afternoon, when Frank and Pearl went to pick the last of the choke cherries that would be rotting soon with the weather changing. Electa Caroline, Laura, Pearl, and their aunt Elizabeth planned to can the rest of the summer berries and fruits they could get picked before the frost ruined all the crops for the season.

Fall was approaching quicker than Silver Lake residents were prepared for. Having beautiful sunny autumn days usually meant harsh cold winter nights ahead. Pearl's parents were hopeful their home would be finished soon. Her mom was thrilled at the idea of having a new home, especially since she grew up in an old musty log cabin home that barely kept them warm in the winter. Pearl had never seen her mother happier then when she was in the McFarling's Mercantile picking out material for her new curtains, ordering their new furniture, and thinking about buying some of that new fancy modern wallpaper out of the Sears, Roebuck & Co. catalog.

Pearl took a deep breath, smiling to herself, as she looked around at the blue dusk settling like a blanket over the deciduous pines. She was relaxed and at peace with her life, enjoying her time with Frank. Such a beautiful evening Silver Lake had offered them. She had always loved this time of year. Her heart full, she inhaled all the delicious scents surrounding them and tasted autumn's nutmeg, cinnamon, and pumpkin that swirled in the dry crisp air. She drank in the sweet mixture.

Frank finished filling up the last of the wood buckets they brought with them, and then decided to take a break and eat some biscuits she'd made them that morning. He moved the ladder away from the tree he'd just finished and wiped his hands on his old work trousers, fresh choke cherries tickling his tongue.

"Mmm mmm!" Frank licked his lips and winked at Pearl. "I can imagine these dark cherries made into a sweet custard." His eyes had a voice of their own, begging her. Another handful went into his mouth.

"Sure Frank, anything for you." Teasing, she picked up a cherry and threw it up towards his mouth. Because he was six feet, four inches tall she didn't throw the cherry high enough, so he bent his knees and swooped in just in time to grab it then pulled her towards him, lifting her up off the black heeled boots she wore and almost knocked over one of the buckets.

69

Pearl squealed playfully, hitting at his shoulders and yelled "Hey, no fair…you put me down this instant!" Laughing, and as an afterthought, she smirked and added "Mr. Marion Frank Bunyard!"

A shocked look covered his face "Oh! Now you've gone and done it, my fair lady." He pulled her even closer to him, feeling every curve of her youthful warm body against his. Crows flew overhead cawing at one another, emulating Pearl's scream.

She was so relaxed and at ease, loving when he teased like this, he spun her around like a rag doll laughing at how light she was and planted a loving kiss on her rosy cheek, reluctant to put her down. He could tell by the spark in her eyes that she had an idea, and before he could ask what it was, she said, "Tell me another story of Wintoka and Thunder Cloud, please?" Now, she was begging. "And I promise, I will make you the sweetest cherry pie you ever tasted." Batting her enthused, sparkling brown eyes. How could he say no?

"Deal, but there's a catch." Frank chuckled. "I want two of them." He leaned over, all joking aside, and kissed her soft lips, sensually running his thumb over the curve of her bottom lip and reaching for her chin then guiding her mouth up to meet his. Sparks flew in every direction as Pearl melted into his strong, hungry and powerful embrace.

Chapter Eleven

Wintoka ran the whole way home, stopping only once. She approached the reservation where loud yelling and commotion was taking place by one of the crudely built huts. Taking big gulps of air, trying to catch her breath, she heard her mother scream, followed by her father's firm warning. She didn't know which scared her more but knew when she heard her father raise his voice, especially at her mother, nothing good came of it.

Wintoka listened to her name being yelled and looked around to see if anyone else was close by. She didn't want to get caught snooping around her own home, that would look suspicious, like she was guilty, but she wanted to see what was going on before she barged in and tried to pretend she wasn't with Thunder Cloud earlier that day. Her stout grandma Chilali, with obsidian black hair pulled back showing wiry thick gray strands accentuating her high cheek bones, lived close by with two of Wintoka's uncles, their wives, her grandsons, and Wintoka's arduous cousins, Red Eagle and Black Bear.

Wintoka would know Grandma Chilali's chanting and humming anywhere. It was a tactic she'd learned as a little girl when she watched her grandma calm the family down with that soft gentle voice of hers. She knew her grandma was over at her parent's hut dealing with whatever was upsetting her father. Besides, Thunder Cloud Chilali was Wintoka's favorite person.

The loving old woman was always there to protect Wintoka against her father's harsh punishments when she got caught being mischievous. Hunting Bear was so much harder on his oldest daughter, yet he would allow her younger sisters, Awentia and the twins Wanishewa and Sheshwana, to do whatever they wanted. Wintoka knew it was because of Thunder Cloud and being friends with his family from when the Modoc's lived on the reservation with the Klamath years before.

They were lower class than her family, and Hunting Bear wouldn't tolerate her and Thunder Cloud being friends. When he caught his oldest daughter playing with the young boy and several of the other Modoc children, who were usually Thunder Cloud's cousins, it usually meant a stern punishment. She never understood why her family taunted, hated and humiliated the Modoc's who were always good to her. She loved them like she did her own people and always felt a kinship with them. No matter how many beatings Wintoka took, it would never stop her from loving Thunder Cloud.

Thunder Cloud's grandmother, White Bird, reminded her so much of her own grandmother, and was always convivial to the war Chief's young daughter pulling her up onto her lap when she was in a circle telling the children stories. Loving the child, Grandmother White Bird played with her dark black long hair while Thunder Cloud watched, and knew, even as a young Modoc, there was a closeness between his grandmother and his best friend. Wintoka shared a familiarity and friendship with the old woman she herself couldn't even explain. She missed the comfort and attention her old friend gave her when Thunder Cloud's family followed the leadership of their Chief, Captain Jack, back to their old village and ancestral lands.

Reaching into the warm air she pushed aside a clump of dry tree leaves to try out a different view. She hated living on the reservation. Everything about it was infuriating and backwards, not the way her people were supposed to live, being bossed around all day and told what to do by that creepy Agent Knapp.

A loud scream pierced her thoughts, sending shivers up her spine when she heard her mother scream her name again. 'What are they saying?' She was close enough to hear the fighting but couldn't make out exactly what it was all about.

Feeling like a fish out of water spying on her family, she decided to be bold and go see what was going on. 'After all it couldn't be that bad, right?' she was hoping, pretending to feel in control. Her left eye flashed with a nervous twitch and she lifted her hand up to stop it when a small black bat swooped down in front of her in the dusky evening catching his dinner.

Trying to calm her breathing, she kept talking to herself when she heard a twig break close behind and then felt the nudge. A brown and white spotted pony greeted her. With perfect understanding, the yelling and fighting inside her home was clear to her now. Wintoka knew exactly what was going on and who was behind it, getting her father all riled up and as fast as she realized it, she was marching towards her home, when the front door opened and Red Eagle ran out, almost knocking her to the ground. Their eyes met, creating angry sparks, closing the short distance between them. Knowing he'd just ruined her life and provoked her father, Red Eagle proudly displayed his deception with all the confidence of a young Klamath buck. 'How did he see Thunder Cloud and me today? Had he been following us before tormenting Little Horn?' It all made sense to her now. She'd wondered how their clothing wasn't discovered. 'Stupid!' She was mad at herself. How foolish of them.

Her chest tightened and strong muscles tensed with anger. Acid rose in her dry throat. Trying to hold her head high, she kept walking towards the hut, glaring her cousin down as he walked away, sneering at her, their dark eyes locked in fierce battle, with younger Black Bear on his heals mimicking Red Eagle's bravado. Wintoka knew her life would be over as the daughter of a Tribal Link Klamath war chief and she would forever be banished from the reservation the minute her father's fist slammed into her face.

Chapter Twelve

Hours of slow and painful walking all night led Wintoka towards Thunder Cloud's wickiup. Eyes almost closed, puffy and swollen, she stood there trying to make out his home, sad, numb, and empty inside. The tall tickly cracked dry grass brushed up against her welted, bruised, and bloody long legs, hitting the elk bladder she carried with some dried rabbit meat and berries against her side. Luckily, grandmother Chilali generously snuck her some food. The decorated elk bladder her grandmother had made and the clothes on her back were the only things she owned now. She flicked a fat ugly beetle off her shoulder, watching it land on the rough cracked ridges of some tree bark below as memories of the previous night came back haunting her.

Wintoka's mental and physical energy was depleted. She gave in, no longer able to fight the lassitude, so she found a cleared spot to rest under in the shade of a Cottonwood close by Thunder Cloud's home. The dappled tall grass around her hid her fatigued, beaten, and bruised body while curious iridescent dragonflies explored overhead. Before she knew it, she was giving herself permission to lay her wary body down and let go of all the fear, hatred, anger, and guilt she'd been drenched in since the previous night.

Mid-morning transitioned into afternoon when Wintoka eased herself into the present. She sat up, wincing with a jabbing pain in her side that took her breath away. She knew her father must have broken at least one rib, but she wondered if there were maybe two or three more. The young girl spent much of the afternoon tending to her broken body and spirit. She saw someone coming towards her, interrupting her thoughts, and tried to hide herself better. Scrambling, she accidently made more noise than she meant to, but it was too late. The boys already saw her.

Poking at her with sticks to make sure she wasn't a spirit, they asked her what she was doing. With big brown eyes they looked over every bruise and abrasion on her battered body. They knew who Wintoka was from years of seeing their brother sneak off with her, and always knew when he was hiding her out around their wickiup, but they'd learned to never intervene for fear of Thunder Cloud's anger. Never seeing her close up or a female so wounded, they were naturally curious.

"Balaq hak batgal Thunder Cloud?" she croaked. The boys answered that he was at their wickiup skinning a deer he'd shot with his bow before dawn, but they would hurry and go get him as she requested. La'as scratched his toe with the stick he used to poke Wintoka with, and then threw it down into the dirt. Wintoka watched as Thunder Cloud's younger brothers looked back and forth at one another and then turned and ran off. She thought about how much they looked like their striking older brother, only just a couple of years behind him in age.

"Wintoka!" Thunder Cloud gently scolded her. "Q'ay noo S? Aywakta, I don't understand." He saw the sadness and fear through her swollen purple eyes before he looked her badly beaten body over. Blood drained from his face. "Wintoka!" Compassionate words flew from his raw and tender soul. Thunder Cloud scooped her up into his protective arms and carried her to his family's home so they could nurse her back to health. She was so overwhelmed with gratitude and love that she could now let relief cleanse her damaged spirit. Blinking back stinging tears, she looked up into the sky and watched as an eagle circled overhead, keeping watch over her.

Frank!" Pearl practically yelled, getting caught up in the story and about scared him half to death. "You mean, she never could go back to the reservation? That was her home!" Goosebumps danced up her spine. She was feeling like she knew Wintoka's heart and was beginning to have her own relationship with her. "Oh, this is all so sad."

She sat very still, listening to Frank's unerring wisdom and the explanation of why the Klamath's wouldn't allow their daughter, especially the daughter of a war chief like Hunting Bear, to be associated with Modocs, much less love one of them. They were a waring tribe. But Pearl was still having a hard time digesting the sadness and understanding it all—she hadn't even heard the slow beautiful melody sung by nearby birds or noticed the sun was dimming on the two of them or that they would soon lose their daylight and the little warmth the sun was still offering.

"My grandfather was a great defender of the dwindling Modoc tribe and had a lot of respect for them. He said when he first moved here, he did what he could to help their tribe, and believed we were to honor that this was their mother earth, their homes and their families. Too many mercenary settlers and ranchers wanted the land for profit and didn't see a need to share land with the Modocs." He'd never realized it before, but watching her care about them meant a lot to him, and knew it would to his grandfather, too.

Frank knew he couldn't live without this amazing, beautiful woman in his life, especially when he saw how kind and tender her heart was. He laid there under the shade of the falling orange sun with a lustrous pink and purple hue, relaxed, looking at her, thinking about how glad he was he had asked her father's permission to marry his daughter.

Frank's nervous thoughts about how he would propose were interrupted by Pearl's voice. "I knew I loved your grandfather when I first met him. It's good he cares for the Indians and tried to make a difference. It makes me proud to know him, Frank." Pearl was touched by his grandfather's compassion.

Frank had eaten most of the cherries they'd picked while he talked, but Pearl didn't care, or even notice. She was too engrossed in this amazing story of pride, hatred, loyalty, and the most intriguing of all, the love that outlasted. She would have to scold Frank for the choke cherries later, and remind him why there wasn't any pie. She smiled to herself.

The weeklong wedding celebration ended sometime that morning for the newly married couple. Neither Thunder Cloud nor Wintoka knew when they fell onto their tule mats in her father-in-law's home. They were tired from dancing and exhausted from the celebration given in their honor. Another fire and dance would start up again later that night when the sun circled around the earth one more time.

Wintoka was Thunder Cloud's new wife and shared the wickiup with his family. As a gift for marrying into his family, the tribe helped prepare a feast of waterfowl, fish, dried pine nuts, and special elk meat that was prepared with a blend of seasonings saved only for unique occasions, such as a wedding. Tightly woven and decorated tule baskets were symbolically placed on a tule mat around the fire on the fifth and final evening of celebration. Gifts of beaded necklaces, barrettes, and carved fir wood trinkets were given by Thunder Cloud and his family to Captain Jack and his two wives in honor of leading the ceremony and uniting Wintoka and Thunder Cloud earlier that week.

Wintoka and Taw-Kia, who was quickly becoming Wintoka's closest friend and confidant, were gathered around the fire painting symbols on each other's faces, and their horses nearby were being painted by her mother-in-law, Grandmother White Bird, and Thunder Cloud's aunts. All the women were in high spirits. The Modoc women were feeling blessed to have Wintoka's amazing wisdom and kind spirit among them. Many remembered the sweet, curious little girl all those years ago when they lived at the same reservation and knew her and Thunder Cloud would be together one day.

Giggling and clucking of the Modoc tongue and loud excitement could be heard all throughout the Modoc camp. Wintoka and Taw-Kia had just finished doing each other's hair when they saw someone close by in a large group of pine trees watching them. The afternoon sun bounced off a U.S. Army button on a blue shirt, giving the soldier's hiding spot away.

There was quick and frantic movement of women, children, and elderly as they took cover when Captain Jack rode into the camp. "What is going on?" Wintoka was terrified, feeling vulnerable and insecure for the first time among her new family.

"I do not know, stay, I will find Thunder Cloud."

Captain Jack and Thunder Cloud's father, Great Bluff, had set up a perimeter to surprise attack the soldiers, unbeknown to Wintoka and Taw-Kia. Captain Jack scowled at the two young soldier boys who were surrounded by fierce Modoc warriors. He was carrying his hatchet and spear on his horse, along with his rifle at his side. Spitting out the words of a man who was deadly serious, he said "She is of us, she will not go. You go, now."

Fear struck Wintoka, kicking her straight in the stomach. She found Thunder Cloud's eyes were letting her know she was safe, and he would fight to his death for her. While Thunder Cloud and Captain Jack battled it out with the soldiers, Taw-Kia ran as fast as her lame foot would allow and got Lightning, Wintoka's wedding present and favorite horse.

"This is official business," the first soldier boldly stated, raising his shoulders like he had endorsed authority. "Agent Knapp has requested she goes back to her own tribe, so there will be no trouble on the reservation."

Instinctively Thunder Cloud yelled "NO!" vengeance filling his eyes. "She is Modoc wife now! YOU GO!" He threw up his arm, pointing at the soldiers to leave the way they came. Thunder Cloud's eyes burned into the soldiers' arrogant expressions. Private First-Class Bud Abbott sat on his United States Army's shiny black horse, not realizing the danger of Thunder Cloud's words.

He was looking Wintoka over, thinking to himself how he could take her with force and then have his own fun with her before they returned her to her family at Fort Klamath, while his partner, Private Samuel Collins lusty dark eyes were following Wintoka's long legs. Unaware she was looking around for an escape route, scared beyond words, Wintoka used bottled up fear as her motivation and anger, offering her determination and strength. She jumped on her horse Taw-Kia had brought and hid in the brush close to her. She kicked Lightning's side and took off with precipitous speed. No one was taking her away from these people who were her family now.

She knew the Private's words were deceitful, and they were untrustworthy men who were given much control and power. Thunder Cloud was trailing her for protection before the soldiers could even react. Wintoka steered Lightning through the large rocks and sporadic pines, fiercely dodging whatever obstacles that might slow her down. The overconfident soldiers had just enough time to jump on their horses and they were off in a race with Wintoka and Thunder Cloud. Following with heated revenge, Great Bluff and Captain Jack were behind them in a flash.

She was not going back there, so she could be tortured and hated among her people. She did not belong there anymore. She was a Modoc now, and nothing else in her life mattered more than getting away from these men who not only wanted to ruin her new life but harm her body in ways that were unforgivable. Remembering the things she unwillingly witnessed many times by soldiers on the reservation, while the fathers, husbands, and reservation agents turned a blind eye, was enough to keep her riding all through the night if she had to.

Chapter Thirteen

"Oh fiddlesticks, Frank! Look how dark it is. Father is going to be vexed." Pearl was worried and didn't want her parents to be angry with her or be unnecessarily worried. Time had gotten away from them while Frank told her stories. She quickly rushed around, getting the food basket together and grabbing what was left of the cherries.

"Merciful heavens, I'd say. Better get you home." Knowing Pearl's father knew she was with him this evening, and knew he was going to propose to his daughter, eased Frank's mind. He and Pearl's father, Charles, had mutual respect and trust. Frank was just hoping Charles would make sure Electa Caroline knew her daughter was safe. He didn't want her having undo stress.

Pearl set the cherry buckets on the dirt by the back door next to the old metal milk can, and then told Frank she would be right back, to go ahead and have a seat on the swing while she ran inside to tell them she was home. Frank sat a few minutes waiting for her, thinking about how cold the weather had been these last couple of weeks, and how soon the snow would start.

He was trying hard to keep himself calm by thinking about things other than how he would propose. Lost in thought about his parent's farm and what he would need to prepare and protect it for winter, he looked up to see Pearl walking towards him. The sight of her made him quiver with excitement and anticipation. He couldn't even remember what he'd been thinking about two minutes before. She always had the same effect on him that made him feel like a foolish love-struck schoolboy.

Wearing a thick white cotton sweater over her relaxed yellow cotton dress, hair back in a loose curly bun, she had a glass of fresh lemonade Aunt Elizabeth just made that morning and was a picture of pure beauty and elegance. Frank's eyes stayed on her until she settled in next to him, where the two of them sat silent for a moment. She laid her head on his shoulder as the swing gently rocked, taking in the tranquility the calm evening offered. He quietly sipped on his lemonade. The bright full moon lit the country setting while the creaking sound of the swing hummed with the sounds of frogs and crickets. Laura wanted to join them, but Pearl told her not tonight. She would be able to another time. Pearl felt like being selfish tonight and wanted Frank all to herself. So, Laura sat inside sulking by the multi-colored rock fireplace with her mom and Aunt Elizabeth, who crocheted and visited by the firelight.

Laura was always left out, but she liked Frank too. He was always so nice to her. She didn't want her older sister mad at her though, so she picked up her quilt square and went back to work on it. Feeling Laura's disappointment, Electa Caroline quietly whispered, "It won't be long until we can give her our gift, Laura, right?"

A smiling Laura caught her mom's sparkling eyes and the corners of her mouth slowly turned up. It was a surprise her mother and her were working on for Pearl. They had talked about Pearl's wedding day before Pearl even knew it was coming up. It was a secret Laura and Electa

Caroline shared and kept to themselves. Of course, Aunt Elizabeth was in on it too, encouraging the excitement from time to time when Pearl wasn't home. She was gone with Frank most of the time. Their mom knew this was a good way to keep young Laura out of the young lovers' way and would help make her feel important, knowing a secret her older sister didn't even know yet.

"Mmm, that hit the spot! What a treat. Thanks." Frank sat down the glass next to the swing. Anxious feelings told him it was time to ask before the evening slipped away from him. Frank had rehearsed what he wanted to say many times over the last couple of weeks while working on the horses in the stable or out riding and checking his parent's property.

Finally, Frank decided it was time. 'Here I go,' he thought to himself, wiping his sweaty hands on his trousers and stopping the swing to turn towards her. "Pearl," Frank started out saying her name like he sucked in all the love the world had to offer. She turned towards him to see why he was acting a little foolish, when he gently reached for her hand. "There's something I'd like to talk to you about. I've been pondering on it for a long while now." His hands were shaking. She listened whole heartedly. Something was happening to Frank that was completely unfamiliar to him. "I don't want you to give me your answer until I'm done asking." He reached up and put a runaway curl back behind her ear. She leaned into his warm hand while he continued, "I feel we are matched perfectly, Pearl, and I will be a good husband, if you'll have me?" He shifted and squirmed around on the wood swing uncomfortably. This was harder than he expected. With his voice cracking he started again. "I will never seek to change anything about you, and will love you always." He was so sincere;

Pearl's heart was melting with each word. She could feel the heat from Frank's body next to hers as she stared into his electric blue eyes. She was increasingly sympathetic towards him, because she too felt just as nervous about his question as he did, and she was sure he could hear her loud heartbeat with every breath she took. It felt so close to her throat. Pearl wanted to hear those words a thousand times. She squeezed his shaky hands. "I love you, Pearl." Frank murmured as he leaned in and tenderly kissed her. He was thrilled by the passionate way she responded and knew he'd just received his answer.

"Yes Frank! I will, I mean," she got all flustered and started to giggle. "Yes, I will marry you." she answered with little girl enthusiasm. Eagerly the two embraced in a long-devoted hug, that was quickly interrupted by Pearl's sister, Laura running outside letting the wood screen door slam behind her, interrupting any intimacy the two shared. Pearl's parents and aunt and uncle soon followed to see all the excitement. Charles was delighted to have Frank as a son-in-law, and eagerly congratulated the young couple giving him a firm handshake. "I don't have a ring yet, Pearl. I'm working on getting that, and will have one by our wedding day."

She gave her mother and Aunt Elizabeth a big hug before the family invited Frank inside, to visit before he needed to head home and share the news with his family. Charles, Frank, and Uncle Will walked behind the women, who had their arms around each other chattering with excitement the whole way back to the small, cozy house as their long skirts flung up dust behind them. Coyotes imitated one another in the distance as the full moon lit up the cheerful little Silver Lake town and all the lizards, frogs, and chirping crickets were settling in for another cold autumn night.

Chapter Fourteen

It was a beautiful Sunday afternoon with yellow, brown, and green leaves swirling around in the cool, crispy autumn air, when Frank was in his parent's barn fixing some broken cattle feeders. As usual, Spot was at Frank's heels, cautiously watching and waiting for some love.

The memory of Pearl's light lavender fragrance, her beautiful honest eyes, how much fun she was, and how much he loved every minute spent with her flooded his mind. Sitting there in the tool room, reflecting on his girl and their upcoming wedding, he knew why he felt something was missing from his life months before he met her. It was her all along he was missing. He couldn't imagine what life in Silver Lake would be like without her. Just thinking about her sent a chill up his spine.

He felt like he could reach out and feel her soft cheeks, her delicate but strong hard-working hands, and knew she would make a great wife and wonderful mother. Frank had always admired the tender loving way she treated her sister. She was such a compassionate person, and would be an amazing woman by his side while building his dream ranch and living their lives together. Thinking about how she was shockingly witty sometimes made him laugh out loud, with huge smile crossed his mouth. Yep, she was his girl, with a gracious spirit, spirit other women admired and only dreamed of. She was one of those people who stood out in a crowd without even trying and had no idea it was happening.

The hair on Frank's neck stood alert when he saw shadows move to the right of the room where he was working. He was so busy daydreaming of Pearl that he was unaware someone came into the barn. "State your business," he demanded with insistent boldness when he saw petulant brown eyes stare back at him.

Thunder Cloud walked out of hiding, his two brothers following close behind, and Frank walked cautiously towards the three men. It had been months since he'd seen them. For a few moments no one said anything, but stared at a lizard that darted up the wall, stopped, flicked its tail, looked back at them then took off. Unsure tension filled the unfamiliar space between them.

He made the old dog, Spot, stay behind, but felt reassured that if something were to happen to him, Spot would alert his parents or eventually get one of the neighbor's attention. He took a long deep breath, opening his mouth to talk, then heard the dog's deep, low growl next to him. "So much for being a good dog," Frank said under his breath.

Not sure what Thunder Cloud needed, he asked, "Is everything alright, Thunder Cloud?"

No one answered until Frank softened when he looked Thunder Cloud and his brothers over. They were skinny, gaunt looking, and obviously were there in need of some help. Sad, empty eyes searched the barn as if to confirm Frank's thoughts. He ventured closer to the men.

"Thunder Cloud?" Frank said again, gently pushing Spot away with his boot.

Thunder Cloud slowly replied "Food."

Frank knew the men in front of him knew and understood English well, but Thunder Cloud didn't care for ranchers around to know this. He got more out of the stupid, land-sucking white people when he and his brothers pretended not to always understand. It was one of the many ways they'd learned how to survive.

Thunder Cloud, Pony, La'as, and Pony's wife Taw-Kia were the only Modoc's left not living on the reservation. They stayed to themselves for fear that the government would try to push them where they did not belong or move them halfway across the country, to Oklahoma, in cattle cars like most of their family had been after Captain Jack's hanging at the end of the Modoc war. If the Federal officers from the Agency were to find any Indian bands by themselves, they were to be treated as hostile Indians and taken immediately into custody. The small inadequate band was forced to seek help from time to time and knew this was one of two places to get the help, understanding and compassion they yearned for. The other was Frank's grandparents' home, George and Louisa Duncan.

Once they all moved outside, Thunder Cloud finally shared they needed food and some supplies, as the hunting had been bad and the snow season was settling in soon. There wasn't enough food to prepare for winter storage. A forceful gust of wind played with crispy autumn leaves that danced around the windmill. Thunder Cloud took his gaze off Frank for a curious moment and looked up at the top of the platform, and all sets of eyes wondered if the rickety windmill was going to come down on them.

Before they got skittish and took off like they usually did, Frank thought it was best to act fast. "I figure we have what you need. You stay here," Frank said, pointing to the ground then holding his hands up in the motion to stop and stay put. He turned and ran towards the house, looked down to see a huge gopher hole and jumped over it just in the nick of time, guessing he should fill that in soon before someone broke an ankle.

Sarah Emmaline was bent over a fire pit set up out back of their old farmhouse, stirring a large kettle where she was making soap. His mother was just about to add the lye to the boiling mixture of animal lard when she heard her son's anxious voice. "Ma, Thunder Cloud is by the barn. He says they're hungry and I'm sure they are. I ain't never seen them all look so skinny. Can you help me really quick before he gets skittish like he's known to?" He rushed the words through the air trying to gather items.

"Lands sake! He's here? Now?" she replied with surprise. His mom stopped stirring and looked around. Jesse was out in the field, herding sheep with a neighbor. It was just her and Frank on the property.

Sarah Emmaline dried her hands on a once starched white apron and quickly gathered some grains, sugar, dried black beans, bacon, coffee, and some dried beef from the storage room off the small kitchen while Frank grabbed a couple old quilted blankets out of the chest in the upstairs loft he shared with Otto, to help sustain them through the winter.

Taking large steps back to where Thunder Cloud and his brothers waited, Frank handed them all the provisions he hoped would help get them through until they needed more. Thunder Cloud's wordless smile was thanks enough for Frank as the group of brothers turned and, swift as an arrow, blended into the landscape. Frank took his hat off, scratched his head, and stood there in wonder, pondering where they always disappeared to.

Chapter Fifteen

uring those first few weeks after Frank proposed to Pearl, the weather turned a nippy cold and snow was starting to cover the town of Silver Lake, dropping a couple feet every few days. Frank and Pearl wrote secret love letters to each other and slid them into each other's hands when no one was watching. Pearl loved getting his letters, and soon the two of them were making up secret codes only they knew the meaning to.

Late at night, after Laura was sound asleep, Pearl would pull the love letters out, hidden under her bed. Loving every word written, she read them over and over until she fell asleep.

My Dear Little Pearly,

I thought I would write you a few more lines this evening. I intended to go to town today, but it has been snowing all day, so I did not go. Will go up in the morning if it quits storming. I've been working hard on our house. Excited to see what you think of it. Glad I was able to buy a small ranch to sustain our family in the years to come. I can't wait to start our lives together.

How have you and Laura been? Working on the quilt, that's a secret? Well Pearly I have wrote all I know, and I expect you will get tired of reading this letter. I could write some more but I don't want to disgust you with this letter with too many questions. I would love to see you just for a while, if not always. I could sure enjoy a talk with you dear. It's a fine thing to be able to write a little if a fellow can't write good, I don't know what in the world I would do if I could not write to you. And if you didn't write to me, I would sure die. Well I will close for this time. Write soon and a long long letter, yours as ever

bye bye, FB

On the outside of the envelope he wrote: *Apples are good, and peaches are better, if you love me, answer this letter.*

Pearl slowly and as quietly as possible folded up Frank's letter that she found in her quilting basket earlier that evening, as the wind slipped in through the loft's small window where she and Laura slept side by side. She couldn't believe it had been over a week since she'd seen Frank.

Pearl knew Laura was involved in helping Frank hide letters around. Those two were clever, and Laura loved being part of the game as he made it fun for her. It was probably Laura's idea the letter got put into the sewing basket. Knowing sleep must come sooner or later, she shut her eyes and turned over and got comfortable before wrapping her right arm over her sister's small snuggled-in body, and pulled her close to her, a huge smile covering her tired face.

The small ranch house was ready to move into with shingle siding, broad wood window frames, indoor water, and even a newer-used blackened cook stove Frank took out a small loan on, as a gift for their wedding. He had been over there inspecting the new property and house, making sure everything was in order, so he could show it off to the soon-to-be new woman of the house.

Overwrought with excitement he couldn't stand it anymore, so he jumped on Juniper and headed over to his future-in-laws new house they just finished building, and found the sisters hanging freshly washed clothes on the rope inside the house by the wood stove. Giggling, having a merry time, Pearl was singing and doing a fun two-step dance she'd learned from her best friend she had left back in Eugene City.

"Oh please, teach me that," Laura energetically begged. Pearl's smile brightened as she waved her sister over to where she was.

"Come on over here." They dried their wet hands on Pearl's apron when they heard a rider coming down the dirt road.

"Aww," Laura whined with displeasure. "Now you won't teach me," she said frenetically under her frown, and let go of Pearl's hand when Frank opened the front door, poking his head in.

"Afternoon ladies." He tipped his hat first to a cantankerous Laura. "Would you have time to accompany me to our new home, Ms. Hardisty?" he asked.

"I'll finish up the clothes, Pearl, so you can go," Laura tried to sound convincing, even though the scowl carved in her forehead spoke for itself.

Frank calmly turned his attention to his future sister-in-law standing next to his fiancé. "Oh no, Laura." Frank shook his head "I shall not have the woman of the hour left behind!" He winked at Pearl "I was really hoping you could assist me by helping Pearl and me about where to put the spring house that I still need to build."

Pearl's face relaxed. She felt warm affection for her man at how thoughtful and caring he was.

"Really?" Laura's spirits soared with a bright smile. "Let me go ask Mama if I can go." She picked up her skirts and ran as fast as she could, yelling, "Mama!"

Electa Caroline was already walking down the newly laid steps towards the couple standing by the clothesline when Laura almost ran right into her. "Afternoon, Frank." Electa Caroline gracefully approached him as she picked up laundry where Pearl and Laura left off.

"Afternoon ma'am." He nodded to his future Mother-in-law, tipping his hat. "I was wonderin' if I may steal your girls for the afternoon so I can show them the ranch house?" His cheeks reddened a little when he added "Reckon it wouldn't be proper if Pearl and I went alone." Quiet tittering filled the room, lightening the awkward feeling swirling around.

"Oh, by all means, go on. How very exciting, Pearl." Electa Caroline was thrilled for her daughter. "Go on and I'll finish up what you girls have left," she said to her daughters. Her eyes followed them as they went to get their ponchos. "You must, I insist, stay for dinner when you bring my girl's home, Frank."

The young man knew she never took no for an answer, "Yes ma'am," Frank respectfully replied.

"Beef stew is cooking now, beets, and jelly cake for dessert," Electa Caroline yelled out, turning her head while shaking out her husband's freshly-washed undershirt.

"Thank you ma'am, that sounds delicious." Frank guided Laura up on Juniper while Pearl went to saddle Midnight.

The ride to the ranch house didn't take too long, considering everyone rode fast with anticipation. "We'll let ya off your horse first, before I make you close your eyes." Frank winked down at Laura, loving how the young impressionable girl went along with everything. She put her warm, small gloved hand up to her mouth and giggled at her sister's excitement. "All right now, you promised, remember?" Frank smiled real big, guiding her inside the front door, Laura on his heels.

Step by step Frank walked Pearl in to the new kitchen he'd remodeled with the help of his father and grandfather, who worked tirelessly day and night to get it all completed before the wedding. Pearl's father, Charles, and her Uncle Will also pitched in when they could get away for a few hours a day. When Frank allowed her to remove her hands and open her eyes, she let out an excited scream that pierced both their ears.

"AHH!" she shrieked with pure delight. "Look at that! It's a Home Comfort stove!" Laura slapped a hand over her mouth, just as surprised as her sister. This was the first time Laura was at the house and she knew Mama didn't even have anything as nice as this. She'd never seen a finer stove in her life and neither had her sister who, with happy tears and shiny cheeks, jumped up and down with excitement, hugging her little sister and pointing out all the built-in shelves above it. Her heart was racing fast. She looked at Frank with watery grateful eyes that silently said, 'Thank you.'

"I knew you'd love it. Grandfather had it shipped here all the way from San Francisco, California. It's used, but the folks who had it never used it much."

Pearl's long skirt swished around her small feet. "It's marvelous, Frank!! Simply marvelous." She couldn't believe all the work everyone had done on their new home, and never even knew her father and uncle had any part helping, especially when they were so busy themselves getting her parents' house ready.

The ranch house was a little small, but a perfect beginner home for them. "You like it, Pearly?" Frank asked, lifting her up and wrapping his strong arms around her, giving a tight hug.

"It's the best, Frank! Thank you!" The two snuck a passionate kiss while Laura was exploring the rest of the small home. Pearl slipped a letter into Frank's hand while she had the chance. He immediately put it in his back pocket and bashfully smiled at her before Laura walked back into the large ranch style kitchen.

Frank was exhausted. It had been a long day. He finished up dinner at his future in-law's home and quickly rode home in the cold evening, planning to retire to bed early. He had a big day planned early the next morning, moving the entire livestock he'd recently purchased in Lakeview to his new ranch. A small cattle and sheep drive he would normally do on his own if it was springtime. But he was nervous about getting all his animals to Silver Lake safe, with the weather turning, so he decided to hire two drivers along with one of the neighbor boys, Tim, who had been hanging around the ranch house while they were fixing it up.

Under heavy quilts in the cold room, watching his breath in the night air, Frank lay dreaming of his sweet Pearly girl. Remembering the letter, he forced himself to re-light the oil lamp on the stand beside his bed. Chilled and shivering, he ran across the cold hard wood floors to find his trousers. Once Frank found what he was after, he hurried back into the comfort of his warm bed and quickly opened it, cherishing every written word as he tried to get warm again.

My Dearest Frank,

What would my life had turned out like, if not for you in it? These last couple months have been the happiest times of my life! I am eager and often find myself impatient to start our lives together. Mother said we could surely use her and daddy's feather mattress, so we do not have to purchase one. It's rather old and been used over the last 20 years, but at least it will be something to start out with in our new house and what a great gift. It will fit perfectly on the wood frame you made.

Mother was using it as an excuse to get a new one. I'm sure of it. Mama always thinks ahead, doesn't she? Every time I am in the McFarling's Mercantile, I think of all the fun stuff needed for our new lives together and how grand it would be if I didn't have to worry about cost. But my dear, I assure you I will never be that type of wife. I am very frugal by nature. I take after my old grandmother Hardisty and her careful use and re-use of everything she has owned.

I have almost completed our honeymoon quilt. When I started it last year, before moving from Eugene City to Silver Lake, I never dreamed of my life changing so much. I am grateful to have you in it, and to soon be happily married to the most handsome man God ever created!

Yours Forever,

Pearly

Unknown to Frank, Pearl was reading his note as the very same time. Laura must have put it under her pillow after they got back from the house. Frank was so sneaky and made finding his notes so much fun, not to mention romantic.

Miss Pearly Hardisty,

My dear girl. I will now try and write you a few lines to let you know that I haven't forgotten you in our busy times. You are on my mind every moment and I look forward to the day, which is just a few of them away, that I can call you my wife. I don't want to share you with anyone else. I am foolish at times thinking that way, but cannot help it if I am. You know I am foolish anyway, but love is love and cannot be changed. If I had to live the rest of my days without you it would be death to me. I don't think there is ten minutes in the day but what I don't think of you. You're first in the morning and last at night. I can see you now, standing there on your parent's steps watching me ride away tonight. I knew that I had to leave you behind, but the best of friends must part at times. Well dear, it is getting late and again, I have much work to attend to in the morning. So, I guess I will close for this time, I could write to you all night but I suppose you would get tired of reading it.

Hoping this letter finds you well.

I remain as ever your own boy, bye bye FB

Chapter Sixteen

ocks tumbled along the dark, dirt road out front of the Mercantile as Abbie Jean's blackened leather boot kicked another rock, watching it bounce along. Her head turned down trying to avoid the strong cold wind rushing past her. "Burrrr," she whispered under her breath, pulling the knitted shawl tighter around her shoulders under her poncho.

She was pouting from a mixture of boredom and sadness. The only sounds surrounding her in the bright full moon night were the scant shuffles of field mice, and owls that were watching and waiting to catch one. Everyone else in this quiet, peaceful farm town had been asleep for hours and would soon be up and ready to start the new day. Abbie Jean made a habit of sneaking out and walking about the streets when she couldn't sleep or when her moods shifted, feeling like life might be more exciting outside her four-bedroom walls. This night she'd been thinking about Pearl and Frank as she walked around, wishing things could be different. She wasn't the only one moping around town feeling sorry for themselves tonight, however. Misery always has loved company, and was known to show up at random times.

"Woot woot," The sound of an impersonated snow owl, was all Abbie Jean heard before she felt a rough tap on her shoulder as she was rounding the corner at the O'Neil's Tobacco shop. Somber in her own thoughts, she didn't hear anyone come up behind her. Reaching deep inside her throat to scream, but the scream was stifled when she saw Otto quickly put a finger to his lips to shush her.

"You bout' done and scared everything including the devil outta me, Otto!!" she whispered with sass and shock. Once she was done being angry at him, she was excited he was in town, but wasn't about to show it and give him the satisfaction.

"Oh, I doubt it. You are the Devil," he replied and laughed at his own joke. "What in sprite's name are you doing out here, alone, in the middle of the night?"

She shrugged off his question. "I don't owe you anything, especially after you were a jackass all those months ago! I don't forget so easily." She glared him down, raised her head, tightened her mouth, and folded her arms.

He was loving it. "Oh, I see how you want to play. I always did like my girls sassy."

Otto stopped walking backwards in front of her, forcing her to stop, then peered directly into her sensitive eyes. "What are you doing here? After you acted a fool at the dance and left me alone for everyone to stare!" She was getting bottled up anger out, finally, and didn't care one bit what he thought of her now or did she care to be proper. She was still hurt and terribly embarrassed from his behavior. Her arms were crossed still. Tears burned her narrowed eyes. "Remember?" She wasn't whispering any more. "Fourth of July night? The dance…. that was," she paused hoping he was hearing her pain, "That was supposed to be fun?"

Otto watched her anger rise. Of course he remembered. He was ashamed of what he did to her now, especially when she said it that way, but at the time, he'd never thought anything about her. Just his own anger and humiliation. Besides, he had his mind on another woman back then. Lifting a cold hand up to his chin, rubbing fingers over thin stubble, he watched Abbie Jean closely. She seemed different to him than the last time he'd been with her. She'd grown up on him.

Sensing his strange actions, she asked him what he was doing in the middle of the night in Silver Lake, anyway. He lied, saying he was there to get an early start at helping Frank. Not sure if she took the bait hook, line, and sinker, he changed the subject. "The question is...what on earth are you doing outside on a stormy night like this?" Otto circled her one more time, stopping directly in front of her again, looking straight into her deep serious ice blue eyes, adding, "All alone?" with true sincerity she'd not expected.

Profound light grayish-blue eyes that didn't laugh at her with the insensitivity she was used to from him, but told of a sorry man who was honest about his concern and was thoughtfully studying her. She would have liked a few more of those sincere, kind moments with Otto. It felt amazing. She found herself willing to stick around and see what the night brought. "What happened to your head anyway? You look like a horse trampled you," she asked, minus the sass.

"Oh," Otto put his hand up to his head where he was injured. "Reckon too much drink and not enough brains will do that when you lock horns with old friends and gamblers." He turned so he was side by side with her, putting his arm on his hip then looking into her questioning expression, and motioned for her to put her arm through his. She did and smiled up at him.

He turned them around and started the walk back to her house when she stated, "Especially when you cheat'n em', eh?" and the two of them shared a laugh which immediately relaxed previous tension between them.

Surprised by how comfortable she was around him, it suddenly occurred to her he was being kind, gentle, and acting like he really cared how she felt. They went on exchanging pleasantries like this over the next couple blocks, really enjoying one another's company.

Coming to an end too soon for both of them they came up to the steps on the outside of the house that lead to her room. "Abbie Jean, it has been my pleasure walking you home." He took her gloved hand in his and put it to his lips, kissing them ever so gently and then he smiled, causing her knees to weaken and her heart to skip a couple of unexpected beats. Sparks twirled up and down her spine. "Well, pretty lady, not sure where this is going but I hope it happens again."

It was the first time in Abbie Jean's life she was silently stunned and never moved her head or eyes. 'Is he asking me out?' she wondered, 'And flirting with me?' She was a little skeptical, not wanting to be embarrassed or hurt like she had been not all that long ago by him, but she was really enjoying his company.

Otto jumped up on his horse and trotted back to Lakeview, knowing his life was about to take a turn and change for the better. Abbie Jean turned back to watch him ride away, whispering a hushed goodnight where only the night heard.

Chapter Seventeen

en dressed in their Sunday best were standing around forming circles and were anxiously waiting for the big moment, listening to soft whispering voices mixed with tense laughter in the back of the old church.

"Oh mother! I've never been so nervous or so happy." The shaky bride couldn't stop the butterflies fluttering in her tummy. The pretty white, cold snow outside the plain tall church building was stacking up high along the wood siding, while the heavy old bronze bell proudly hung above the church ringing as the chilly winds brushed by, announcing to all that a wedding was about to take place.

Pearl's long ivory silk wedding gown was simple but elegant, and made her look like a princess out of an old storybook. Electa Caroline was proud that her eldest daughter was wearing the very wedding gown she'd wore years before, even though they had to hem it up several inches and alter the mid-section, as Pearl had a smaller frame than her mother.

Ten-year-old Laura was standing at Pearl's side, ready to walk down the short distance between the church benches carrying a small silk pillow with a simple silver ring tied in a knot with white lace. Electa Caroline made sure everything was ready before she gave Louisa Rinehart, Pearl's grandmother-to-be, the go-ahead to start the music. She looked her daughters over one more time before excusing herself to sit with their father who was waiting for her. "You are a beautiful bride. Pearl," she murmured, and tenderly hugged her nervous daughter, then wiped large tears from her eyes. Preparing herself for this day the last couple weeks finally caught up with her and she was overcome with raw emotion.

Walking down the aisle with his beautiful bride tightly snuggled up to him, happy the wedding was over and everything had gone as planned, Frank looked around and saw the guests and decorations for the first time that day. Frank saw his younger brother and with Pearl beside him they walked towards Otto.

"How long you been here?" he asked, surprise with just a hint of worry in his voice when he saw his brother in the very back by the coat rack, standing straight as an arrow with his hands folded over his puffed-up chest. Relief washed over Frank when he thought his brother had forgotten the most important day of his life. He was genuinely glad his little brother made it.

"Long enough to see you two get hitched. Congratulations, my brother. I'm sorry I got into town so late! The storm was on my tail, following me the whole way here." Otto grabbed Frank and hugged him. Frank stumbled back a little, startled by the energy Otto had. Gently pulling away, eyeing him over, Frank was aware Otto didn't smell like liquor, which pleased Frank more than his brother ever knew.

"Well, no matter Otto, glad you made it." Frank slapped his brothers' right arm. "Hey!" Frank was full of enthusiasm and excitement. "We're heading to the Grange Hall for a reception dinner. You're coming over, right?" Frank looked down at Pearl, carefully watching her reaction, treading lightly, remembering the awful last encounter all three of them had together. But he wasn't giving up on his brother, especially after finding him freshly bathed, nicely dressed, clean and sober today.

"Miss out on Grandma Duncan's Dampfnudeln?" He dramatically shook his head, "No way." Then he turned his attention to Pearl, who stood next to her man smiling at Otto, biting her lip. "Welcome to the family," Otto genuinely offered.

He was so different than the last time she'd seen him, maybe he was different when he wasn't drinking. She'd never had the opportunity to see him sober though, so she would keep an eye on him. "Thanks," she said, returning an authentic, gentle hug from her new brother-in-law. Laura had been peering from behind her sister's gown the whole time

"Laura, would you like to come with Frank and me to the reception?" Changing the subject, Pearl turned away from Otto, before it was obvious to those closest to her just how uncomfortable all this unsure kindness was making her.

Electa Caroline happened to overhear Pearl ask Laura to ride with them and quickly piped up, "Now, Darling," Pearl's mother stepped in, giving Laura a look, hoping she would remember the plan they already discussed before the wedding began. She had been observing the situation from a tenuous distance.

Laura glanced at her and remembered then stumbled over her words, quietly declining, "Oh, no, but I thank you." She said looking at her mother. "I'll ride with mama and papa"

Pearl figured there was some reason her mother didn't want Laura to ride with her and Frank, thinking her mom just didn't want her little sister to be a burden. Pearl modestly guided Frank's attention back to her, away from Otto and said "Frank, I think we should be going," and nodded to the coat rack behind Otto, suggesting it was time to get her poncho.

The young couple were the last ones in the church, still enjoying the excitement and energy remaining. Frank turned, giving his full attention to his bride, and bent over and gave her a loving kiss on top of her head before guiding her long, warm fur poncho over her wedding gown. The warm gift was from her grandmother Elliot and only worn once before her wedding day.

Joining hands, the newlyweds exited the church together as Mr. and Mrs. Frank Bunyard, and were surprised when they stepped out into an excited but frozen crowd. Loud cheers came from all directions. Grandma Duncan waddled over, losing her feet in the snow with each step, and walked up to her new granddaughter-in-law and gave her a warm loving hug, arms only reaching to her upper back "Herzlichen Gluckumsch" Grandma Duncan clucked.

Pearl caught the gift behind unfamiliar words. "Thank you, Grandmother." She might not know German, but she saw it in Grandmother Louisa's kind eyes.

Pushing through the crowd, Liam McFarling was driving a large graceful team of Clydesdales hooked up to a freshly polished black buggy that was adorned in white and light rose-colored satin ribbon blowing behind like it was late to the party, running to catch up. Abbie Jean stood nonplussed with mouth open wide staring, surprised by what she saw. She groaned softly to herself, watching her father pull up tight on the reins as he drove the massive team up close to where the married couple stood waiting. Bitterness filled her veins. She stood there tapping her brown leather boot covered with white fluffy snow, impatiently waiting for the crowd to clear so she could start home. Insecurely, scanning the group of onlookers once more, her heart jumped when a pair of familiar soft gray-blue happy eyes appeared before her.

Between looking at her and watching his brother escort his new sister-in-law up onto the buggy, Otto seemed genuinely happy today, dressed in a clean flannel shirt and new trousers. She wondered how much he had to drink already. Or maybe, she wondered, just maybe he was being himself without any drink, just like the night he found her walking the streets. Maybe he is really changing after all, and that thought slowly started to warm up her chilly jealous heart. She looked at him again and this time smiled back.

The cheering crowd soon cleared out and were on their way to the Silver Lake Grange where the reception was being held, or on toward their cozy homes for the remainder of the day. The weather was turning worse outside, and most of the farmers who didn't have ranch hands thought it better to get their livestock taken care of early on this stormy October Saturday afternoon.

The thoroughbred Clydesdale team galloped along, slowly taking their time while the couple snuggled together, warming their feet on steaming hot bricks beneath blankets on the floorboard. Not even the freezing wind mixed with icy-snow smashing against their rosy cold cheeks could ruin their afternoon. All Frank could think about was the night ahead, and as he looked into deep brown eyes the color of soft fur and knew she felt the same way.

Chapter Eighteen

Powerful chilly winds caused the warped old wood shutters to slam against the rough siding on the Granges exterior. Temperatures had dropped at least five degrees by the time the wedding was over, and the party had moved over to one of Silver Lake's oldest buildings.

Abbie Jean 's parents, Liam and Maeve McFarling, were good friends of the Bunyard's and wanted to give a nice wedding gift to Frank and Pearl on their wedding day, so they offered to drive the newlyweds to their home after the wedding dinner and reception. It was an extra special gift for them because the couple would get to spend the first night of their lives together in the comfort of their own home.

The McFarling family didn't leave it at that, however, they went the extra neighborly mile and made sure all of Frank's newly purchased livestock was fed, watered, and cared for so Frank could focus on his wedding with the reassurance that all of his animals were taken care of. Liam had always liked Frank and the two families had lived in the same town for many years. He was happy to help do what he could to make sure Frank and his new bride had a wedding day to remember.

The enormous Clydesdale team was moved into a stable across the street by Liam himself after he dropped Frank and Pearl off at the reception. He wanted the team to be close enough he could hitch up the carriage when the newlyweds were ready to leave. There was another large stable just behind the Silver Lake Grange where the guest's horses were cared for by a young boy Liam hired to help.

The ten-year-old kid was one of Frank's cousin's sons who lived close by. Abbie Jean's father knew the boy was slow at processing life, thanks to having a loud, abusive and hysterical mother and a father who'd skipped out when he found out his son was mentally challenged shortly after his birth. Liam had to be very explicit when giving the boy directions. Ira wasn't always a reliable kid, but would help Liam, who was kind to him. And Liam knew the kid tried to please everyone and always did his best, which Liam appreciated, so he cut him a break, wishing his mouthy, critical mother would do that same. Ira had a gentle and honest temperament Liam wanted to see continue to grow, so he nurtured his damaged spirit when possible.

Ira did as he was asked and was in the middle of brushing the horses and planned on feeding them next when he heard a haunting wolf cry from the outskirts of town that bemusedly overwhelmed him, causing him to shake. Ira mumbled to himself how much he hated wolves. They made his muscles tense up and his throat tighten. He swallowed hard and wanted to get his job finished and get safely inside with everyone else. He really, more than anything, wanted to watch the married couple dance. He liked Frank alright but loved watching his new wife; she was the prettiest thing Ira had ever laid eyes on.

Ira was working as fast as he possibly could on all the guests' horses, trying to do a real good job like Liam told him to, but the evening was quickly turning too cold before he could finish up brushing and feeding

113

every horse. He had hoped to be back in the Grange before now and was overwhelmed with a fear and loneliness that was as deep as the night was dark in the high dessert.

"You's gonna be jussssst-jjjjjusst, fiiinnneee gals." Ira's voice shook, his lip started to quiver, and the scared boy started to sob while he stroked the horse's thick black coat. He'd noticed that most of the horses had been agitated since they'd been put in the stalls and knew something wasn't right, and it terrified the hell out of him, making his eyes twitch with nervous reflection. He'd worked with horses all his life and knew they felt warnings humans couldn't. Whenever the animals got jittery, he promptly followed suit.

Shaking his head, not sure what to do, he paced until his knees locked up with fear and goosebumps covered his body. His head started to pound something fierce; he was so cold and so terrified he kept that looking at his surroundings, and felt something just wasn't right. Even though the young boy processed life slower than others his age, he had a special connection with animals, feeling like he understood them more than most. Frozen with fear, he stayed in one place watching the horse's reaction to whatever was causing enough nervous tension to fill every stall.

"Well tttthhhiis ainnnt'tt do-do-doin me no gooo=goo'd," Ira's frozen lips sputtered and spit trying to convince himself it was time to get moving and get out of there fast. The horses would have enough food and water, and as for brushing them, forget it. That was the furthest thing from his mind right now.

He took a long deep breath trying to calm his nerves and looked around the stalls one last time with both hands on his unsteady knees. "Stttop th=thh=thhaat!" Ira screamed at his body, wanting his legs to loosen up so he could run when it was time. That's when he saw something large move above him. Whatever it was crouched down low in the loft, where hay bales were stored, so it was hard to see exactly what it was. The oil lanterns rocked in the wind, causing shadows to dance all around the stable, confusing Ira.

Ira felt pressure from large, yellow canine teeth and felt hot breath on him before they tore through his jacket at the base of his neck where veins bulged, working overtime. He was overwhelmed by the intense pressure from the beast's heavy body. The monster was dragging the young boy across the stable floor with incredible strength. Ira tried to reach out and grab whatever he could get ahold of to stop himself from being dragged. The last thing Ira saw before passing out while the strong creature terrorized him was a beautiful young woman delicately covered in a dark wool overcoat and a matching fir cap walk through the Grange's front door, affectionately laughing with her date who was holding her gloved hand. What happened to be the worst night for a young boy was an amazing dream that was coming through for another.

Chapter Nineteen

itter cold air rushed through the door following Otto and Abbie Jean inside, playing a game of follow the leader. Fighting to get past the couple who just entered, it circled around the room taunting everyone in its path. Pearl slipped out a nervous laugh from the icy wind rushing up her wedding gown. She leaned into her new husband, holding onto the dried flowers delicately pinned in her hair, heads turned to see who was coming in late.

Otto was trying hard not to be the inebriated brother he was once known as. He was out to impress the townsfolk along with his family today. It was 'the first day of the rest of his life'. He'd heard his Grandfather say that before when he was lecturing Otto about changing his habits and controlling his life, but didn't understand the true meaning behind it until now. He repeated it to himself as many times as he needed to get through the afternoon. Otto was proud today, and it showed. Proud he wasn't hammered and proud to be with Abbie Jean. There had been lot of insalubrious gossip after the last time he was with her and, reflecting on that now, he was saddened he hurt her and her reputation. It was only right of him to do everything he could to make up for that horrible night. His demeanor was composed and methodical, squaring his shoulders, standing straight. From now on, it was important to him to show he was out to change any bad opinions.

Otto and Abbie Jean slowly scanned the room, looked at each other and shrugged, then gave one another a knowing smile. Abbie Jean removed her black leather gloves while Otto helped her out of her dark black, heavy wool coat and hung it up after shaking off the heavy wet snowflakes.

Frank gently pulled Pearl's arm and the two of them walked hand in hand up to the pair who had just entered through the grange's heavy door. "Otto," Frank exclaimed "You made it!"

Otto received Frank's handshake that turned into a brotherly hug. A smile worked its way around Abbie Jean's mouth. She leaned in and gave Pearl a gentle hug. It felt like the start of something new for all of them.

Pearl's face lit up, beaming with happiness, smiling from ear-to-ear. "Thank you for coming out to help us celebrate in this dreadful storm." Her face was warm with love for them both. "Oh, this is just wonderful." As the words flowed from Pearl's mouth, she bent towards Otto, giving him a sisterly kiss on his freshly shaven cheek.

Simultaneously, Frank and Pearl were both thinking how strange and different this day was compared to the previous time all four of them were in the same room.

"Well nigh, lookies waaat ye 'av 'ere lad." Grandfather's gruff voice bellowed through the Grange. He stood to greet the couple and show his appreciation for the effort Otto was making. "'Oy' bout I play me fiddle for yer." And he grabbed his finely-tuned instrument while Otto pulled out his harmonica and started playing alongside his grandfather. With excitement in the air, the reception picked up and soon everyone was doing circles, holding skirts up high, and kicking their feet to the tune of an old Irish jig. The room was quickly warming up and all the couples, families, and friends attending the small reception were making some fun memories together.

After a half-hour of dancing they took a break and granddad pulled Pearl aside. "Yer know Lassy, you're perfect for dat old boy roight dare," nodding towards Frank who was walking away from a group of old farmers he'd been discussing his recent purchase with. Frank's sparkling baby blue eyes had been eyeing his young bride the whole time the two were apart. Sparks were flying from across the room when their eyes met, setting off fireworks.

"You flirting with my gal, old man?" Frank asked, walking into the conversation. He was approaching his two favorite people. Frank reached for Pearl's hand and asked if he could steal his beautiful bride back from his grandfather for another dance. After George Duncan got a second wind he said, "Oi'm ready Lass," and he stood and yelled out, "Let's dance!" loud enough for everyone to hear, and grabbed his fiddle from the old country.

"Come on my dear Abbie Jean, Otto... Let's go." Pearl pulled at Otto with renewed enthusiasm, who turned and grabbed the cup of hot tea out of Abbie Jean's hand and set it down on the stained wood table, decorated with food trays, and they dashed out to dance. Everyone who could dance was out on the scuffed hardwood floor. Older folks watched the younger ones enjoy the fun, tapping their feet to the rhythm by clapping, cheering them on throughout the evening.

The long autumn blustery fun day was coming to an end, the guests were winding down, getting ready to head home. The bride's parents held hands as they watched the newlyweds climb into the carriage Liam McFarling had pulled around front for them. "Thanks again Mama, Papa!" Pearl searched the small scattered crowd "Everyone!"

The small group of family and friends who ventured into the storm outside to see them off cheered once more as Liam slapped the reins down on the Clydesdale team leading the carriage to the young Bunyard's new home. They were off, ready to begin a new life together as Mr. and Mrs. Francis M. Bunyard. But the night wasn't close to being over for Louisa, Electa Caroline, Aunt Elizabeth, and Sarah Emmaline, who had all the clean up ahead of them.

George Duncan leaned back against one of the old poles outside the building and watched the smoke rise above his pipe as he puffed on the sweet-flavored tobacco. Otto and his father, Jesse, were sharing small talk as the men-folk often did after the family activities.

"Otto, where ya living at these days, boy?" His father's words came out a little sharper than intended, so he tried to soften them up by quickly adding, "It was first rate of you to attend today, son. I know your brother was real excited you came."

Otto's astonished smile lit the dark night, thinking how nice it was to please his father for once. It was a rare moment the three generations were sharing. 'And for once,' Otto thought to himself, 'It's me getting the attention, not Frank.' And he smiled really big at that feeling, like he'd taken another corner in his new life and was rightly proud of himself.

The men were interrupted before they had time to visit very long. "Has anyone seen little Ira James?" George Duncan's niece, Eliza, asked with a hint of panic in her loud shaky voice as she stomped with purpose out onto the front porch, causing it to rumble.

Ignoring his dramatic, bantering cousin, Otto continued, "I'm staying at the same motel in Lakeview, working for old Fitzgerald's ranch there on the West Side." His father scratched at his whiskery jaw, listening to and impressed by every word. "I'm bettin' on moving back to Silver Lake soon and be Frank and Pearl's foreman out on their new ranch. We was gonna start hiring real soon, maybe three ta four hands."

Jesse struck a lucifer against the heal of his boot, blocking the strong wind from the match with his callused hands, and nodded approval to his son and sucked his pipe like it was nobody's business.

The men felt Eliza's bulging eyes while the wind guided fresh snowflakes swirling around them. Jesse turned towards his son's cousin, seeing she wasn't going to excuse herself from their talk until one of them at least responded to her. As politely as he could, Jesse finally replied. "No ma'am, can't rightly say I seen yer wee lad." Then spit tobacco juice over his left shoulders into the white fluffy snow and watched it sizzle steam into the cold night. "Mighty sorry." Her Uncle George and Otto mumbled that they hadn't seen Ira James either then went back to talking amongst themselves.

A couple of the men were all thinking the same thing, but no one would mention it out loud. They thought Ira James was just fine, somewhere playing in a corner alone, stuttering to himself as he usually did when forced to be in a large crowd, so they went about conversing and ignoring her. All except Grandfather Duncan, anyway.

Come to think of it, he hadn't seen the kid since earlier that day before the wedding. Then again, this could be a way for Eliza to get the attention she always craved. For some reason George had a strong suspicion his niece wasn't borrowing trouble this time. He sensed the heavy concerns she carried tonight, and her uncle quickly dismissed all the unkind thoughts he'd previously had about his petulant niece and asked when the last time she saw the boy was, which interrupted the conversation around them. He owed her at least that much. It wasn't the young boy's fault his mother was squalidly.

"Well now, Uncle George," she started out moving her large chubby hands in the air before landing them on her massive hips, "I reckon it was right after that beautiful wedding this afternoon. He was helping that odd little man, Mr. McFarling, with the horses." The men shifted where they stood, uncomfortable. "Why he is always pestering my little Ira James, I'll never understand." Her deep hunter green shawl fell. After noticing the uncomfortable look the men had, she quickly pulled it back up on her shoulders and tied it in front, covering up exposed cleavage, and continued, "He's a meddling bilk as far as I'm concerned. Now, big Ira, Ira James's' daddy, Ira James Cody the second, God rest his soul," she made the cross sign in front of her, "Said I was a fishing for a whole world of hurt if I ever said anything to upset that bug-eyed wife of his, Maeve McFarling." The buttons threatened to pop an eye out should the thread give way. "Why, she'd have the whole group of them at that woman's auxiliary club talking all hogwash about me and my poor little Ira James."

It was so hard for George, Jesse and Otto to keep up with her hands, mouth, and cleavage. Jesse rudely walked away before Eliza could fill her lungs up with air again. He'd had enough of her. Frank and Otto's father tolerated very little drama in life that he didn't have to, much less his wife's niece.

George looked over at Otto's shocked expression, his eyes as big as saucers watching Eliza theatric performance, and chuckled out loud.

"Well, Eliza. We'll git us a group tah-gether and search fahr de lad." George and Otto gathered some men and set a plan up, then split up, heading in different directions with lanterns held out in front of them leading the way.

Several men headed towards the stable to see if he was hiding in with the horses, figuring that was a good place to start because Eliza said he was helping Liam McFarling with grooming, feeding, and watering them. Everyone knew the boy loved horses and spent a lot of time out with them.

Otto and George started around the outside of the stable searching when Jesse branched off and went inside. Turning the corner, he sensed the horses' stress. It was apparent something had upset them, and he could feel it before he even saw their behavior. Looking up at them he tripped, stumbling over something. Lowering his lantern to the ground he saw a torn and bloody child's jacket. He picked it up, rushing to find the others, aware this was more serious than anyone first thought. They'd need to track whatever it was that took off with Ira and would need to hurry before it was too late and they lost the tracks.

Soon the men had a plan together, but before they could start out they were caught by Eliza again. Reluctantly, Jesse asked, "Is this here Ira's jacket, Ma'am?" Ice crystals were forming on his handlebar mustache.

"Oh, my boy!" Eliza screamed, attacking Jesse's arm. Her knees went weak. Concern and fear grabbed at her tortured heart. Between the frozen ground, new snow, and hungry wildlife, they knew the chances of finding Ira were limited, much less finding the child alive. There was a new storm heading towards Silver Lake as they prepared.

Sarah Emmaline wrapped her freckled grandmotherly arm around Eliza's fleshy body and gently guided her back inside for some hot tea and honey while the men worked on finding her boy. During what felt like a lifetime, no one said anything. Abbie Jean, Grandma Duncan, and Electa Caroline all rushed to assist the shaking upset mother.

Chapter Twenty

The temperature dropped frightfully fast, hitting record lows on Frank and Pearl's wedding night. New fresh snow was never safe coming down fast on hard frozen ground. Frank was worried about everyone getting home safe and thought about all those they left behind at the reception to clean up. He felt like he should be there, harnessing the horses and making sure the carriages transported the guests home to safety on this dangerous, frozen ground.

Liam tied off the reins and jumped down off the bench up front and tried not to slip. He unlatched and opened the carriage door for Frank, who then turned around and helped his cold bride down, whose face was wrinkled up frozen trying to avoid flying cold snowflakes coming at her. The couple repeatedly thanked the McFarling Mercantile owner for not only driving them home but being so generous and neighborly, starting them a fire and helping alongside a few others feeding and taking care of their livestock so they could have a relaxing, carefree wedding. Liam watched as the couple headed to their new home and smiled through chattering teeth to Frank, who turned and waved goodbye.

Frank looked behind him once again to verify Liam was upright, turning the corner on Duncan Lane heading towards Main Street, without the Clydesdale team or carriage giving him trouble. It was hard to handle powerful controlling beasts such as these without pulling a heavy metal carriage behind it, sliding on challenging icy roads, but Frank could see Liam had it under control, so he turned back to his new bride.

Closing the front door tight against the wind trying to force its way inside, shutting out the world and its frozen soul, Frank turned to embrace the most beautiful person he'd ever laid eyes on. She was all his now. With gentle affection he helped her remove the long heavy poncho she was wearing and hung it up close to the fire so it would dry. "You warm enough?" he asked his wife, moving towards the woodstove. Bending down, his knees snapped and popped in harmony with the wood stove when he tossed in extra logs.

"I am," Pearl responded, not believing how relaxed she was actually, when it seemed like she should be anxious or nervous. She walked up next to where he was kneeling and put a cold hand on his shoulder and massaged it for a moment. Flipping the lock on the wood stove handle, Frank stood and turned his body towards hers.

The fire sparked and crackled, throwing warmth their way. Pearl found his hand and lifted it to her soft rosy cheek, rubbing it in a circular motion. "Mmm," she purred. "Frank, I love you so," she stated, and leaned into the warmth of his body. Her voice was gentle and tender. He loved that about her. She wanted him as much as he did her. There was a burning desire filling up the space between them.

A comfortable smile worked its way around Frank's lips, confirming his happiness. He whispered back, "I love you, too," and, with more tenderness than he'd ever given anything in his life, he led the woman of his dreams, his new bride, to their bedroom for their first time together.

Frank and Pearl hadn't been in bed long when there was a loud and urgent knock on the front door that felt like it would wake the devil himself. "Who'd you s'pose that is?" Pearl held onto the warm quilt comforting her. She wasn't asleep yet, but was relaxing and snuggled up to her husband's firm warm body, thinking about how wonderful the day had been and overcome with love and emotion for the intimacy they'd just shared.

Frank looked worried, knowing that type of knock meant business. Something bad must have happened if they came calling on him and his new bride with a severe snowstorm out there.

Instant regret set in when Frank left the warmth of Pearl's ardent body and the comfort of the heavy quilts over them. Sitting at the edge of the bed in his long johns, he hastily threw on his clothes, pushing tired feet into cowboy boots. He turned once to look at Pearl, who gave him a worried, apologetic shrug before he headed through the bedroom door and quickly opened the front door, curious to see what was going on.

Wet inhospitable wind and snow invaded the small ranch house. A cranky "Burr" escaped Pearl's lips when she jumped out of bed once she heard familiar voices. Rushing around the room in her ribbed cotton gown, she found her robe and pulled it on then headed to the front door where Frank stood listening.

Her new brother-in-law, Otto, her Uncle Will, Grandfather, and her own father were getting men together for a search party, her Uncle Will told Frank. He shared the little information with Frank he had, knowing he was a good man and they would be able to count on his help. Even better, they knew his sweet new wife would support him leaving her on their first night together to search for the missing boy, and would do whatever she could to assist the family in finding Liam.

Pearl shivered from the cold, moving her fingers through her thick wavy long brown hair, knotting it behind her head before handing Frank his rifle then kissing him a long, hard goodbye. "I will have ham, hotcakes, and coffee ready for you and the men upon your return. You will find Ira soon, I just know you will." She was pushing the words out of her mouth, not wanting to say goodbye like this to her new husband of only a few hours, but knowing she didn't have a choice. No one wanted to be out in the harsh numbing cold weather, she was sure, but especially not a hurt, challenged, innocent child who more than anything needed to be found alive.

Pearl pulled the thick drapes back on the living room's large front window and watched as all those strong, brave men she loved so much saddled up, freezing cold but determined. Frank's horse was already saddled and ready to go by the time they woke the couple up. "Father is always thinking ahead like that," she mumbled to herself. A smile crossed her glum face. Frank turned around and looked in at her high up on his horse, giving her his full attention before riding off as if to say he was sorry. She stood there alone, feeling the enormity of it, and waved to their backs.

Leading a pack horse with supplies, Grandfather turned the corner out on to the main street, following Frank. Pearl wished she could have fed them and warmed their bodies with strong coffee before they left, but she knew no one would be able to sit long enough to eat. They would only worry about getting out there and searching. Now was the time to find fresh tracks and uncover the old ones. "Oh," Pearl sighed heavily to herself, lowering her shoulders, "This is just dreadful," and she wished she was with her parents at their new home, not here at hers alone.

Her heart lightened a little, setting down the picture of Frank she had been staring at after they left. It was a gift he gave her before the wedding. She set it down on the slightly crooked nightstand and leaned back on the bed, running her hand over the quilt she was lying on and stared up at the ceiling.

It was the very quilt she had worked on for so long. So many hours spent thinking about an unknown future that was ahead of her when she was still living in Eugene City. It was the quilt she traveled with to her new town, Silver Lake, and the very one she'd hid in her trunk up until now. "I never thought I would be married to such a marvelous man," she whispered to a quiet cold, lonely room. The time they'd known each other had been short and their courting brief, but their love for one another would always be strong, she knew.

Pearl dressed and splashed cool water on her face from the basin that was sitting on a small parlor stand, before combing her hair into a tightly wrapped bun atop her head. She went to her new kitchen and lit a couple more oil lamps and candles before she found her apron. She wrapped it around her thin frame, feeling the coolness of the empty little house settle around her. She couldn't deny she longed for the warmth of her bed and husband beside her. She found herself even missing Spot, who had jumped up on Frank's horse as they headed out. Spot always sat atop Juniper like he was the king.

Eager to have the rest of her stuff unpacked, her kitchen washed, cleaned, and the wood floors scoured, she wanted everything done before Frank came home. Adding more kindling to the cook stove to start some fresh coffee, she looked around and started a mental plan of what she needed to accomplish, but the morning would first need something warm to get her started.

A few hours later the sun rose from the horizon, the sky was clear and full of possibilities. It was a peaceful quiet morning after a terrible storm. Thick snow covered the landscape. Pearl found herself sick with worry and fatigue as the morning slowly crept by. Cleaning up the dusty, mouse-ridden, abandoned house was nothing compared to the stress and constant unease she experienced when no one had come calling with information.

Feeling pure exhaustion, she sat down and got comfortable in the old wood rocker next to the stove near the front of the window's warm, bright sunlight welcoming her. She took a deep relaxed breath and looked outside to see if anyone was coming. Heavy, tired brown eyes started closing as she finished massaging lavender oil into her sore, blistered hands, and then took another sip of hot lemon and honey tea she'd just made. She rocked, relaxed, and sipped, then looked around the clean room and smiled. Proud of what she accomplished, she finally closed tired heavy eyelids and slept.

Later when she woke, she reached over for a log when sore muscles screamed pain. Slowly she grabbed a couple logs to throw in the crackling old wood stove that was hungry for something to burn before resting. She was grateful for Liam, who took care of making sure they had enough chopped firewood when he started the fire the evening before. A terrible thought filled Pearl's heart and mind when she shut the gray iron doors, latching them. It was probably little Ira James who chopped and stacked all the wood for them before Liam had him help with the horses.

"Oh dear, that poor child!" Tears swelled in her worried eyes. Leaning her head back she heaved a heavy sigh for all the unknown frustrations she couldn't control while the rocker gently guided her back to the nap she desperately needed.

Chapter Twenty-One

Waking to an awfully stiff and kinked neck was the least of Pearl's concerns when she opened her eyes and finally focused. She'd been sleeping so hard. The chill in the morning air from letting the fire die down was only minor compared to the cool, aloof, mysterious black eyes that were staring back at her. Shocked and surprised, Pearl came out of her rocker at once, dropping the afghan to the floor. Panic quickly rose in her throat, trapping words from forming as she scooted back as far as she could without hitting the wall.

Who was this Indian in front of her, looking at her with such intensity it was surreal, yet she began to feel like she knew him? Where did he come from and why was he there in her house? Had he been watching when Frank left and planned to attack? Why was he looking at her in this familiar way? She was outraged and extremely offended by the way he just stared. She could feel him reading her soul. Fear and concern finally helped Pearl find her voice.

"What do you want with me?" she demanded, trying to use force if she was going survive this unwanted intruder in her house.

"Me," the Indian replied, pointing to his chest, "Have hurt child." Thunder Cloud nodded towards the only bedroom in the small ranch house.

Keeping her eyes on him, her head turned in the direction he indicated and soon her eyes followed suit and she saw slight movement on her bed where the door had been propped open. It hit Pearl like a ton of bricks. "OH MY!" she yelled at the top of her lungs and ran to the boy. Thunder Cloud, who stood with such ease and grace, seemed amused by her excitement.

Taking just a few short steps, Pearl was in her bedroom, looking at the young boy's torn and bloody, badly bruised small body. Feeling grateful he was still alive, but at the same time sick to her stomach over the thought of what the child must have encountered, made her feel queasy.

"Ira, dear?" With shaking hands she lifted his hand in hers and crossed her other hand over the top. He was cold. "Can you hear me?" She had met the boy a few times before and had witnessed his unusual character as he played in the streets by himself, but honestly didn't notice him much at the wedding. Now she understood why.

The injured ten-year-old groaned. "Yes," and tears slid down his swollen face. Once opened, his eyes darted from Pearl to the Indian back to Pearl, before resting them on the wood windowsill, where a large violet-black crow sat cautiously watching.

Ira groaned again and Pearl wanted to check his injuries, hoping the men would come back soon so they were not only safe but could get a doctor out to her house— the sooner the better by the looks of Ira. It looked like some broken bones and miner stitches, so far. The boy was lucky. Ira opened his tired light golden brown eyes again and looked away one final time. He wouldn't lock eyes with anyone again the rest of the day. She was sure he sustained injuries you couldn't see with the naked eye. Pearl turned back to say something to Thunder Cloud in the front room, but he was right behind her. She'd never even heard him approach. Sensing that she wasn't only safe in this man's presence but that she knew him, she let her guard down some. There was something so familiar about his behavior and movements. When he was watching the crow outside, she snuck a peak at him, inspecting every mysterious feature on his body, amazed by what she could see of his tribal tattoos on his thin frame.

Before Pearl went to fill the water pitcher, the Indian gave her a basic summary of what happened. Out scouting for food near town, he followed a male cougar into the stable behind the grange where the reception was happening. He explained how he knew the boy was in there, so he wanted to make sure he was safe but not scare him. By the time he got there, the animal was gone and so was the child, so he followed the tracks, and after killing the cougar the storm came in with such force there was no choice but to get him to shelter out of the worst of it so he could be safe until he could find somewhere to take him. Pearl understood by the way he chose his words that he was unsure where to take Ira. He couldn't let anyone see him; it was too dangerous being seen in town, especially with a hurt child. After he got Ira to a safe shelter, they hunkered down until morning while he treated his injuries with nearby herbs he made into medicine. It was the best he could do with limited resources and help.

"How awfully kind of you to care so much. My husband and some other men are out looking for him right now."

The Indian smiled at her. He thought she was nice, and was a good fit for Frank. Pearl gave him a kind smile and said she would be back in a moment; he could have a seat and she cleaned off the chest at the end of the bed for him. She was going to get them some water and supplies to start doctoring the boy. When Pearl returned the boy was the only one in the room, his eyes were shut and looked like he may be in a comfortable rest. She didn't want to disturb him. She laid a tattered, worn-out quilt over him. The Indian had vanished, but how? She hadn't heard a footstep, a door, or even a window cracked open.

Scanning the room again, she turned to check the front room when movement out the bedroom window caught her attention and she turned back to see several crows flying away.

Pearl stood there in the room puzzled, holding a bowl of water, gauze, and some supplies under her arm. She smiled at the mystery of how he entered the small house and then disappeared a hero. She was so happy Ira had been found and was alive, now all she had to worry about was the men getting back safely and getting word out to the doctor and Ira James's mother.

Pearl set the supplies down on the bed next to Ira and headed back to the kitchen, leaving Ira to his much needed rest, and just started getting things together to make some broth and tea when she heard horse hoofbeats outside in the front yard riding in, and was thrilled to hear Spot's barking as they got closer to the house.

Now that the blizzard had quieted down, Silver Lake could finally get back to cleaning up the damages and take care of livestock and property. The teakettle spit and sputtered coffee aroma throughout the house, drawing Frank and his granddad inside, tempting their taste buds. Pearl saw them walking up the steps and let out a huge sigh of relief and looked up to the heavens above, giving a silent prayer of thanks. The glowing smile on her face said it all. The sun went to work adjusting itself above the clouds, setting off beautiful warm rays sprinkling happiness on the day ahead.

"Frank," Pearl couldn't hold her relief and excitement in. She ran and jumped up into arms he held out for her. "I have the grandest news for you!" she exclaimed.

Frank's frozen hands held her out in front of him at a distance that spelled concern. Grandfather was greeted by her with a kiss on the cheek but still stood nonplussed by her happiness and excitement at a time like this. They still had no boy and found no tracks or a body to bring back. The heavy snowfall covered everything, working to their disadvantage.

Grandafather and Frank started to question Pearl when they heard a groan come from the bedroom. The men concurrently turned to look at one another, then gradually walked to the bedroom and stood staring at the bed, dumbfounded by what they saw. "Ira James!" Frank exclaimed "Well, I'll be damned. Am I happy to see you boy!" Ira just groaned with swollen eyes and drool slipping out of his mouth. It was agonizingly apparent that the pain was a lot to bear for the child.

Grandfather was relieved to see him safe and sound, but couldn't help cracking a joke to lighten the mood and got to laughing at himself. Frank saw that sparkle in his eyes and quietly asked, "Old man, what's so funny at a time like this?" Grandfather couldn't resist, and Frank knew it. "Lassy, 'how'd yer like sharin' yer marriage bed on yer weddin' noight wi' another paddy?"

Frank chortled and they both turned to Pearl to watch her reaction, and then smiled at one another like little boys who just got caught. It was just as they suspected; Grandfather received a red-faced glare which made the guys laugh even more.

She ignored their fatuous snickers and went about the room cleaning up, tucking the beds sheets in and checking Ira's fever one more time while she waited for them to compose themselves. "Old man!" She pretended to reprimand Frank's grandfather, smirking under her scold as she wagged her index finger his direction. "Frank and I aren't worried over how the mattress should be used our first night together," then motioned to Ira, "When this poor lad has been injured and is now laid up." It was Frank's turn; she turned her wrath on him and finished. "We are far more worried about keeping him alive than making more little lives."

A proud smirk covered her face as she turned away and went back to the task at hand like the men weren't even there. 'As tired as these men should be, they're still men!' Pearl thought to herself, listening to them hoot and howl for several more minutes before she shooed them out of the room and reminded them of the sick child in the other room. Although Frank was enjoying the entertainment, especially after being out in the cold searching on his worn-out frozen horse all night, he admitted to himself that he was a little shocked by what his new wife said, but knew that's what made him love and respect her even more. She wasn't witty very often but when she was, she was on fire, and he enjoyed every minute of watching her shock others with her comebacks.

Weak groans came from the bedroom again, alerting Frank and Grandfather Duncan that Ira James's mother needed to be notified. "He's in pretty bad shape."

Frank warmed his hands by the woodstove while Grandfather sat down on one of their only chairs, the rocker, and relaxed his cold, tired bones before breakfast, enjoying a few puffs on his dark pipe.

"I see you met Thunder Cloud," Frank exclaimed, sure that his wife had already figured it out. Pearl came around the corner holding a bowl against her stomach, beating eggs, and asked, "So that was really him?" Smiling to herself she knew it had to be, but wasn't a hundred percent sure at the time.

"He's a quick one. Had to learn how to be safe around Silver Lake after the Modoc War and when hiding." Frank rubbed his rough red hands together.

"After we eat I'll head over to my folks', where Eliza is staying, and that will take care of letting Otto know he and Papa don't need to meet up to go lookin' again. If you want to head in and let Doc know Ira is injured, he'll need a buckboard to carry the poor lad." Pearl then remembered her father and uncle had been out there searching too, and asked Frank and Grandfather about telling them. "Eye, grand idear. I'll stop by and let yooehr Pa and uncle know."

Chapter Twenty-Two

A s if to confirm what he was thinking about, Frank turned around and found Pearl already looking at him. "I wonder how many marriages start off as fun and exciting as ours was?"

Pearl was sitting next to the oil lamp on the small maple wood table. It was only their second night together; both were hoping it wouldn't be anything like the first. "Frank, I've been wondering all day about Thunder Cloud." She re-positioned herself so she could get a close look into his tired blue eyes "Where does he stay if he's not on the reservation, and how on earth did he know how to help with your cousin or where we live?"

So many unanswered questions she'd been thinking about, remembering his intense obsidian eyes and the way he stared at her when she woke up. She didn't have time to do anything but care for the poor injured body until help arrived and they transported him. Once the sheets on the bed were laundered and the house spruced up, Pearl spent the rest of the day helping Frank around their ranch house, fixing doors, and cleaning out dark cooled spaces for their vegetable storage. They had so much to do still and would need Otto's help if they were going to make progress before a harsh winter took over as it did every year in Silver Lake.

"Well, my wife, what do you say we retire for the night and put this day behind us. I am plum worn out." Frank held out both of his strong calloused hands to help her up. She gladly allowed him. "Would you like me to answer all those questions as we ready ourselves for bed?"

As if to say 'Of course!' Pearl offered a great big smile. Frank had been feeding the wood stove all day, keeping it warm in the small ranch house. She didn't shy away or hold back when he led her to their bedroom, where he slid her work dress off her tired body and put a long cotton night gown on that offered warmth and comfort.

"There," Frank's soft and tender words tickled her ear as his gentle hands released the tight bun from her hair, making her heart skip a beat. Shaking it out, she rolled her head around side to side, relaxing and freeing the day's tensions. Her freed hair let off a light romantic fragrance of lavender, tantalizing Frank's nose, arousing him, and he murmured "Mmmmm..." and nudged up next to her, causing a strong ache and desire for him in her groin.

Once he was in bed tucked in close, Thunder Cloud's story was about to pick up where it left off while Pearl relaxed her head against Frank, letting her hair cover his chest as she laid against it, listening to his heartbeat. She loved lying next to her warm husband who was lovingly stroking her shoulders and lightly caressing her arms as she listened to him pass on the stories his grandfather told him. Sharing time together in bed, they talked and relaxed and, when feeling like it, explored one another, giving intimacy time for comfort and reassurance. Before the story started, a strange noise distracted Frank, but instead of startling Pearl he pretended everything was alright and continued.

Chapter Twenty-Three

"You ou mean to tell me that Captain Jack killed one of my best soldiers?" The Klamath reservation Agent was outraged. A stunned Private Collins was thinking about what Thunder Cloud had done to his friend and comrade as he watched the offensive behavior unfold before his eyes. "You boneheads! Letting Wintoka out of your sight and then cowering to those filthy heathens! How could you?"

Before Frank got too far into the story, he looked down at Pearl, making sure she was still awake. She peered up at him relaxed in his arms, with an expression on her face that she was waiting to hear more, when Frank said, "Agent Knapp was one of the vilest Indian Agents in the west. He was known for his hostile and disrespectful treatments towards Modocs, Klamath, and the Piute from the Lakeview area. He was a terrible man and had a passion for inflicting pain and misery on them." He finished up telling her how he felt, moving his fingertips up and down her soft arm. After softly kissing her sincere and inviting mouth they got cozy side by side again as husband and wife, best friends and lovers. Frank picked up where he previously left off.

Afraid for his life, Private Collins stood facing the angry giant who towered over him, scared of what was coming next. Collins, already shook up because of the danger he just faced, barely escaping with his life up against all those Modoc warriors they didn't expect to challenge. Making them mad was not a real bright idea and he couldn't understand why getting Wintoka back was so important to this mean, arrogant monster they called Agent Knapp. She was just some girl who was kicked out of her family and tribe.

They should let her go; besides, why should they care what these red niggers did and what happened to them. His mind was drifting with his own thoughts when he remembered that Agent Knapp was talking to him. "NO SIR," he yelled out, standing at military attention, straight as an arrow.

"No SIR...WHAT?" the Agent snarled and spit thick dark chunks of chew into the young soldier's face, causing him to flinch.

Keeping his shaking knees from buckling, the affronted soldier answered with a stern voice he forced from the back of this throat. "NO SIR, it wasn't Captain Jack that killed and scalped Private Abbott, SIR. It was Thunder Cloud, a strong young brave that is Captain Jack's cousin and Wintoka's lover."

Agent Knapp whipped his head around the room, fire filling his intense eyes as he stared at Private Collins. The agent's red face looked like it was about to burst into sweltering hot flames at any moment hearing that Wintoka had been with him. Before the young soldier knew it there was a horrendous pain in his ear drum when he hit the corner of Agent Knapp's desk on his way to the floor. Agent Knapp shook his hand out. It instantly went red and started to swell up. "Get him out of my sight!" bellowed the petulant agent to another soldier who had been observing

141

from a safe distance around the corner. "I will take care of that chief myself, once and for all—and his fool cousin!"

Finishing up with what was just business to Agent Knapp, he yelled out behind him "Private Davison!" and before he waited for an answer, he finished up his demands, "Saddle up my horse and get someone to handle Abbott's burial, have a letter on my desk ready to sign and be sent out when I get back. I'm sure his kin will want to know their lad died a brave soldier." Agent Knapp's puffed up, red faced, and barked out orders he expected to be carried out with precision and accuracy.

Stepping over the Private he had just knocked out, the agent let his mind wander to the beautiful young Klamath girl he was trying to get back under his care and custody. He didn't care one bit that her family kicked her out. He knew better than anyone that Wintoka's family would never take her back. They would rather see the sun turn black and bathe in a river of blood before they saw the daughter who once belonged to them and now disowned forever. There was no forgiveness for what she did.

Agent Knapp wanted his hands on her, at any cost. Just as quick as he thought of Wintoka's soft, silky caramel skin and long, straight black hair, piercing dark eyes that lured him in, he got mad all over again at Captain Jack and how he was always meddling. He remembered Captain Jack's old man, who was just as bad years before when he was chief.

"Pearl?" Frank paused. "Love?" A quiet snore interrupted the rest of the story, the part of the story he was excited for her to hear. Frank was comforted she was asleep, however. He knew she needed lots of rest after such a busy day with the wedding and the reception and then the worry

142

over Ira James missing, not to mention the scare she must have had with Thunder Cloud and Ira James left here in their bed, hurt, for her to have to care for and deal with. He was proud of his new wife and how she handled the chaos of the recent events and knew she was the right one to live on the ranch they had plans to build together.

After watching her for a few more minutes, Frank leaned in and kissed her soft relaxed lips and pulled the quilt up over her, and then slid out of the warm bed without disturbing her. He quietly grabbed his clothes off the arm of the chair then moved towards the door and shut it. That nagging feeling gnawed at him to check the property one more time.

He was out the door with his colt revolver tucked in his trousers and high boots over the top of his wool stockings, checking the perimeter of his house and outbuildings. He felt an unnerving worry in the pit of his stomach and couldn't let it go. The sound of ice crunching under someone's feet caused Frank to turn around. The bright full moon lit up the icy snow all the way up to the main road, where he saw a figure coming towards him. There was something familiar about this person's walk. He seemed to want Frank to know he was headed his way by the noisy steps he was making. At once Frank noticed who it was and knew why he felt that push to go outside and check the property and why that nagging feeling was bothering him.

The men's eyes met, and a feeling of gratitude and appreciation passed between them. Frank startled Thunder Cloud and himself when he grabbed his upper arm and pulled him into a gentle fold of appreciation, shaking his hand. Thunder Cloud's prodigious smile lit up the bright stars in the dark sky. "Thank you," Frank said, releasing any tension Thunder Cloud, or Frank, may have still carried before this evening.

For the first time in both of their lives they felt like they were on comfortable ground as equals, no stress hiding behind any motives, just pure friendship spread out before them. "Are you alone?" Frank asked him as the men stood face to face in the frosty October night. Thunder Cloud nodded. Frank was curious as to why he was here. "Do you need anything? Are you hungry?" It was too late to invite him in for something to eat, but he felt he should do something for this man who risked his life for his cousin.

Thunder Cloud's dark eyes scanned the perimeter then nodded towards the house, "The boy?"

Frank looked in the same direction, meeting Thunder Clouds eyes and shook his head back and forth. He saw that Thunder Cloud was worried about the young kid and was asking about him. "Oh, I am sorry." The question on Thunder Cloud's face fell, Frank immediately realized Thunder Cloud misunderstood so he corrected him. "Oh…no….I mean he's fine, or will be, but he's not here anymore. My grandfather and the boy's mother took him to the doc's house in Lakeview, where the doctor kept him for evaluation. He has some deep cuts that will need to be stitched up and watched for infection, and what looks like some broken bones, but he is alive—thanks to you and your bravery."

Thunder Cloud smiled, happy the boy was alive, and looked down at the ground, relief written all over his cold face.

"I killed her." His thick Modoc accent made his English sound choppy. Frank wondered what it was that tried to kill his cousin's son.

"What was it?" He asked.

"Cougar, very big one," Thunder Cloud responded with a tinge of pride. The men found it easy to talk to one another. Frank was curious about something and decided to ask, "You brought my cousin here to my house because you didn't know where else to take him?"

Thunder Cloud nodded, agreeing, then asked, "Me scare Sn'eweets?" Mixing English and Modoc together he motioned his head toward the house again. Frank was perplexed over what he could be asking and gave Thunder Cloud a questioning look. "Your Sn'eweets? Your woman?" He waited a second, trying to remember the words he was looking for in English. Thunder Cloud asked again, nodding towards the house.

"Oh," Frank understood now and smiled, "My wife. Her name is Pearl. Yes, she is my," then paused, "New wife." The words felt strange on his lips. Frank smiled, and Thunder Cloud noticed the spark he saw in Frank's eyes were of a man who was deep in love. He remembered the look he once had when watching Wintoka and the love that overpowered every other possible emotion. The pain of losing her still tortured him and grabbed at his broken heart.

"Scared?" Thunder Cloud asked, and nodded his head towards Frank's small ranch house once again, where he saw Pearl looking out at them with a warm quilt tightly wrapped around her tired body. These uniquely different minded men stared in her direction as the bone chilling cry from a coyote bounced off the surrounding mountains and sent a chill up Frank's spine.

By the look on their faces it was obvious. They both chose to heed the warning signals and move on calling it a night. The two men shook hands that renewed loyalty and a friendship they would embrace in years to come. "Thank you, again. You did the right thing and we owe you." Frank put his cold hand in his coat pocket. He had always known Thunder Cloud as the fiercely brave warrior, who was twice his age, and had a gentle side he didn't show too often. Tonight, was one of those rare times however; he wouldn't forget about. It was the beginning of a trusting relationship neither had seen burgeoning.

Spot was out of his doghouse and up on the porch wagging his tail as Frank headed back towards home. The faithful dog waited patiently for his return, knowing there was the possibility of a head scratch. Climbing up the icy steps, Frank felt the stress of the previous night's search fighting the cold blizzard and the long day they'd just had settle in. The last thing he remembered of the day was the way his new bride snuggled in towards him when he got back home and entered their warm bed. Tomorrow would be another day to share Thunder Cloud's life story.

"Awww," Frank sighed. 'This is heaven,' he thought to himself as his head hit the pillow.

Chapter Twenty-Four

Thunder Cloud, Captain Jack, and all of the warriors slipped out in the middle of the night. A previous tribal meeting among elders made it clear this would be the last time they moved. Setting up traps and preparing to deceive the soldiers and Agent Knapp was all the braves cared about right now. They would be ready for not only the army but for when their women, elderly, and children traveled to meet them at the lava caves.

Back at their home everyone was busy packing and preparing to move from the immaculately built wickiups that had been their homes for the last several months. A black incandescent bird looked down at something simmering over the fire pit from her perch high above. Her round beady eyes followed the beautiful female below with straight black hair pulled back in one long braid, stirring the pot as thick steam drifted around her. The boding crow twisted and turned her head sideways, allowing her small coal black eyes to relax on the thick stew the young woman was preparing for her husband's family.

The crow was desperately trying to get her attention. "Caw caw," echoed as two more black birds swooped in, crowding the leader, mimicking her caws. Ignoring the birds presence, the determined young woman below was afraid to look up at them, much less into the leader's all-knowing eyes. Wintoka knew they were visiting the wickiups for her sake, and their presence was making her nervous.

The glistening black-winged birds were on a quest, which was causing Wintoka to have powerful emotions and choke up. The soon-to-be mother was feeling far from herself these days. She was feeling woozy from the unfamiliar pregnancy hormones and needed to sit down for a spell. Today wasn't the day for this kind of spiritual quest the Crows were trying to guide her towards. She needed to keep going.

Moving forward. It was important to conserve her strength and not give in to grief and melancholy, but she knew she must listen to those who were giving her the gift of insight. When ancestors come back to help, they were doing it because they cared and for the concern and overall wellbeing of the clan.

Re-braiding her hair, Wintoka chided herself for being rude and disrespecting, momentarily forgetting the clan's cultural and spiritual path, she finally opened her heart. Gathering some kindling, she added small sticks to the tripod fire, keeping the temperature even the whole time she cooked. She wasn't one to typically worry, and most of her life she had been known as the spirited young daughter of the powerfully strong and intimidating Klamath war chief, Hunting Bear, but that all changed months ago when she was disowned, forced out of her clan and off the reservation by her own people. Somehow it left her feeling vulnerable, especially that the relentless Klamath Reservation agent was after her, now more than ever. That didn't help her insecurities.

The cawing became louder above her. She set down the cooking paddle she was stirring the stew with and shielded her eyes from the sun to look up. She was shocked when she saw how many more crows there were now filling the sky above her.

Overwhelmed by the disappointment she felt she was to them and to herself, Wintoka gave in to her frustration and violently screamed up at the birds, "Cheet-ake-awan!" and with tight fists rolled up in a ball and a burning throat she sat down and folded over like a tortilla wrapping herself in grief and anger. Grandmother White Bird heard what happened when she had been wandering from wickiup to wickiup, making her way towards her grandsons' wife, and she saw scared black wings flapping wildly in the air. Wintoka busied herself after the outburst when she saw the gentle frail old grandmother coming towards her, embarrassed at her behavior.

The troops were coming onto the Modoc's land by the hundreds, marching under Agent Knapp's command, trying to force Captain Jack and his people back onto the reservation again. The year was 1872, and for several years now the Modoc clan had been pushed around by several different groups of people; first it was the righteous and selfish settlers, Ben Wright's murderous group among them killing many innocent Modocs.

Wintoka heard Thunder Cloud's grandmother close by and looked up to see white-streaked long gray hair that poked out of the blanket Grandma White Bird had covering her head and body. Wrapped loosely and pulled together in the front, she walked slowly and methodically to Wintoka, who needed her more now than ever before. Gently, the old woman held out her soft, wrinkled, cold hands to her frustrated granddaughter-in-law and pulled her close, giving her a reverent hug before guiding her to sit on a large fallen log where Wintoka's tripod fire sat warming their mid-day meal. Cold settled in as the clouds spread out above, covering the sun from giving any warmth, leaving an unnerving sensation behind to hover.

Still holding Wintoka's hands, warming them up as they sat huddled close together, she listened close, and without introduction, Grandmother White Bird went right into it.

"Maidikdak and her two daughters lived in the south. The old woman knew that five chiefs lived in the north, with their father, who was a chief, too. She wanted her daughters to marry those five brothers, so she made them ready for the road. To one daughter she gave a basket of food; to the other beads, nice shells, and porcupine quills."

Wintoka relaxed, finally, and rested her head against her shoulder, feeling like she was a little girl all over again when Thunder Cloud's grandmother would share old Modoc parables passed on from one generation to the next. She was the clan's storyteller, and the kids couldn't hear enough stories. The little Klamath girl was always the first to run and sit on her lap to listen. It was Wintoka's favorite part of the childhood she left behind and missed. Her eyes started to burn; her heart stung. Small tears spilled over watery eyes. Overwhelmed with how life was changing she decided to stop thinking and just listen. She knew Grandmother was trying to share something important with her, and that she needed to focus and not let her mind wander. She sighed, looking at all the little kids who came running and sat around Grandmother White Bird's feet to listen. Watching her every move with big brown round eyes, they were ready as she continued:

If you see a man coming from the east, you will know he is Wus. Don't stop to talk to him. He is a powerful man; he can do anything he likes. If he gets mad, he will turn you into an animal or a bird. Don't go on the west side of the lake. Follow the trail on the east side.' The mom was clear on her directions." Wintoka pictured Agent Knapp as Wus and hated this character already. After all, Wintoka knew 'Wus' was the Modoc word for fox.

"When the girls came to the lake, the west side looked nicer, the trail was brighter. The elder sister wanted to follow it, but the younger sister said: 'Our mother told us not to go on that side.'

The elder sister said: 'You can follow the other trail if you want to. I am going on this trail; it is nicer.'

The younger girl didn't want to be alone, so she went with her sister. When they passed Wus' house she was frightened. She said: 'I feel as if somebody was looking at me.'

'I feel that way too,' said the elder sister. Presently they saw a young man coming toward them.

'What nice girls those are,' thought Wus.

When he came up to them, the younger sister said to the elder: 'Don't stop. Go right on. This is the man our mother told us about. Don't speak to him.'

But the elder girl stopped. Wus made her stop. The younger went on a little way, then she turned back; she was afraid to go on alone.

'Where are you going?' asked Wus.

'To the chief's house,' said the elder sister.

'What chief is there out this way? I am the only chief here. I am the chief of this world.'

'You are not the chief we are going to. That chief never travels around. Our mother told us there was a bad man on this side of the lake. His name is Wus; he doesn't smell good.'

'I know that man.' said Wus. 'He is not bad. He has power and can do anything he wants to.'

'We are not going to stop here,' said the elder sister. 'We are going to the chief who lives in the north and has five sons.'

'Go on, if you want to,' said Wus. When the girls started, Wus watched them till they went out of sight. He was saying things in his mind. As they traveled, they became old women, with humps on their backs; their bodies shriveled up. There was no flesh on their bones, they could scarcely move. Their hair turned white, and their teeth fell out. Their beautiful clothes turned to dirty straw, their strings of beads were twisted bark, their baskets looked old and broken and the roots in them turned to moldy skins, The shells and porcupine quills were bits of bark.

The younger sister said: 'We didn't go the way our mother told us to. That man was Wus; he has done this. If we had gone on the east side of the lake, we shouldn't have met him. We should have done as our mother told us; she is old, and she knows more than we do.'"

Wintoka was starting to see why Grandmother chose this story to share. She was trying to teach her that it was important to listen to what the crows were telling her. They knew, they were wise and given the gift to guide by the creator. Even though Wintoka didn't want to leave yet because they weren't ready, it was important to get to the warriors and warn them about the soldiers. But there was more, she knew. Grandmother White Bird always had several hidden messages wrapped up in one fable.

"After a long time, they got to the chief's house. The five brothers were out hunting. The chief didn't know what to give the women to eat; he thought they were too old to eat roasted liver (old peoples food). When he gave them some, they pushed it away. They lay down to sleep, and while they were sleeping the five brothers came. They knew Maidikdak's daughters and knew who had made them old.

153

The youngest brother asked: 'Did you give these women anything to eat?'

'I gave them liver,' said the old man, 'but they couldn't eat it; they haven't any teeth.'

The young man was glad they had come; he sat down and watched them. About midnight they turned to beautiful girls. In the morning, when they woke up, they were old women again.

The chief said to himself: 'what kind of a man is my son? Why does he stay by those dirty old women?'

The young women heard his thoughts and they felt badly. At last they crawled up and went out to wash in the river. The elder sister said: 'If we swim, maybe it will make us young again.'

They took off their clothes and old torn moccasins and began to swim. Right away they turned into beautiful girls; their long hair floated on the top of the water. As they swam, they talked and laughed, for they were glad to be young again. They made fun of their father-in-law and said: 'That big chief thought we were old women; he fed us liver!'

The young man heard this and said to his father: 'You fed those girls dirty liver. Did you think they were old women?'

The girls kept diving down in the water and coming up, and soon they began to change. They became green-headed ducks and floated off toward home. The young man felt badly; he didn't want them to go.

Old Maidikdak heard them coming, and when they were near the house she said: 'My daughters, you didn't do as I told you. I told you about that bad man. If I hadn't this would be my fault; now it is yours.'

She tried to catch them but couldn't. At last she went under the water and caught hold of their legs. She pulled off their feathers and they were girls again.

The next morning the young man said to his father: 'I am going to carry my wives' clothes and beads and porcupine quills to their mother.'

When he got to Maidikdak's house the two sisters were off gathering wood. The old woman saw him sitting on top of the house and she asked: 'Who are you?'

'I am one of the five brothers who live in the north.'

'Are you the youngest?'

'Yes, I have brought back your shells and porcupine quills. Wus changed your daughters to ducks.'

'Come in, son-in-law, my daughters have gone for wood.'

The young man was glad. When the girls came, he said: 'I have left my father and brothers. I will live here now.' Ningadaniak."

Grandmother White Bird stood up slowly, shoving Wintoka's hands away from helping her. Stiff and painful knees popped and cracked as she started to move. She stopped and pulled her blanket tight around her old, frail body, then did something that surprised everyone watching. With renewed vigor she lifted her walking stick up above her head, pointing it towards the sky and, with unbelievable strength and determination, she began chanting a prayer of thanks to her ancestors who sat atop the wickiup and trees watching her after several reverent moments. Then she went on about her business, humming softly to herself as if nothing had happened, picking up where she left off before she told the story. She went back to wandering from hut to hut again, chewing on her gums, working them back and forth until spittle dripped from her open mouth. Wintoka felt as heavy as a buffalo sitting there, quietly trying to concentrate on her plan, the one she knew Grandmother laid out before her.

Putting her cold hands on her growing stomach, she thought about Thunder Cloud's baby and knew what she must do, and she would need to do it soon to save their warriors who needed her now. They were in more danger than they knew. She needed to get to Captain Jack and the warriors to warn them they didn't have as much time as they thought. Soldiers were on their way and coming fast.

Chapter Twenty-Four

"They have been close by all morning" Nina whispered under her breath as her daughter-in-law walked up next to her.

"I know. I saw them too," Wintoka replied while helping Nina line the baskets with straw and tule leaves so they could carry the food they had already made.

"I saw our ancestors were visiting you, yes?" Nina waited to see what her daughter-in-law would say. "Yes, and you saw Grandmother tell me one of her stories?" she responded, already knowing her husband's mother knew. Nina nodded her head yes as she tore the tule apart with her teeth. "She is telling me I must do what is hard for me and what the crows tell me. They are old and wise and know better than I do," Wintoka said with pride in her voice.

Her mother-in-law noticed and smiled, nodding her approval. She looked up while working to see soldiers surrounding them everywhere. "They think they are sneaky like a snake and don't know we can see them. They underestimate us Modocs!" This especially infuriated Nina. Wintoka could tell by the way her nose twitched and the harsh tone she used when she spoke. "Watch us with eyes like the hawks that hover over their pray, waiting to pick them apart. I am sure those soldiers enjoy watching us women, our elders, and our children while all along knowing they are here to war with us and we are alone now." Nina had seen it too many times before.

A terrible thought then hit Nina. "What if it isn't just the soldiers out there? What if that boastful Agent is watching, trying to take you back to the reservation again? Wintoka! We must leave what we cannot pack up this moment and go, for your safety." The women knew they needed to move quickly.

Nina went around camp letting everyone know it was time to leave, whatever they could not finish packing up and gathering in those few precious moments they would need to leave behind. "Gmocatk. Come Grandmother," Wintoka put her arms around the disoriented worried Grandmother. Over the last several months Grandmother would change from time to time, and you never knew which woman you were talking to. One who was witty, smart, and alert, telling folktales while loving all the little naked children running to sit with her; or the Grandmother who was in front of her right now, confused, scared, upset, and with no idea who anyone was or why they were packing. She didn't want to leave her home. The last time she moved with them into her son's wickiup was the last time she was moving; she knew it back then and knew it with an even stronger conviction now.

Wintoka stood watching Grandmother White Bird struggle with internal conflict, wondering how she could help her when movement behind her caught Wintoka's full attention. Beyond a large fallen Ponderosa pine several yards away was a stout thoroughbred carrying a shaggy blonde-haired red-faced lump of a man, with a long grungy beard and small bronze binoculars fixed to his eyes. The trained stallion sat very still under the man's heavy weight. Grandmother White Bird squinted up into the unfriendly grayish sky above, feeling the sharp wind rush by, and pulled her blanket around her tight. She watched as a hawk circled overhead, it's long golden wings unmoving. It was riding on the currents, searching for its prey, and knew something bad was on its way.

Panic rose in Nina's throat when she turned in time to see Wintoka running towards her. The pregnant woman forgot all about Grandmother White Bird or what she was saying to her when she'd spotted the one person in the world who had total control over everything her Modoc family and tribe did. Knowing he was coming for her and that all the warriors were at the lava caves, voice cracking with fear, she quietly told Nina she would head out first with Thunder Cloud's younger brothers. They were only a couple years younger than him and would be good protectors for her. Taw-Kia, Captain Jack's cousin, volunteered to stay back with Nina and distract Agent Knapp and any soldiers that may figure out Wintoka was missing among them and go after her.

Everyone was informed of their part, ready to act with a plan in place, they continued to pack and prepare for a quick move. While plans were being made and excitement filled the camp, grandmother White Bird meandered from wickiup to wickiup looking for a place to lie down and relax. She was exhausted from sharing her story with Wintoka and the children.

Chapter Twenty-Five

Laura was about as warm as she could get, all snuggled and sound asleep in the back of the covered wagon, with warm bricks and heavy quilts securely tucked in around her. She was exhausted. It had been a big day for her, riding all the way to Lakeview with Pearl and Frank. She would have gone anyway for the adventure, but was feeling extra lucky because her sister made sure she got time to visit her new best buddy, Ira James, who was staying at a nursing home for elderly and developmentally disabled and those recovering from injuries and surgeries like his. Even though a little more than two months had passed since the attack, Ira still required care at the nursing home.

Frank was anxious to get the work started on Otto's bunkhouse and replace the livestock shelters that were dilapidated. He knew taking the extra wagon and horses would slow them down, but he didn't have a choice. They had to stay with friends overnight anyhow. Time was flying by and the seasons were changing fast. Fall was already behind them and Christmas was just around the corner.

"That poor young girl," emphasizing her words Pearl sympathetically shared her feelings with Frank regarding Wintoka. "That was a lot to take on for such a young pregnant wife." Especially after all she had been through.

It was nice to spend some quality time together being able to hear more of the young Modoc couple's world. Life was busy for Frank and

Pearl, getting used to their daily routines and married life, but Wintoka and Thunder Cloud were never far from Pearl's mind. She felt them, wondered about them, and worried over them while doing her chores throughout the day, especially since she'd had the chance to meet Thunder Cloud. She was even caught daydreaming about the young Modoc couple as she was in a conversation with her mother or at their quilting gatherings. They were a part of her life now, and she felt connected to them as much as Frank had always been.

Pearl sat quietly staring out at the beautiful but cold white snow as it drifted towards them. Finally finishing her sentence, "And to find out Wintoka was with child and living that nomadic life. Oh, I just can't imagine, Frank. Those people being displaced and having to move all the time, they didn't deserve that." She unconsciously let her own hand slide onto her stomach deep in thought. "Burrr," she whispered. "I'm so cold." A shiver slipped into her poncho and up her back, causing her to shake. Still holding her stomach, she could see out of the corner of her eye that Frank's head was turned her way, studying her every move, eying her from stomach to face with a questioning look. She felt his demeanor change as they rode. 'Oh no,' Pearl feared, 'I can't let him know just yet.' And as inconspicuously as possible she moved her hand away.

Hearing voices in front of the wagon where she was lying, Laura slowly woke up from a dream-like slumber and rubbed her eyes, as icy cold wind brushed by her. They were pulling up to the house just as she sat up and yawned, 'It's the perfect time to cut off any questions,' Pearl thought with a tinge of relief for the distraction; she hoped Frank would forget what he saw.

161

Throwing off the heavy quilts, sensing the awkwardness between her sister and brother-in-law, Laura rushed up to Pearl and leaned against her. "Is everything alright sister?"

"Oh yes, puddin, everything is just fine." Taking a deep breath Pearl paused before adding "I'm just freezing cold and wish I was sitting by the fire right now. Don't you?" and gave Laura a sweet tender hug. Embracing the young girl seemed to calm both their individual fears. The horses snorted and stomped in protest of the coming storm. "Tell Mama and Papa hello for us, and let them know we will take care of the extra wagon they let us borrow and get it back to them just soon as possible." Pearl's soft gentle finger tapped the tip of the little girl's cold nose and finished instructing her sister. "And we'll get together for a visit soon. Alright my girl?"

Laura nodded to her older sister and hopped down with Frank's help.

Pearl was nervous to be alone with Frank now, her stomach filling with butterflies by the second. She was sure he'd figured it out by the look he gave her. She didn't mean to put her hand on her stomach; it was just an instinct while thinking of Wintoka and the hardships she was experiencing while dealing with a difficult pregnancy. She felt Frank's eyes on her again. A jangle of nervous energy tore through her, making it hard for her to stay still. When she finally worked up the courage to look over at him, she knew he'd been staring at her. A surprised but teasing crooked half-smile and his warm blue eyes sparked with unquestionable happiness. The adorable, innocent look he gave Pearl made her snicker out loud.

"So, it's true then?" he finally spoke. She nodded her head and told him she'd missed her monthly twice now since they'd been married and had been sick almost every evening, hoping he didn't notice with everything going on with the ranch. She was stressed and worried he would be unhappy about it.

The two of them then started laughing and by the time they got control of their trepidation, Frank pulled her so close to him she could feel his warm, shaky body and said, "Come here woman." Pearl didn't even care that the blankets slid off her lap or that she was shivering uncontrollably, and totally forgot all about the bitter chill circling them when she heard what he said next. "You have made me the happiest man in the world!" It was something she would remember the rest of her life. He was so kind and loving when he spoke, his voice gentle and concerned. She couldn't help but melt at the sound of it. "I didn't think it was possible to feel any luckier than I already do with you as my wife but now," he paused for what felt like a long time, "We're going to have a family, Pearl." A huge smile lit up the world that surrounded them.

Relief washed over her. She'd been so afraid he wouldn't want children so soon when there was an overwhelming amount of work to be done on the ranch. Things would be hard, and they would need help, but for now she could sit back and breathe a little easier, knowing that he not only knew about the pregnancy, but he was thrilled to have a baby and start their family.

Holding Frank's hand, watching him smile at her, she knew this man next to her would support her through life no matter the challenge.

Leaning back against the hard wood bench she took in a deep, relaxing breath. Subzero frosty wind filled her lungs and she let out a sigh of appreciation.

✦

Chapter Twenty-Six

Two young, petulant soldiers were left to watch over the clan's property a few days after the Indians had abandoned their homes and headed towards the lava caves to meet their braves and warriors who had been there preparing for battle. The scoundrels who were sent by their commanding officers were instructed to set the wickiups and huts on fire, making sure nothing was left behind. Scattered around the Modocs wickkups were broken belongings and debris, evidence of a quick escape. The soldiers each grabbed a stick and went to pilfering what was left, piecing together the Modoc's story of their lives that was gone forever.

"Hopkins!" Private Jacobs yelled up over the top of a small wickiup that probably housed a newly married couple or a small family. "Catch." But before Hopkins could look up to see what he was talking about, a flying tule moccasin smacked him upside the head, knocking his kepi hat off his head, upsetting fiery bright red hair.

Madder than a wet hornet, he yelled, "You dimwit, you hit me with one of those cherry nigger's slimy sandals, God-damnit-all." Hopkins spread out his thick freckly white fingers and precipitously ran his fingers through his hair, trying to put the curly red strands back into place, making Private Jacobs laugh out loud at his friend's foolishness. Hopkins had distinct full hair, this was true, but the way he primped it made him the laughingstock of his brigade. He fussed over it more than a teenage girl preparing for her first date.

Hopkins shot a glare towards his comrade and grabbed a stick he found from a tripod his horse kicked over just moments before. Private Jacobs jumped out of the way of Hopkins stick as it came swirling towards him. "God, you can sure be a blowhard Hopkins," Jacobs yelled, moving out of the way.

Furious, he followed him into the dark wickiup. As the soldiers entered, they heard a dry raspy sound close by, making them forget their bantering. Hopkins put his finger up to his lips to shush Jacobs until their eyes adjusted to the dark and they could see clearly. Both were afraid but neither wanted to admit it. Jacobs left eye blinked rapidly followed by several nervous twitches.

The mid-morning dew was lifting, and the winter sun drifted by when Private Hopkin's threw down the small stick he had been carrying around and picked up a large blunt piece of wood, making his way to his partner who had just finished lighting up a cigarette.

"Hey, bone brains." Jacobs threw his partner a look offering him one of his cigarettes as their eyes adjusted in the dark confined space.

The private shrugged before thinking twice then shook his head, "Naw, I'm good."

The raspy moan was heard again, sending chills up their spines. The two friends moved closer to the door where they froze in place. Alarmed, they shot quiet looks of concern to each other. "This place is really starting to freak me out," Private Hopkins whispered to his comrade. He was standing as straight as a gun barrel, rigid, nervous, and suddenly felt he needed to use the latrine. Jacobs puffed harder on his cigarette, trying to decide where the noise was coming from, when they heard an American Tree Sparrow answer her mate's call in a branch hanging over the wickiup where she tenderly covered three small eggs in a sheltered nest.

The snap of a twig inside the wickiup sent them spinning, Jacobs dropped his burning cigarette. "That ain't no animal, Jacobs!" he screamed. "Well, I'll be dammed!" And as if on cue they both moved back slowly when an old woman shuffled under the dried tule mats.

Private Hopkins' eyes were fixed on his buddy who was shouting, "Oh good God! Look, it's mammy Modoc." The ignorant young man nervously laughed as words flew out of his bemused mouth, spitting a large chunk of chew in her direction as the old woman before them started chanting a Modoc death song. The jangle of nervous energy made it hard for them to stay still. The wise grandmother knew what was coming and expected the worse; she'd been mentally prepared for it, and started chanting a song that would help calm her as she was dying, giving her strength to go with honor.

It was clear the old grandmother was senile and ready to pass on. The young soldiers witnessed just how bad off she was when she slowly crawled out towards their voices, getting their first look at her. A thick milky white substance, giving a ghostly appearance, covered her eyes when she looked at the soldiers. Grandmother White Bird had one leg in this world and one in the next.

"Hey granny, you were left behind, weren't you?" The reckless soldier went from stating the obvious into a song he thought would be funny.

"Aw, you poor old ugly thing ain't ya, granny?" He slapped his hands, emphasizing the word granny to the tune of Yankee Doodle Dandy and jumped up and down with renewed energy, making a game out of it. Entertaining his buddy and comrade, private Jacobs danced around her with an enthusiastic spring in his step as Hopkins watched. "Lost her family and don't know what to do." Then holding his hand over his heart giving his best performance, chest puffed out he finished with, "Oh....this poor old ugleeeee grannnnny," and reached up to the sky, screaming into the clouds the last words. Both soldiers howled and laughed so hard they nearly fell over. They were having more fun than they could have imagined being in the west on assignment out in the middle of Indian Country.

White Bird was terribly exhausted, taking her lasts breaths, which infuriated them. They wanted to be rewarded with a reaction. They looked down at her and saw she was immobile and just lay there, not crying, not talking or begging, just indifferent to everything going on around her. That's when the soldiers saw red and the kicking began. They took turns, squealing like the pigs they were, delighting in all the fun. Private Jacobs lifted his leg and slammed it into her side. Then Private Hopkins took a turn and disappointment set in when the young men only heard air escape from her lungs when administering the harsh blows. She was a remarkably strong and brave grandmother whose spirit was ready to say goodbye. She refused to play into their game and make as much as a peep knowing it would excite them.

Thinking they got bored, she breathed in relief and peace when she heard her abusers finally walk away. Taking a deep breath, White Bird relaxed and fell into a comfortable rest where she dreamt of strong black stretched-out wings guiding her across the cloudless open sky, where she proudly soared for all below to see. A few minutes later she was jolted awake and felt disappointment when she realized she was still alive.

The soldiers weren't talking. She couldn't hear anything and was so tired, fading in and out of time and life. Something made a 'humppphh' sound as she felt the weight of it fall upon her back. Her lungs tightened, crying for air, they were full of dust and smoke, making her thirsty. She couldn't remember the last time she had something to drink. Swallowing wasn't an option with all the smoke now. She knew she must just lie still and be as quiet as possible, it would all be over soon, but she couldn't help the desire to hum. It was time. Her death song got louder along with the weight of something else being dropped on her. She picked up the distant sound of drums she heard from the other side and followed it. Staying strong, the loving, forgiving, and kind grandmother felt her family's love and strength as they came to her, one by one, to lead her to the spirit world.

Reaching out to feel around her she touched the hungry flames burning through the tule mats, aggressively searching to consume her body. The pain wasn't like anything she'd ever known. The ringing, drumming, and chanting in her head got louder and more intense with purpose. Her spirit was spinning, circling all four corners of the earth. The whole time White Bird was feeling her body on the outside, she was seeing herself on fire below. She was already gone, just as the soldiers laid their last tule mat on her burning body.

"That should do it." Wiping his hands on his United States uniform, Private Hopkins told Private Jacobs who was stirring the burning tule mats around, making sure each one caught fire. The stench of her burned body overpowered the air around them. The soldiers finished up with the burning of the tee-pees and wickiups and kicked over anything and everything that would allow them to let loose of their guilt and anger all at the same time, as they walked away from the dreadful, horrific mess they'd just made.

Riding their horses back to camp where they would brag for days on end, Hopkins and Jacobs laughed and joked about the fun they'd had when a loud cry from above forcing them to look up. High overhead a gentle golden eagle with black piercing eyes circled, making sharp tight movements. Time slowed the soldiers' heartbeats and quieted their mouths as dozens of shiny black winged crows escorted the soldiers back to their command post, the emancipated eagle leading the way.

Chapter Twenty-Seven

Traveling was hard going for the pregnant mom and her two brother-in-laws, who headed out hours before everyone else, stopping only twice for a few minutes of rest and sleep. The boys took turns guarding her, taking their job seriously while Wintoka napped when she couldn't push on. They needed to get to Captain Jack's stronghold to tell them how many soldiers were coming and get her to safety away from the sinful grasp of Agent Knapp. Before they could reach the group, however, they were seen by guards Captain Jack had posted everywhere. Word was quickly passed around through the chain from one warrior to the next so by the time Wintoka, La'as, and Pony reached Captain Jack, Thunder Cloud, and his father, they were prepared and ready for Agent Knapp and his bloodthirsty soldiers. It gave Wintoka time to slow down and not rush the rest of the way, which was a nice respite. She was cramping and sick most of the time on their trip over the two days it took to travel.

It was strange for Wintoka to feel like her world was slipping away. She had always controlled her situation and felt empowered by her new tribe. The mood was dark and the evening dreary as they approached the camp the next night. The warriors had been preparing for their first of many battles with the United States army.

An excited Thunder Cloud approached Wintoka, thrilled to see her, glad she was safe, he wrapped his strong arms around her from behind. Being with his wife and feeling her body against his again was so rewarding. It was the first time she'd smiled over the last week and she turned around, allowing relief to wash over her as she fell into his gentle welcoming embrace. The tired young wife laid her head down against his chest and inhaled a breath of thankfulness for his strong presence. Feeling the warmth of his body against hers was doing her a world of good. She needed nothing more right now, nothing less.

Wintoka thought of her baby, all snug and safe in her stomach, and felt the dependable love from her Modoc brave made her ache for stability. She was grateful for this moment of attention and much needed love and affection, knowing it unfortunately wouldn't last too long. The joy from his embrace was lost on everyone around them, making the young couple feel alone long enough to sustain them.

Two days later the rest of the clan showed up at the stronghold and was informed on what was happening now that the Modoc war was officially under way. The first night they were altogether again with everyone under one large cave. Everyone, that is, except Grandmother White Bird, who had been searched for as far back as a day's ride to see if she fell behind. With no luck they were forced to give up and let her spirit go in peace, knowing it's what she would have wished for.

Bellies were full, and the warriors got support and hugs from their women and children before Captain Jack called all them together in a circle for council. The guards who had been posted throughout the lava caves also attended the meeting with information they'd gathered. They found that their biggest enemy since day one, Agent Knapp, was pushing soldiers forward. Little by little, step by step, the dirty leader was trying to force his men past the four-hundred-yard perimeter Captain Jack set.

While the warriors counseled, their families were getting settled in. A small cave bat swooped down in front of several little kids who were bent over laughing at one of the animated dogs, who was rolling around in some old dusty coyote bones. A little hand tugged on Wintoka's snug deer skin dress with shredded tassels. She looked down to see a little brown-eyed girl who'd escaped from the group of kids. The sweet child looked up to Wintoka, pleading for some attention.

"NuNu," Wintka whispered, watching the little girl. NuNu wrapped both her hands around Wintoka's legs and whimpered. Her sister-in-law's heart melted. "Ginaatdal'gepgi. Come up here." She pulled the two-year-old up and embraced her. She loved Thunder Cloud's little sister, but sometimes those big brown eyes made her long for her own younger sisters and it was all she could do to compose herself and keep the grief from consuming the memories she was forced to leave behind.

NuNu squeezed Wintoka's neck one last time before being set down on the lush green fern that carpeted the cave's hard cold flooring. The cave was so immense it would comfortably fit the almost one hundred seventy men, women, and children. The little girl took off after her big brothers to watch the tribes Shaman, Curly Headed Doctor, wrap the cave's perimeter with a long red-dyed tule rope. It was promised that everyone who passed through the cave's entrance was protected from the white man's bullets.

He was fascinating to watch, and the children followed him wherever he went because he practiced magic, which they revered as sacred.

Captain Jack was informed that there were dozens of white army tents springing up on the outskirts of the lava beds and, after much thought, he announced, "We celebrate being together tonight." Then looked around from warrior to warrior before adding, "Tomorrow we battle and send the blue coats back to Boston!"

All were in agreement, and for the first time in weeks, and now all together with family and their clan, an unusual excitement filled the chilly air.

"Rose, come." Captain Jack indicated he wanted his daughter and only child to sit next to him. He was still in the large circle of warriors discussing plans when he found his large eyed, round faced, shy girl sitting alone, scratching pictures into loose rocks and dirt with a stick he'd sharpened for her.

The grandmothers were watching the babies and little ones, helping them gather supplies around the caves that they could use during their stay. While teaching the next generation their secrets, almost everyone had Grandmother White Bird on their mind, knowing now she must have chosen to stay behind and prepare herself in quiet to go to the next world, where she would watch over those she loved and guide them best she could during these difficult times. The old woman must have felt she would slow the tribe down ,and knew it was time to make her decision. She was not openly discussed again, only missed and thought of. It was time to move on, and tonight they would celebrate her life and everything she gave of herself, along with preparing for war and asking the old spirit Chief Kumash for strength in battle. The warriors broke up council, feeling good about their plans, and passed the pipe around a couple of times, making sure everyone had a turn showing unity in all things.

Rose sat on her father's lap, getting some rare attention and love from him this evening while he spent some time enjoying and admiring her sweet, quiet demeanor. Rose felt her father's eyes on her and turned towards him, and with chubby five-year-old hands she reached up and gently touched her father's cheeks. The little girl lovingly smiled then, returning the quiet affection between them. Captain Jack laughed out loud and picked her up and carried her over to his younger wife, who was also Rose's mother.

Evening settled in and darkness fell upon the lava caves. Wintoka, who'd rested up and felt better both mentally and physically, and Taw-Kia, who was all ready for a pow-wow, started the dance around the large fire in one of the caves not far from where they'd set up camp. Bellies full, spirits renewed, it was a great feeling to be all together again. Thunder Cloud, Captain Jack, and Diami led the powerful and all-knowing spirits to their war dance as great plumes of smoke rose into the still calm air. The large fire, made with sagebrush, greasewood, and juniper, crackled and hissed as waves of excitement sent sparks of electricity around the cool winter's evening. Quiet drumming coming from a small group gathered in a circle away from the fire began getting louder as the war dance intensified.

Soon others joined in, and within moments most were feeling their progenitors' spirit soaring through them while they gave their worries over to those who walked this land before them. As they danced, bare feet felt the sacred rhythms, and with hands held high above their heads the warrior's chanted war songs while the women danced in circles, swaying their hips, waving their arms and, together in the strongest of unions, they called forth strength from the war gods and ancestors.

On the outskirts of the lava caves dozens of small fires were keeping soldiers warm. Most had either gone to bed on the cold frosty night, leaving the rest to relax, smoke their pipes, read, or talk amongst themselves in unified groups. But regardless of the activity chosen, they all heard the same thing: Captain Jack's band of Modocs, who were preparing for battle. Jingling sounds from dark bare feet pounded the dry dirt below with lances made of shells and dried scalps, long brown, blonde, and black hair still connected to the shrunken skulls, the sounds could be heard for miles throughout the army camp.

Agent Knapp thought it ghastly, although he'd heard it during ghost dance ceremonies on the reservation, but never with as much fright and intensity from the drums and war dance as there was tonight. No. This was different he had to admit to himself. It would be a miracle if anyone slept that night, but one thing was for sure—they would never forget the intimidating and unnerving sounds the Modocs made calling forth native spirits that chilly January night.

Chapter Twenty-Eight

The following morning brought a new set of problems and concerns as the men awoke after a rough, sleepless night. Thick fog rolled in just before the break of dawn, and the soldiers were turned around and confused where Captain Jack's stronghold was. Worried about where the battle would begin, panic set in among the large platoon. Many wanted to return later when they could see better and gain a better position on the enemy, but they were ordered to continue with their battle preparations. Against better judgement and bad gut feelings they followed the directives from their chain of command and moved forward into position.

In the meantime, fathers and grandfathers helped paint the warriors' faces, preparing for the first battle of the Modoc war. Thick black lines were drawn on heavy white paint covering their faces, making the warriors ferocious looking but, more importantly, they felt fierce and invincible on the inside. How one felt when preparing for battle was powerful. Their chief, Captain Jack, learned it from his father, who was chief many moons before his son, when the white man was just beginning to fight them for their land. Power of the mind was a great tool when fighting the enemy, whether the enemy was white, Indian, or the soul within in your own body.

Captain Jack, Thunder Cloud, his father Diami, Captain Jack's uncle, and the rest of the large group of warriors stripped themselves of most of their clothing and tied thick rawhide around their knees, ankles and wrists. This would not only protect their bodies from getting torn up on the sharp jagged lava rocks, but also give them an edge on the enemy by helping them move fast, making it seem like there were more than sixty warriors to the Army's almost three hundred.

On the morning of January 17, 1873 the army advanced in thick dense fog and unfamiliar territory among strategic, skilled Modoc warriors, who went to great lengths to protect their women, children, and elderly who were huddled in secured caves where they were protected from enemy gun fire.

Agent Knapp was among the soldiers commanding orders to mostly young and immigrant soldiers who listened to his uneducated nonsense directing them to shoot. Artillery rounds were bouncing off lava rocks everywhere, giving away their position. Captain Jack made a bird call to Thunder Cloud, who was crouched low, shielded behind a passageway, signaling him to move to a different post. The warriors moved around under the nose of the army who thought they were fighting five times the warriors they were because of this intelligent and unified tactical plan.

Newspapers all over the country shouted the Army's lost battle, infuriating Agent Knapp even more. As soon as it was over the women scavenged the dead soldiers for things they might be able to use while the men took all the ammo and rifles, which helped them build a stronger defense for the next battle.

Chapter Twenty-Nine

"Laura, you must focus, dear," Electa Caroline tried telling her youngest to speak up and practice her lines. Pearl and Electa Caroline were trying to help Laura memorize her part in the Christmas pageant, which the primary children had been working on. The Silver Lake Ladies Auxiliary Club had planned it for Christmas Eve this year, and Laura was thrilled that Ira James would be home in a few days and be able to stand next to her as Joseph.

"I am sorry mama. I am just so excited!" Uncharacteristically, Laura stretched out her arm and theatrically spoke to an imaginary audience and with built-up energy ready to explode, she practically yelled, "I can't believe Mrs. McFarling chose *me*!" The excited ten-year-old was on top of the world, dreaming of how much fun she was going to have acting the part of Joseph's wife, and in front of everyone she'd come to know since moving here to this small farm town. "I never would have been given this chance if we were still living in Eugene City." The sweet young Laura squealed with honest exuberance that neither of the women staring at her with eyes as big as saucers had ever seen displayed in this unusually shy girl before.

Laura was small in stature for her age and always wore her long silky light brown hair braided down her back. She was usually so quiet that it was hard to believe this was the same child. The dreamy little girl twirled into her mom and grabbed her around the waist, hugging her tight. "Thank you, mama." And before either of the women knew what was happening, Laura grabbed the bucket on the kitchen floor and was out the door on her way to feed cold, hungry chickens who'd been impatiently waiting for their fodder all morning.

"Burrrr," Pearl said, pulling her sweater around her waist as the door closed. "Hope she doesn't catch a cold out there doing her chores." Pearl adjusted herself on the wood stool, cutting the crusts off the pies she and her mother had been baking all morning for the Christmas party auction. The toasty warm house seemed to hug her as she sniffed cinnamon mixed with apples and nutmeg, a scent she had always loved, one that reminded her of cozy fun Christmas holidays together and fascinating stories her parents shared before heading to bed on Christmas Eve. Pearl always missed her younger brothers this time of year, and knew her parents felt their loss too.

Electa Caroline gently interrupted Pearl's private memories by asking how she was feeling these days. "Are you tired honey?" Her mother tried to remember what it was like being pregnant. "Or craving anything?"

Pearl was relieved they were alone. It always was a little uncomfortable to her when others talked openly about pregnancy and such things. Electa Caroline wasn't as old fashioned as her own daughter when it came to the truth and experiences in a woman's life. "I guess, a little of both." Pearl paused thinking about how she was feeling.

This was the family's first year spending the holidays in Silver Lake and it was turning out to be one of their best Christmases ever. The excitement in the air was as thick as a toasty marshmallow swirling around in a warm cup of hot chocolate. The upcoming Christmas pageant was the talk of the town. Everyone in Silver Lake and relatives from the nearby farms made it a priority to attend this extra special holiday event. It was a tradition as old as the hills. All the old folks sat around sipping dark coffee, sharing stories about the old days and catching up on all the new gossip around town. Other than the Fourth of July, it was one of the only times they had to visit without stress from farm chores and could truly relax.

The women had been baking pies all week and working on helping Laura with her part, and it had been a nice chance for mother and daughter to catch up. Since Pearl had her own home now, Electa Caroline missed her presence terribly. She was incredibly proud of Pearl and the way her life was going and she truly adored Frank, loved him like a son, but Electa Caroline and Charles terribly missed having their eldest daughter around. Missed her calm, and loving demeanor. Missed the adult conversations she equally enjoyed with both of her parents. Pearl was smart but also had compassion for others and helped a lot with Laura, who often needed special one-on-one attention that took a lot of extra time neither parent could always dedicate or had the forbearance to give her.

"Darling, sit for a spell while I get the house cleaned up." Electa Caroline bent over and picked up several books and a knitting basket that were taking up space on the old creaky wood rocker that sat by the warm wood stove.

"I'm sorry, but I am plum worn out, Mama." Pearl yawned, quietly exhaling, grateful to put her swollen feet up.

Electa Caroline leaned down and swiped the stranded wisps of hair to the side of Pearl's forehead that were always loose, and said a silent prayer of gratitude for this daughter in front of her that would bear her first grandchild. Grinning from ear to ear, it was written all over her face that she was excited to be a grandma. Electa Caroline walked away and started in on the mess in front of her. The men would be home soon enough, and daydreaming about grandchildren would have to be saved for another day. 'Enough lollygagging for now,' Electa Caroline thought to herself. It was time to dig in and get her kitchen in some kind of order before preparing dinner.

Chapter Thirty

"**I** don't know about you, Frank, but I am famished," Otto yelled over the 'eeemmuuu' sounds coming from several annoyed sheep who wanted their feed. The men were trying to rebuild one side of the barn that was leaning so far over that if it snowed any more it would tumble to the ground and probably crush several sheep. The guys were trying to salvage what they had to work with to keep the cost down and save time.

Frank's in-laws invited him and Otto over for dinner, so they were trying to hurry up, as both men were starving. It was the last time they'd all be together before they celebrated the holiday at the Christmas pageant on Christmas Eve a couple of days away. Electa Caroline knew how hard the men had been working and how determined they were to accomplish shelter for the livestock, even if it meant they worked straight through the day in this bitter cold and harsh weather with little rest.

Frank yelled back over the loud animal noises, "Same here, Brother! I'm hungry enough to eat one of these here sheep."

Otto couldn't believe what he then witnessed when he saw Frank grab one of the lambs and leaned down, putting his arms around the bulky animal and bit a mouth full of fur, acting like he was taking the bite out of the mangy animal. The two men laughed and continued to laugh until their sides ached with more than just hunger pains.

Otto playfully slapped Frank on the back, the men still in fits. "You're killing me, no more!" Otto gasped for air, "I can't witness any more sucking face with your girlfriend." Trying to get air, he leaned over and put his hands on his knees. Still wheezing and gasping for another breath while he jested, "Enough is enough." The men were giddy with unfamiliar discomfort from long days of hard work and delirious from hunger. "Come on, Frank... Let's go get us some grub."

The brothers shut up the barn doors best they could and headed over to where Pearl had spent the last few days cooking and baking with her sister and mother.

The family was already sitting around the table when the men showed up. Steaming hot plates of mouthwatering yams, cornbread with sweet butter dripping off the crunchy edges, and a large round of roast beef surrounded by a mixture of colored greens Electa Caroline and Pearl gleaned and canned not even three months ago from her sister-in-law's garden before they moved into their new house.

"You outdid yourself, Mother." Frank said, leaning in to lightly kiss her cheek, still getting used to calling her mother. The men sat down to join the family. Pearl felt a warm hand over hers under the table as her husband slid into the open place next to her. She held on to it tightly and squeezed it back, then leaned her head over onto Frank's shoulder, showing her appreciation and love for him.

Charles quietly watched the interaction between them, appreciating what he'd just witnessed. He really liked Frank and was getting to know him well, appreciating him like he would have a son, and besides, Charles enjoyed watching the jovial fun the two brothers shared when together.

Charles wanted to hear all about the repairs and building projects and what they were working on. Dinner passed with easy conversation and friendly talk about the goings on in their small corner of the world. "Grandma Duncan just finished up the last stitching on the auction quilt. She told us Saturday when the family got together for breakfast at the Lone Pine Ranch," Pearl shared, scooping up a piece of homemade apple pie that was being passed around the table. Finishing up a mouth of flaky pie crust, Laura chimed in saying she couldn't wait to see what a crazy quilt looked like. After all, it was the talk among the Silver Lake women in town.

The talk turned to some overheard gossip Otto shared with everyone about the Christmas pageant. "You hear that old man McFarling is all bent out of shape because his wife was angry at him for not fighting to move the pageant to the little room above their mercantile?" Otto shoved a mouthful of yams in between sentences, thinking to himself what an amazing cook Pearl's mom was, when she chimed in saying she wasn't surprised because that family always had to outdo everyone no matter who it was or why. Frank finished the conversation by saying it was too small to fit everyone in there anyway, and besides, its Abbie Jean's little dollhouse.

Otto kicked Frank under the table.

"How is she doing these days anyway, Otto?" Pearl asked, winking at Frank. They loved teasing him when they were all together, poking fun of their relationship just because they could. It was something to rouse Otto about, now that he was a changed man. Pearl was observing Otto's reaction and thought to herself, 'Gosh he looks so much like Frank. Such handsome men,' and smiled to herself.

Pearl thoroughly enjoyed being around him lately and was so glad, for her husband's sake especially, that Otto let go of drinking and made amends with everyone he was at personal war with.

The small cozy living room smelled of fresh popcorn mixed with hot cocoa and mint. Aunt Elizabeth, who'd been especially quiet most of the dinner, said she'd heard that Abbie Jean was planning a big surprise for the kids at the Christmas Eve party.

"She is?" Otto looked at his brother's wife's new aunt who he'd known his whole life, surprised. "First time I've heard about this," he said.

Pearl poked her finger on the needle she was using to string the popcorn for their Christmas tree "Ouch! That didn't feel good," and looked up to see Laura scooting over next to her older sister, who was now sucking on her pinky.

Hot air filled Pearl's ear when Laura whispered, "What do you think it is, Sister?"

Laura didn't dare ask out loud in a room full of people, afraid she might actually be heard. Pearl's warm arm reached around her sister's small body and pulled her close to her. "I don't know sweet girl, but sounds pretty amazing huh?" She kissed the top of her head then turned and looked around the room that was full of people she adored and loved with all her heart.

'This will be the best Christmas ever. Our first year here, with so much to look forward to in the new year.' She put her hand on her stomach and gently gave it a little hug. She was so happy and full of life. Frank happened to catch what his wife was doing and by her glow radiating happiness he sensed what she was feeling, and it didn't take long before the two of them found one another and locked eyes. Sparks shot through the room, which seemed to close in on them as if they were the only two in that space, in that moment, at that time.

Chapter Thirty-One

S aving as much space to park for those riding in from the small towns that surrounded Silver Lake was a necessity because there just wasn't enough space for so many buggies to park around the Chrissman Bros. General Store. The Bunyard family had arranged on riding to the Christmas Eve party together, except for Otto, who wanted to be dropped off at Abbie Jean's so he could escort her to the party. But she'd planned on being there a few hours before to help with the decorations, and besides she needed to finish up her surprise for the kids.

Abbie Jean's parents never really got over the fact that their independent, headstrong daughter chose to be with the Bunyard boy, but they had noticed a considerable difference in him and came to really like him more than they cared to admit. Otto had not only kept his promise of sobriety and staying out of trouble while courting their daughter, but went out of his way to demonstrate he was worthy of her time and love. The most important thing to Maeve McFarling was the fact that no one judged her daughter while dating him.

The transformed, easy-going young man came to care a lot about Abbie Jean, and saw her potential as she was maturing. They put away the unkind things that occurred at the Fourth of July dance and were able to move past the last several months. Abbie Jean wasn't the bad girl she liked to show off after all, Otto had learned. She still had an edge to her that he secretly thought sexy and attractive because he couldn't help liking the 'bad girl' image she sometimes surreptitiously let escape. That's why the two of them got along so well together. They understood the recklessness in one another no one else could. Otto knew Pearl's influence on Abbie Jean was an important part of what changed her, too. His sister-in-law had a natural kindness to her that she gently brought out in others, but did it in such a graceful manner it encouraged people to be better when they were around her. It was just one of the many reasons she always had a crowd surrounding her. People loved the sweet, loving, forgiving, and genuine soul and friend she was to everyone.

Otto couldn't wait to see Abbie Jean and what she had planned for the children. Curiosity was getting the best of him. Doing for others and going out of her way. This was aberrant of her, a behavior he was falling more and more in love with.

Laura, on the other hand, had not been herself for several days due to the anticipation of her part in the play, and also because she was so happy to finally have a close friend, one who understood her quiet unique ways. Ira James was her very best friend in the whole world, and the two of them had formed a bond deeper than friendship. She felt great to finally have someone in her life who understood her, even if he was a little goofy at times and the rude older boys made fun of him.

It was time. December 24th, 1894, 6:00 pm and everyone was set to go, women in their best festive dresses and men in their best flannel shirts and trousers. The Chrissman Bros. building had festive arched green wreaths over the small windows and homemade quilts hung on the old whitewashed walls.

Looking down through the window high above at the guests exiting their buggies and tying up horses to available posts below, Liam McFarling watched with an empty growling stomach as men with their chatty women and excited little ones walked towards the entrance that lead to the only set of stairs the building had. He was almost done with the few last-minute jobs he'd been given. Lighting all the lanterns, saving the largest Rochester oil lamp for last. It was much too fancy for the old building, but had been shipped all the way from back east as a gift by Mr. Chrissman's rich uncle.

Scratching his freshly shaved chin, looking up towards the ceiling, Liam thought how it looked too low and a little unsafe. He'd been upstairs many times for dances and celebrations and had never noticed it so low. "Well, I'd best get to work moving it up a little higher," he said to no one in particular, and went to grab some tools he'd brought for little odd jobs he knew would be asked of him.

He was interrupted by his daughter's stressed voice. "Papa! I would like some help with the last box I need brought in." She finished a little softer with, "When you get a moment, please."

He yelled over his shoulder at her that he'd be right there while he searched for a bench to stand up on to move the expensive lamp up a couple of notches. Stepping up onto the wood bench he heard voices coming into the decorated room that smelled like succulent turkey and juicy ham. Liam turned and smiled, stepping back down off the bench to greet them. Frank, Otto, and their father, Jesse (who wasn't particularly pleased to be there), walked in with heavy boxes of pies and wrapped Christmas presents.

"Ev'nin' Liam," Jesse said in his deep dry voice, tipping his hat. "Looks like we're in for a night of some real entertainment." He nodded to the rows of benches where the pageant was going to take place.

"Reckon so," Liam said, stumbling over the bench he'd just moved to get to the oil lamp, forgetting it was there and why he was using it. After greeting the men and shooting the bull for a few moments, Liam turned back to finish what he was doing, looked at his hands and then around the room forgetting why he'd had the tools in his hand in the first place. "Eh...? Land sakes, what was I doing?"

Shaking off the feeling he was in the middle of doing something, the small balding man with gray sideburns decided to mosey along and help his daughter. He grabbed the handful of tools, hiked up his pants, and walked off, promising himself he'd try to remember why he needed them later when he wasn't so busy. It was something important he knew; he just couldn't remember what.

More guests were beginning to enter the warm inviting building with heavy coats and high boots leaving clumps of snow behind them. Soon the building was full of family, friends, and neighbors from all over Lake County.

Chapter Thirty-Two

There were more than one hundred and seventy-five people there by the time the dinner and auction ended. After dinner the men stepped out for a smoke while the women helped prepare the kids in their costumes and the rest helped clean up the dinner. Pearl helped wherever she could, when she felt like it. She'd been awfully tired lately and the waves of nausea were extra bothersome tonight.

"Come Laura, I'll help with that," Pearl said to her sister, who was in the corner of the room where they partitioned off an area for the children to get in costume.

The shaking ten-year-old with big excited eyes stumbled over the material on the floor. "I don't know if I can do this Pearl," Laura quietly whispered, looking up at her sister with pleading eyes.

"Oh, honey" Pearl said calmly, knowing she had to do whatever she could for Laura's sake, even if she felt like vomiting right at her feet. "You can do anything you want to do, and you remember we are all here smiling and happy to be watching you." Pearl smiled with genuine concern and rubbed her little sister's back. "You are the person they picked for this part because they have faith you'll do a wonderful job." Pearl told her, trying to keep a positive note in her voice. "You have worked really hard on your lines. Besides, you have Ira James here beside you and he really needs your support too. You earned this, Laura." She stopped to catch her breath and stop her head from spinning. "Try to enjoy it."

Laura smiled, looking around for Ira, and found him getting ready around the corner from her which gave her all the confidence in the world she needed.

The kids were so excited that Santa was coming after their pageant that they had a hard time containing themselves, which caused a little extra friction in an upstairs stuffy room that wasn't nearly large enough for the almost two hundred people it was holding.

Electa Caroline put together the stage along with Grandma Duncan, Abbie Jean, and Aunt Elizabeth. Meanwhile, the men were still enjoying a refreshing break away from the excitement upstairs. Pearl excused herself with a look of panic that caught her mother's eyes. Electa Caroline asked from across the room if everything was alright.

"I'm fine, just going to sit for a spell and get some fresh air outside." The young pregnant wife gave her mother a reassuring nod.

"Night sickness always got me too. Poor darling," Grandma Duncan said to Electa Caroline.

"Yes, I'm afraid this is going to be a rough one for her," Electa Caroline responded with a straight pin in her mouth, bending over the front row of the benches making a stage to pin some leftover red material together she had from making her new bedroom quilt the previous summer.

"It's a boy for sure with that night sickness," Aunt Elizabeth chimed in, asking afterword what she could do to help now that all the dishes and food was put away.

Abbie Jean stood not even two feet away from the women, trying to overhear what they were saying, but the rustle and noise of the children was so loud she finally gave up. She couldn't stand being left out of any adult conversations and felt the need to know everyone's business.

Covering her mouth, trying to hold down the saliva that insisted on coming up, Pearl forced a swallow and started running down the stairs, pushing through the door that led her straight into a group of men. Deep, muffled voices talking over one another discussing the new farmer's almanac that would be soon coming out. They saw her whirl around and lose her dinner when their tobacco smoke hit her nose. She couldn't hold it in any longer.

Frank turned around and saw who it was. He immediately rushed to her side to give her some support. About thirty men all, too close for her comfort, realized what was going on and moved away to give them some privacy.

"I'm so sorry. I just couldn't hold it in." Pearl was terribly embarrassed, her face flushed from vomiting and red with humiliation.

"Come here." Her gentle six-foot-seven husband pulled her into his strong supporting arms and shielded her. Frank couldn't have cared less who was watching, he just wanted to make sure she was alright.

She hunched her shoulders her lower lip started trembling. She didn't want this tonight. She felt like she was spoiling a perfectly fun evening. She just felt awful, mentally and physically.

With tight lungs crying for air and cleaner breath, Pearl gave everything she was feeling over to her husband who she'd never been so grateful for. Relaxing under his comfort they heard Abbie Jean's strong voice yell out that the pageant was ready to begin. "Are you alright to go back in, or do you want me to take you home?" A finger gently touched her chin lifting it up so he could see her reaction to his question.

Watery brown eyes told him she wasn't about to let Laura down. "Not with this big moment in her life, Frank, I can't do that to her," Pearl shook her head. Besides, she was feeling so much better now that she'd let it all out and the nausea had passed.

Back inside the overcrowded but cheerful building, Laura, Ira, and the other children watched with big eyes as the rest of the attendees settled in on benches set up in front of them. It was jam-packed. Pearl had never seen this many people all at once in such a small space in all her life. It was almost too much for her and she started feeling claustrophobic, but, remembering her sister, she held her breath for a couple of seconds and shut her eyes until she felt Frank's warm hand over hers.

Abbie Jean sat down at the piano in the corner to play the opening song, "Away in a Manger", and the children laughed when old Mrs. Syers hit the high notes off tune, which made Otto remember the crate of gifts for the children. He was supposed to grab them and take up to her so she could pass them out when Santa came in right after the pageant was over.

He knew it was important to Abbie Jean because the children would be contained together in one corner. Mad at himself for remembering the crate at the very worst moment, he knew he had to do something about it and thought he could do it quickly while the children and audience sang the first song.

He quietly looked around and thought going over the wood bench would be easier than disturbing everyone if he tried to slide past them. Lacking no confidence, Otto sucked in a big breath thinking to himself 'here goes nothing,' and slowly stood, bent over, crouched down as low as possible, and jumped up onto the bench he'd been sitting on. Focused on the task ahead, he started to move quickly through the crowd. Forgetting about the beautiful Rochester oil lamp, he bumped his head right into it, causing hot oil to spill over and splash his unprotected face. He flinched backwards losing his balance. Burning flames raced after sizzling hot oil, catching him off guard. Before anyone knew what was happening, almost thirty percent of Otto's face and body was burning. Laura and Ira looked at one another in terror then back at the Rochester oil lamp that was swinging side to side throwing flames all over like it was a piñata tossing out free candy.

At once, the audience stopped singing and froze in shock and disbelief. "OTTO! STOP!" Frank screamed over the pandemonium. "STOP MOVING!" he yelled this time with more force. The crowd saw their own horror reflected in his burning face.

Intense fear and concern increased among everyone watching. Pearl said a silent prayer before she heard her father's pleading voice, "Stop moving, Son!" Quiet desperation filled his lungs along with black smoke clogging up his airway. "Please, just stop!" the words slid out more to himself this time, knowing the battle had already been lost.

Everyone was backed up as far away from him as they could get. His neck, arm and part of his back was already on fire; oil dripped down off his hand where the fire chased after it, playing a game of follow the leader. The mood in the Chrissman Bros. building had quickly changed from concern and worry for Otto to extreme fear and alarm for themselves as the trail of oil and fire went looking for the next victim.

Pearl was holding Frank's hand, standing up against the wall closest to Laura, watching the scene unfold right in front of them. A look of complete incredulity covered their faces, frozen with fear.

Liam McFarling was the closest to Otto when it happened, Charles on his right with Electa Caroline next to him. Reacting quickly, Liam tried to grab the lamp away from the ceiling where it was dangling after it had been knocked loose from the hook, contaminating everything in its path. He thought grabbing it was the only way to control the oil from spilling but ended up doing more damage. After the initial shock, regret set in and Liam was finding it hard to breathe from the heat of the flames, his small body caught fire faster than he could react and in just a matter of seconds his muscles were raw, ugly, and exposed. His movements were slow and sloppy as his brain tried to process everything that was happening causing him to trip into a large woman who was trying to get out of his way. Oil quickly spilled all over her long fluffy skirt and before she even knew what occurred she was engulfed in flames, her life soon coming to an end.

The room lit up like a Fourth of July fireworks show with hungry, aggressive flames rapidly spreading faster than they could be stopped.

Frank found Pearl and turned her to face him, trying to get her attention. Her eyes were fixed on Otto and then Liam. She was stuck in time and felt like her head was too heavy to move it and look away. He told her firmly to focus on what he was saying. Everything was happening so unbelievably fast and he knew getting her attention, even if it meant he had to yell at her, was the only way to save her life. "Get your sister and get out now! Do not look around for anyone. I will make sure the rest of your family gets out."

There was no time for Frank to give any more directions. He knew how serious this was and knew he had to think fast. Once he saw her and Laura move towards the stairs his adrenaline kicked into high gear and he ripped off his jacket and threw it onto Otto, who was screaming, making high pitched sounds like a suffocating wild boar trapped inside a hot inferno of pain. Frank gasped when he saw his only brothers exposed and twitching cheek bone, the muscle exposed to the naked eye and layers of skin around it already peeling back.

Finally, after a little scuffle, Frank got a hold of Otto and sternly pulled him down to the floor where he was trying to cover the fire that was torturing his sibling and best friend. It was hard to see through the thick heavy black smoke that was greedily spreading. Being so close to where the children were performing gave Frank an idea. He grabbed some red material off the little makeshift stage, where Laura, Ira James. and all the other little kids had been performing just moments before, and wrapped himself in it, crouching low to the floor. Frank turned and twisted so he could see what the people around the room were doing. He was now lying down on the floor next to Otto where he had him covered up. Frank was able to get a clear view from the floor down low.

"What on earth are they doing?" Mad as hell, he couldn't understand why no one was moving, getting out of this perdition. Something must be blocking the exit. His heart lurched with a pain that intensely ached, knowing they were all doomed, trapped inside hell's firestorm.

He saw his brother was quiet and felt for a pulse. That's when his father-in-law, Charles, appeared again at his side, trying to help get the situation under control. The men left Otto, who was still alive but had passed out from the shock of the pain, and together they moved over to a small window and were getting ready to kick it out when all of a sudden a loud blast punctured their ears followed by screams from adults and children alike. The fire was too much for the small window upstairs, which shattered under pressure from the heat.

Frank lifted his large boot and kicked out the remaining glass. The window led to a balcony that was rotted and hadn't been used for several years. Smoke getting denser, turning a chilling thicker black, it was rolling around now attacking the lungs of every family member and friend who'd gathered as a happy excited group just hours before.

Frank and Charles had help from Pearl's Uncle, Will, who was doing what he could to control the situation on the other side of the room when he realized there was nothing more he could do for Liam McFarling. He was gone. His body gave in to the fire that had engulfed his small gentle frame just moments before. Will had no choice but to leave the hysterical Maeve by his side and go help others, who would listen to his advice.

The large, strong man ran over to help wherever he could when he saw what Frank and Charles were doing. They needed all the help they could get once that window was open, black billowing plumes of smoke fighting to get out too. It looked like there might be some help below where men who were outside smoking when the fire began heard the screaming above. From that moment on they were rushing around, trying to get a ladder from the building underneath.

The men at the only window upstairs were grabbing people right and left practically throwing them down the ladder into the safety of strong men below who were starting to feel like they had momentary control, if even for a few seconds. If that's all they were allowed was just a couple of seconds to save lives, they would gladly take it. Every second counted. Every second given meant another life saved during the holocaust that haunted Silver Lake forever, making it the last Christmas Eve ever celebrated in the small town.

Chapter Thirty-Three

Frank knew there wasn't much time to help every person out of one single window. He promised Pearl he would get her family to safety, and no matter what it took he planned to do just that. Even if it was the last thing on earth he did. Electa Caroline and Abbie Jean were some of the first he'd helped down the ladder. They were followed by a woman who made his heart pump extra hard with relief when he held her arm. Overwhelmed with gratitude by the sight of his very own mother, Frank hugged her quickly before assisting her outside to the ladder where Abbie Jean and Electa Caroline waited to help her once she got down, which wasn't an easy task for an older woman with a long dress to catch up her footing.

It was exceptionally hard to keep track of everyone he had seen go down the ladder, with all the fear, chaos and dark smoke overwhelming the distressed people, especially with the nasty smell of burnt flesh hanging in the suffocating air.

Frank stopped what he was doing for a minute. 'Pearl,' he thought to himself, trying to scream her name aloud, but nothing would come, no matter how hard he tried. Frank reached up and grabbed his throat, tried to swallow and get some air, massaging his Adam's apple. Deep, black smoke robbed him of his voice and panic overtook the rest of him when he turned to see who all was left. Pearl looked so frightened, innocent, and disoriented when he saw her trapped with a group of people who were pushed up against the exit door, crushing one another trying to get out.

'Dammit, she didn't get out in time.' Pandemonium and confusion were overtaking the people who were left. 'We're all going to die if we don't move quicker.'

Frank rushed over to Pearl and Laura with red material shielding his eyes and covering his mouth. Screams and the roar of fire were piercing their ears. He wasn't sure who all he was pushing or stepping on to get to her, but he knew one thing he was going to make sure happened: he was getting her out.

Pearl felt her wrist being pulled by a rough and abrasive hand. She didn't know what was going on, but she knew that the burn and sting in her eyes wasn't anything compared to the pain in her wrist that felt like it was being crushed into several small fragments. Fighting against her assailant wasn't doing any good. He wasn't giving up. His grip was stronger than anything she'd ever felt in her life. In the moment of panic and fear all she could think was that someone was trying to move her out of the way so they could get closer to the exit door. She wasn't about to let Laura and her unborn child die in here while they got out, so she fought with all her strength, but it wasn't enough. She had nothing left to fight with and was losing. Close to passing out from lack of air, exhaustion and overwhelming fear, she had no choice but to give in and stop fighting but continued to hold firmly on to Laura's little hand, who was holding on to Ira James's arm with all the of strength she could muster. Once she let herself give in, she immediately felt the person pull her fast and realized she was getting close to an open window.

"Ouch," she blurted out because she couldn't take it anymore. There was dampness in the air, and she leaned into it letting it bathe and refresh her spirit, allowing her lungs fill up with clean air. 'Air!' she thought to herself. At the same time, she saw it was Frank who had been pulling her. As pieces of the building came crashing down around her she realized he was the one fighting with all his strength and persistence to get her and the kids to safety. "Oh Frank." She softly let out under her breath. "My hero!"

Pearl's heart cramped at the sight of Otto, who was laid on the rotten balcony where men were trying to tie him up so they could get him down the ladder to safety. The ache for him was so surreal. She was terrified and overwhelmed by everything moving around her so quickly. The two kids, Ira James and Laura, held on to each other for dear life. Relief and love washed over Pearl as she watched them move down the stairs to safety. It was her turn next. Frank sent her down the stairs with swift gentleness as he worked with speed and endurance to get everyone he could out of the raging fire before the building collapsed. Her mom was already safe outside and down there waiting for her when she took her last step. Pearl had never been so relieved or happy to embrace her mother, but there was no time to hold one another. So many people were terribly burned and injured, and many had smoke damage and were dying right in front of them. Some even jumped to escape being burned alive.

Pearl turned her sore, stiff neck muscles and looked up into the window where she saw Frank, who was still rushing people down the stairs right and left as fast as he could get them going. She was so afraid he wouldn't get out in time, when there was a loud crash below where she had been standing with Laura and Ira James just seconds before. The balcony her father and Uncle Will were standing on to help people down gave out. Years of neglect, rot, and the heavy weight proved too much.

Pieces of rotting burning wood, debris, and bodies came crashing to the blackened snow below. Pearl ran to her father when she saw him in a pile of mangled bodies. Charles couldn't move. He was stuck with her uncle on top of him, both legs twisted underneath the pile of wood, nails, with a mix of human body parts.

"Help!" Pearl screamed with all the strength she had left. Her stomach cramped with intense pain from straining to yell. She felt someone beside her, but it was hard to see who it was with the black smoke surrounding them. The heat from the fire trailed the siding and moved down towards the pile of broken and bruised bodies that were tangled together from the fall.

"I can't move," Charles screamed over the roar of the flames above them.

"I know Papa, I'll get you out somehow," she said, looking closer at who was beside her, coming to her rescue. It was one of her favorite people, and what a relief it was to see him. Her husband's grandfather's strength was undeniable. Pearl felt an amazing love and gratitude for this man next to her; she would have been happy to give her life over to him in that moment. George Duncan, along with a handful of other men who came to her aid, helped pull her father and his brother, Will, to safety. Electa Caroline and Frank's grandmother, Louisa, were already assisting the injured and had set up a crude hospital across the street at an empty saloon, where Charles and his brother were immediately taken.

Electa Caroline hugged her husband, telling him he was going to be alright, hot grateful tears running down her raw, hot cheeks. He was out of danger his wife said, without a lot of hope looking at the defaced leg. She smiled sweetly at him, hiding the fear she felt deep within. She set her fears aside for later; there was enough to be done now with what she'd been given to work with. Time would decide how they fared after this miserable, terrifying nightmare was over and they could assess their loss.

Chapter Thirty-Four

The roar of the flames eventually silenced the cries within. Laura and Ira had been taken to a room in the back of the saloon where Electa Caroline kept them out of sight and wrapped them up in blankets someone found under the counter. They would be alright and safe where they were for the time being, Laura's mom reasoned. Besides, she didn't want Laura or Ira James to witness any more than they had to. There was enough death and destruction to fill their subconscious with nightmares throughout their lifetime, no need to subject the innocent kids to more.

Ira James snuggled up to Laura, who held the blanket up for him. Both kids couldn't control the shaking that controlled their cold and tired bodies, lying on their sides facing one another. A big shiny tear chased another down Laura's black streaked cheek and fell onto the hard-cold table below, making a small puddle.

Laura pulled Ira James up close next to her like she would have a little brother who was scared. He was terrified, and who would blame him after what he'd been through in the previous months. "Th..th...thannnk yooouu Laura," Ira James barely got out. His teeth knocked against each other making a hard-clicking sound as he shook. "Hey Laawwwra," he managed "Do'oo you think Ott'ttoo is dead?"

Ira James had never seen a dead body and couldn't stop thinking about how horrible Otto looked the last time they saw him. It was the most frightful sight he'd ever witnessed with all that skin burned and peeling back, black smoke rolling out of his body like it was exhaling dark evil ghosts who were searching for new bodies to consume and torture.

"No," Laura whispered, trying the best she could to comfort Ira James as she was the stronger one of the two. Rubbing his shoulder with her gentle but cold little fingers that cared so deeply for this best friend beside her, she sighed, happy his shaking was subsiding. She took a deep breath, which helped to relieve her nerves too. "Pearl told me that he was alive, but he passed out from something adults call shock." She adjusted herself to get comfortable on the hard table that was warming up a little. Someone built a fire in the fireplace not far from the room they were hiding in. "I think it means if they don't like something they faint," Laura said after she thought about it a minute.

A few moments went by, then the kids heard a loud scrape from the front door as it opened with a booming urgency, allowing icy cold winds to follow along with the sound of lost, traumatized, and injured adults. One by one they were being led into the once happy place people went to have fun and relax while they washed their worries down with a bottle of Silver Lake's best whiskey. This Christmas Eve, though, it was turned into a room full of pain, broken and damaged friends and family who considered themselves lucky to still be alive.

The saloon was filling up quickly with lots of noise that made the two kids scared and nervous. No matter how much Laura sang to Ira James or the two of them covered their ears, pushing tight against their head to block out the piercing screams of agony, fear, and loss, the noises still found their way into their innocent heads. Laura knew better than to listen to this, but she didn't know how to stop it.

She was thinking of a way to help Ira James before he had a meltdown when a couple rats appeared under the table they were lying on. Aggressive bony rodents with small black beady eyes crinkled up their long intimidating snouts to get a better look at the two sets of eyeballs staring down at them. From all corners of the room rats were appearing. They were known to collapse their rib cages and squeeze under closed doors or through the smallest of holes if they felt threatened. Black, scraggly singed fur appeared everywhere, covering the floor.

"They're trying to escape the heat of the fire and must have had a nest under the Chrissman Bros. building," Laura heard her mother say to her father, trying to calm everyone down. "We'll get them out of here soon. The last thing we need is open wounds and burns getting infected." Electa Caroline was shouting out directions to every able body.

Charles squinted through the pain and looked up at his stressed wife, who was working as hard as she could to organize the distressing sound of chaos and fear. "Electa, that's not something you need to worry about, they're just rats," Charles said through clinched teeth, adjusting his good leg, resting under the weight of his body that was starting to go numb. Charles watched his wife and daughter's new grandmother-in-law, Louisa, along with a handful of other women in the community, work their magic, helping ease everyone's discomfort.

Frank and Pearl's young neighbor boy, Tim, was tending to the fire and bringing in wood as fast as he could gather it. He tried not to look at all the gross injuries and burns, but was happy to be there and help keep everyone warm and water boiled for sterilizing.

Taking charge is what Electa Caroline did best in the face of disaster, guiding others through tragedy and despair. "Grab some of those bottles under the counter behind you, sis." Electa Caroline looked directly at Pearl then wiped black sweat from her damp forehead with a swipe from the back of her free hand. She looked around for a rag or scrap of material to wipe it but found her damaged dress would work just as well.

Electa Caroline was scanning the room and saw Louisa and Grandpa Duncan going from patient to patient, doing whatever was needed to assist them, giving the injured love, water, and support. The saloon was overflowing with people she'd been fortunate to befriend since moving to Silver Lake. These people were not just neighbors and friends but as much her own family as her blood relatives were. They all welcomed her into the fold, their community, without hesitation and with total love and acceptance. She was very fond of every one of them, and it broke her heart to see them hurting. Even Ira James's mother. "Oh heavens!" Electa Caroline was starting to feel the burden ahead of her with that last thought. 'Where was Ira James' mother?' she thought to herself, bowing her head to think about when it was she actually saw her last. Frazzled, Electa Caroline was trying to keep her mind from ending up a jigsaw puzzle and organize her thoughts when all of a sudden the room filled with screams from her youngest daughter and Ira James. Forgetting all about the boy's mother, she ran to where both the children were and instantly felt the hysteria building when she entered the room.

"Aahh... Mama!" Laura screeched, close to falling off the thick wood table where she and Ira James were holding on to one another, scooting back as far as they could. The young girl was panicking, and for good reason. "Mother!" she shrieked again with fear gaining strength only a frightened ten-year-old girl could muster. "Look."

Electa Caroline's eyes didn't need to follow her daughter's finger to where she was pointing at snarling nasty rats; she felt them climbing up her dress. Their hard, sharp, creepy claws dug into her bare skin under her skirt, causing panic to rise in her throat. "Oh Lord!" She was shooing the rats off the table legs they were climbing up.

Not sure she could handle much more of this dreadful night, Electa Caroline was ready to give in to tears that were burning behind her eyelids with each blink when she felt a warm firm hand on her shoulder and at the same time heard, "It's ok darling, you go out to d'ose who need juw'. Grandma Louisa and Grandfather are here for dem. Ve vill take care of dese babies." Louisa nodded to her helpful husband's calm demeanor, giving a relaxing vibe as she spoke. "Ve got dis' here, love." She turned Electa Caroline around and very lovingly pushed her towards the burned and injured.

Electa Caroline could hear Frank's grandfather shoo the nasty creatures out of the narrow room with a broom he'd found, and guiding the bold displaced rodents into another location almost like he spoke their eutherian language.

Electa Caroline reentered the saloon's main room and saw her eldest daughters face, contorted with pain, frozen in time, watching another injured and traumatized victim being brought in as young Tim held the door open. Pearl just stood staring at all the broken, burned people sitting on stools or laid out on tables, desperate for help. She'd never seen so much horror in all her life. Tears fell through her scratched and red, tired eyes.

Standing in the middle of unbelievable chaos, Pearl felt her stomach cramp up again right before another wave of nausea punched her in the gut. She headed toward the saloon's counter where the liquor was stored and was sickened by the smell of death and warm blood filling the room. Swallowing hard, walking past those who were moaning from agonizing pain, a trickle of sweat ran down between her eyebrows. She had to make a conscious effort not to scream out or vomit.

'Oh, this awful smell, ewww!' Pearl knew she'd never be able to get burnt human flesh and scorched hair smell out of her clothes or off her skin, and tears began to swell up. Before she knew it, she was a waterfall of emotion that couldn't be stopped or controlled. Her deep brown eyes burned, and her heart ached, allowing herself permission to let it permeate her soul and wonder about her future: her future with Frank, her family's future with all their loss.

Would Frank survive this? After he fell out of the window would he be able to walk again? His hip was badly broken when the men toppled down covering him. And what about her father and her Uncle Will? Where was Aunt Elizabeth? Pearl was beginning to hyperventilate. Her throat tightened, feeling like a rubber band was squeezing it. Pearl stressed over who all was still in the building when the fire ended their lives. How many children were left orphans now; were there childless parents? Widows, whole families gone?

The questions kept assaulting her thoughts when she heard a horrible screech coming from someone close by. Maybe someone was crying, she thought? It was a frightful and alarming sound, like a large mountain lion being trapped and tortured. She put her hands over her ears and tried to make it stop when she realized her mouth was open and those sounds were coming from her very own mouth. She couldn't stop it; she'd tried but it was too strong, so she gave in and let it run wild until she collapsed onto the floor from exhaustion. She wanted to block out the torture of the night, she prayed her mind and body would go numb, she didn't want to feel anymore.

A sharp cramp tore at her insides, followed by something warm running down her inner thigh. It was more than she could bear. The final straw. To preserve what sanity she may have left, she allowed her body, soul, and mind to let go. She completely shut her eyes once she got comfortable. It was the only thing she felt she had control over. She grieved herself into quiet when she looked down at all the blood soaking her dress. Fearing it was too late, she wrapped her arms around her stomach and hid out-of-view from anyone who may need more from her than she was able to give.

Pearl sprawled out behind the counter and tried not to think of anything. She wished she was in the warmth of Frank's arms and they were lying in bed snuggled up while she listened to his deep calm voice as he shared the rest of Wintoka and Thunder Cloud's story. Letting her mind drift towards happier memories in the first few months of their marriage, Pearl finally relaxed her over-stressed nerves and let go. Wintoka was on her mind while she was carried away from the reality of her world into the challenges of Wintoka's.

Chapter Thirty-Five

The first of April, after many months of battles, the United States army advanced on the lava caves in hopes of ending Captain Jack's stronghold once and for all—but the Modocs weren't anywhere to be seen. They slipped out in the middle of the night, leaving a bewildered cavalry scratching their heads. Agent Knapp threw his hat down. Stark raving mad, he could eat nails he was so angry.

"Just look at this," Knapp said, down on his knees in the cave that was recently occupied by Captain Jack and his family. "They took every last thing with them." He stood up, looked around at some of the carvings on the rock inside and scratched his head before putting his hat back on. "Unbelievable!" He was hoping they may have left some kind of trail or clue to where they went, but they didn't leave even a single piece of clothing or garbage.

"Sir," the staff sergeant tried to get the Agent's attention. "If I may?" The sergeant tried hard to stand straight but the giant next to him was more intimidating in person than he'd been warned about.

"What? Get on with it." Knapp was annoyed.

"The Modocs, Sir, they believe their spiritual god of lava, Kumash, lives here, and because he provided them with so much during their stay, they honored him by not leaving a mess." Sergeant Sinclair proudly shared his knowledge of what he'd learned before traveling out west to assist in apprehending the now infamous Modocs. President Grant wanted them captured, no matter the outcome. The standoff was costing America a lot of money and, as it turned out, it was more costly than Indian Wars before or after.

"Move aside, Sinclair," Agent Knapp shoved passed him. "I don't want to hear your bullshit today."

Sergeant Sinclair didn't let the glaring beast upset him. He knew what he said was the truth, and to be honest, after following the Modocs path over the last month he'd been stationed at Fort Klamath, he thought it was incredible they outwitted the army thus far. They were skilled fighters, thought things through strategically, and were very spiritual, appreciating the gifts Kumash gave them.

Little did Agent Knapp and Sergeant Sinclair know that Captain Jack took his followers and family one way and several other small groups that broke off went different directions because of an internal fight that occurred the night before. A week before a fight had broken out among Captain Jack and some of the braves that thought they knew better than their chief, Thunder Cloud, Pony, and La'as stole horses from a nearby ranch, desperate to get Wintoka out of the caves where she was deathly sick and ready to give birth any time. She was grossly underweight and hadn't felt the baby move for the last several days. Desperation to save Wintoka's life, and hopefully the life she carried, was the most important thing to him. He would have gladly given his life to see her live but that wasn't an option given to him, so he took what was available and quietly moved out in the middle of the night with his brothers, Wintoka, and Taw-Kia, who had no family left alive.

Taw-Kia was giving everything she had to help Wintoka and the baby. Wintoka had been having strong contractions since they left the lava caves. Some of the cramping was caused from severe hunger. Dark circles hung under her once beautiful vibrant brown eyes, her cheeks caved in, and several loose teeth were starting to fall out. The young teenage girl looked like she'd seen a hundred years already, and strands of wiry gray were starting to overtake her once thick black hair.

The young chief led his little family to the very place they escaped from months before. He followed his instinct without a thought to where that would lead them, which also happened to be the very place his grandmother was last seen. Feeling her spirit lead the way, Thunder Cloud knew that they would be safe at their old village where the army would never think to look. Agent Knapp, the United States Army, General Sherman, and all the aggravated homesteaders were so focused on the capture of the man they knew as Captain Jack that Thunder Cloud knew they wouldn't be watching anyone else. Besides, the army thought they were all traveling together so they were following Captain Jack, who was going in the opposite direction.

The day was early, and the vibrant auburn sun set high above the Stukel Mountains that hovered over the worried group who had gathered around Wintoka. There was a smell in the air that sickened everyone. Taw-Kia pulled her hair back and wrapped it with a piece of tule rope, then massaged the exhausted sick mom's temples so she could relax some.

"Pony, we need water." She turned to look at the large eyes peering in the small hut they'd built with the burnt tule mats that were left.

"I go with," thirteen-year-old La'as begged, not wanting to be left behind with the sickness and pain he was witnessing. The brothers knew Thunder Cloud would lose his mind if he lost Wintoka or their baby.

Taw-Kia cringed every time she heard Wintoka grunt. No matter what kind of pain and distress she was in, Wintoka would never show weakness or scream, and even in the middle of giving birth and close to death she was still trying to be strong.

Taw-Kia helped Wintoka stand when it was time. With excruciating pain in her lower back and groin, Wintoka spread her legs apart with her hips positioned directly over the divan made for the delivery. She had never been so grateful for anyone in her life as she was for Captain Jack's cousin, who left her clan and traveled alongside her to help. It wasn't the first time Taw-Kia delivered a baby; she had been trained from the time she was five years old as the clan's midwife with her mother, who had died from smallpox years before. She had a gentle touch, and everything she did helped bring comfort to both the mother and the babies she brought into this world. She couldn't do things the other girls could because of her twisted foot that usually slowed her down. Feeling born for this purpose, she took her role seriously, and many times took on the pain the mothers and babies experienced as her very own. Strength and maturity surpassed her age; she was a loving and natural midwife.

Wintoka's closest friend had already changed out the tule mats several times that morning due to the amount of blood and fluids Wintoka was losing. Time was slowly dragging, and the stress was starting to cripple Thunder Cloud. It had been hours since she started labor and now nighttime was taking over, causing the mood to take on a new worry. The men were hungry, and occupied their time searching for a small animal just to suffice them until they could get more food collected. Needing a distraction, Thunder Cloud stayed close to the wickiup his wife was in while he started cleaning up his old homestead, while he thought of all the amazing memories he had made with the woman he loved so much. He stayed within ear shot of Wintoka in case she needed him.

The dark red clots of blood that were pouring out of the pregnant mother were too much; it was painful for Taw-Kia to watch as thick chunks dropped onto the mats below. "Save your strength," Taw-Kia whispered softly into Wintoka's ear, trying not to disturb her concentration with the contractions. She knew that Wintoka should lie down and preserve what little strength she had. The fatigued mom was turning a shade of white Taw-Kia had only saw when she lost the mother. Sometimes both the mother and baby. Silently, she wondered if Thunder Cloud knew how bad off his wife really was.

Silence washed over the small enclosure. The ceiling was as low as the spirits that filled the space waiting. Wintoka had no more strength to stand and gave in to Taw-Kia's encouragement to lie down.

The next day in the early morning hours everyone knew her life hung on with little hope. The baby still hadn't come and Wintoka was a shade of gray, now coming in and out of life, ready and willing to cross over. It was time. Thunder Cloud was close by, gathering wood to keep her warm, focusing to keep his mind off of what he subconsciously knew was coming, when a scream pierced his ears, sending chills throughout his body like he'd never experienced before, not even when he was in the thick of battle fighting for his life.

Tripping over the wood pile, Thunder Cloud went running to her side. Once again silence filled the small wickiup while he gently stroked Wintoka's small bony arm, reassuring her of his presence. Overcome with strong emotions of loss and hope he immediately choked up when he saw shadows leap and dance around his once beautiful, vivacious wife, pulling her, leading the way while crackling flames lit up the small dark space. For the first time in Thunder Cloud's life he felt fear. A horrible ache took over as he watched his best friend and wife pass into the next world. Wintoka's body completely relaxed as she slipped away into darkness, following the great spirits before her.

Wintoka's spirit had been gone for some time as Taw-Kia worked on preparing the body for cremation. Focused on smearing her with a mixture of ash and pine all over her small bloated, washed body, Taw-Kia was not prepared for what happened next. Singing the death song, sending her spirit off with those who will guide and teach her, the young girl moved Wintoka over on her side when a small dark form slid out from between her legs. The lifeless baby almost hit the blood-soaked tule mats below had it not been for Taw-Kia's quick youthful reflexes. A mixture of grief and shock lay in her hands, wet, cold, and beautiful. Before she could lay the baby girl down on her cold mother another one, bigger than its twin sister fell onto the ground, splashing into the puddle of her mother's birthing fluids.

Overwhelmed with hatred for the United States army that forced this mess on her and those she adored and loved, taking away this beautiful mom and her children's lives was too much for Taw-Kia to bear alone and she cried out for help, then sat and just stared at both small babies, a little bigger than her hand, she'd wrapped in soaked tule mats. By the time La'as, who was the only one close by, got to her she was sitting in the corner sobbing, looking down at the dead twins with a helpless look of confusion and sorrow covering her blood-streaked face.

Hatred, anger, and the pain of loss tore through La'as's heart. Thunder Cloud fled the wickiup where his dead wife lay, never seeing his children born. Pony and La'as stepped up as the men they became that night and helped prepare a cremation spot for their sister-in-law and the twins, glad their older brother wasn't there to see his babies' lifeless bodies.

Chapter Thirty-Six

"It's been an awful long two months, Pearl. You just can't expect to feel better this soon. You've been through a terribly sad tragedy," Frank said, looking at his wife who still wore that grief-stricken look. "We all have."

He went behind where she was sitting and massaged her stiff shoulders. She took advantage of some quiet time with her husband, trying to heed his advice. "I know Frank." She tipped her head from side to side before she reached up to pat his hand. Such a gentle gesture. "At least I'm not so nauseated anymore." Pearl tried to smile. Adjusting himself to move again, Frank slid his homemade crutch under his armpit to get his exhausted wife a small glass of water. "That sick feeling in my stomach every time I moved about was making it so difficult to help you and my mother." Tears sprung to her eyes again, feeling hopeless as they talked. She was so emotional lately and she knew others must be as well. The whole town had experienced the nightmare together. Everyone they knew lost at least one person the night of the fire. The town was filled with horrible sadness and gloom after their shock wore off.

Dr. Daly had been instrumental in helping all the wounded, and the homesteaders far and wide stepped in with supplies, food, clothing, and the most important thing they could offer, support.

News of the Christmas Eve fire spread all around the country, and soon the small town of Silver Lake was receiving all kinds of needed help.

Friends from neighboring counties came to town and stayed to help with farm chores and to clean up the Chrissman Bros. building. It was a critical time for lost souls who survived when their loved ones had not.

Slowly over time, with community support and love, they were able to see the bigger picture and learned to lean on one another to get through it. Death was still fresh in the air and grieving was fragile, as the last person had just passed away after two months of pure agony. With the new month of April approaching, and the snow melting, hope was feeling possible again.

Dr. Daly made a special effort to check on Frank's hip whenever he stopped by for a home visit with Pearl. "He's here, Pearl, you ready?" he asked when the sound of horse hoofs clomping got closer. Frank hobbled over to the door to let the doctor in. A fierce cold spring wind followed Bernard Daly into the Bunyard's warm home. Pearl hadn't left her house in days. She was having a hard time making herself get out from fear of going against the doctor's instructions, but she knew there was so much to be done on the ranch she couldn't just lay in bed and wait. She had mending she could always do, at least, while she rested, and she was grateful for her mother and sister who kept her company on days she couldn't get up when they came to take care of her and Frank.

Leaning in, he gave Pearl a quick hug, then Dr. Daly inquired tenderly. "How's my favorite patient doing today?" Trying to get a feel how things were really going for the young married couple.

Dr. Daly was the one to find Pearl behind the bar on the night of the fire. She was making a sound he'd never heard another human make in all his years of practice. It was a disturbing sight to see, with her hands clamped tightly over her ears and sitting in a mess of blood that covered the floor with blackened ash, making her barely recognizable. He had no idea she was an expecting woman. He thought she'd been injured by the fire at first. After there was some order to the chaos, he went towards her to figure out what was wrong with her.

His heart melted the instant he realized she wasn't burned but in a state of shock and was rambling something about losing her baby. At first Dr. Daly tried looking around for someone who knew if her baby had been in the fire when he saw a very exhausted and worn out woman who possessed a graceful beauty on any other night coming towards him.

"Oh, dear God!" she screamed when she saw the amount of blood covering her oldest daughter's skirt. The broken-hearted mother put her hands up to her mouth, gasping at the sight. "I've been looking all over for her."

Electa Caroline was frantic and started losing the patience she'd been trying to keep together. Hours had crept by since they started bringing in the injured and burned victims. She had already sent Ira James and Laura home with a neighbor who put them up for the night, getting them out of harm's way and giving the children what they needed to feel secure and comforted until they could locate what happened to Ira's mother.

"I asked her to get me a bottle of whisky to help administer to the injured," Pearl's mother's voice was almost a whisper. Grasping the scene before her was painfully unbearable. "Then she disappeared, and I got distracted." She said a little louder, "Oh my poor, poor darling." She looked up with pleading eyes that told the doctor there was something else going on here. "She's in the child way, Doctor."

Dr. Daly's attention became compassionately focused on getting her somewhere he could check the baby. If he could help her keep the baby, it would be a miracle this town would need just at the time they're trying to heal from the horrible sad loss they'd all experienced. A newborn baby would bring the town a happy gift of smiles and love.

"Good afternoon, Dr. Daly. Would you like some tea?" Pearl got up slowly to get the kindling burning in the stove to heat up the water. She felt better physically, she just wished she felt better mentally, but wouldn't dare share that with anyone.

"That would be fine, dear. First, how about we get a look at this little one and see how he's holding up." Dr. Daly guided her to the bedroom and left Frank to take over fixing the tea. "Anymore spotting or cramping recently?" The doctor Asked, moving the pinard horn around on her stomach so he could hear the baby's heartbeat. After he heard the news that made him smile, he put it away and grabbed his stethoscope, putting it in his ears "Breath in," he instructed her, moving it over her heart to her lungs.

"No, I've been really good about staying on my back, lying down and resting," Pearl said, shifting her little bump of a stomach that was starting to show.

"You're taking real good care of yourself, Pearl, real good," Dr. Daly encouraged her while he put the stethoscope back into his dark brown medical bag and snapped it back together.

The dark-haired man with an immaculately trimmed mustache carried his medical treasures with him through the couple's bedroom door to see that Frank had tea ready for them all. Thanking him, he sat down taking a sip.

"You're next, you know," he said, smiling to Frank who sat at the kitchen table, waiting to hear good news. Looking like he was ready to explode, Dr. Daly could tell he should share the healthy news with the father. "Baby's heartbeat is nice and strong." He pulled his chair out before adding, "You're going to have a healthy bambino come mid-to-late summer." Dr. Daly lifted his tea, took a sip and pretended not to see the expectant mother and father exchange a loving smile.

A look of relief washed over both of their faces. "That's great, doc." Frank was smiling ear to ear. It was his turn to be checked for how his hip was healing now. Frank had walked on it too soon, causing the bone to heal wrong. He didn't care if he was going to have a limp when he walked the rest of his life. He was still just so grateful to be alive after the terrible ordeal and all the losses they'd all suffered.

Pearl was allowed to finish up the dishes after using up the rest of the boiling water from the tea, then it was time to lie down again. Even though she wasn't spotting anymore or having those horribly painful sharp cramps, Dr. Daly still felt it was safer to keep her down until she was towards the end of her second trimester.

Pearl could hear the men in the bedroom as the doctor checked Frank's hip. "You need to make sure you're moving it in this motion," the doctor showed his patient what was expected, "Otherwise it will tighten up, making it harder to walk after you get up from resting it." He finished up with the exam then turned with a serious look at Frank who was sitting up on the bed. "Have you made a call to your brother recently? I'm not as worried about him as I am Abbie Jean who is…" His words hung in the air, not quite sure how to approach such a sensitive subject, "Rather ripe." He shifted his bag from one hand to the next and coughed, adding, "If you get my meaning?"

Frank looked rather surprised. "You mean she hasn't bathed?" He didn't understand. "Why?"

The doctor replied, "Your brother is doing really well. His scars are painful, sure, but he is a strong young man, mentally and physically, especially now since he hasn't touched a sip of that moonshine. He's brave, and is going to pull through this ordeal when I wasn't sure his body would let him. But that girl of his, she isn't looking so good, Frank. I'm thinking the loss of her parents was too much to bear, and she's afraid to leave his side for fear of him leaving her too."

Frank was saddened when the mention of her parents came up. He flashed back to the night of the fire and how hard he tried to pull Maeve off Liam, who had already passed from the burns he'd sustained. She wouldn't budge, Frank remembered. She was going with him into the next life and wouldn't let anyone near her.

"Thanks for the info, Doc. I'll see if Pops can get me a trip over to visit them and see how they're holding up, and maybe Mama can work some of her love and compassion on the poor girl."

The doctor handed Frank his crutch and helped him up. "She's been through an awful lot, and to be alone in the world would be extremely hard for anyone, but especially for a young girl that never heard the word 'no' before." Sympathy filled their faces as they thought about Abbie Jean being all alone.

The McFarling Mercantile had been shut down since Christmas Eve, as there was too much on the sixteen-year old's plate to even think about what should happen with the store. She insisted Otto be brought to her house so she could care for him. There wasn't a soul in that town who would even think of arguing with her after news spread that her parents had perished. If she wanted Otto taken to her house to help him heal, who were they to argue with her.

As it turned out, she ended up saving his life because of her diligence and over protective love caring for and treating his wounds. His scars would be horrendous when he was done healing, but she didn't think twice about that. It didn't matter to her. What did matter was that they were together. They'd survived the fire against all odds, and his love for what she'd done for him and the sacrifices she'd made meant more to him than he could even express. Otto never thought it possible to have that much love and devotion towards another person. He'd never experienced it before in his life. All that positive, healthy, and happy love she smothered him with was powerful in helping him heal and he owed his life to her. They were seen as a couple before the fire, and now were inseparable! Abbie Jean would do whatever it took to keep it that way.

Two days after Dr. Daly's exam Pearl's mother and father made a call to visit their daughter and son-in-law. Pearl was delighted to see them and terribly missed being around her parents, Laura, and those in town who she and Frank had received so much help from.

Several churches gathered supplies weekly and dropped them off to Preacher Garrett. There were some helpful teenage boys that volunteered to stay in town and gather and chop wood, run errands, do house chores, feed the farm animals for the families that couldn't provide for themselves. They came from all over Oregon and California. Graciously, the Reverend and his wife put them up at their house, supporting them, and lent their horses to those who needed to travel. The little Silver Lake town wouldn't have survived had it not been for the gift of love and services from those they scarcely knew.

"Mama," Pearl purred, holding her mother in a warm embrace. "How are you and Papa?" she asked as she turned her head to look at her father who was still trying to settle himself into the chair, looking a little uncomfortable.

Electa Caroline whispered back into her daughter's ear, "Oh, you know your father, darling. He's so stubborn he could make the Pope curse." Electa Caroline smiled at her own joke. "He ends up hurting himself when he should be following the good doctor's orders."

The women had a good laugh at her father's expense. "Oh, Mama." Pearl held her mother close to her again. "It's so good to see you!"

She rubbed her mother's back for a moment before Electa Caroline finally got up enough courage to ask, "Has Dr. Daly been back to visit you?" She knew he had been, as all mothers know everything. Suddenly the room got really quiet as anticipation for what she was going to say intensified.

Charles had to force himself to breath when he finally heard his little girl say, "We're expecting a healthy baby late summer sometime." Overcome with emotion, there wasn't a dry eye in the room. Feelings of gratitude mixed with happiness they didn't know possible after all they lost. "Do you need this, Grandpa?" Pearl asked, leaning up against her father who was sitting in the rocking chair Frank's grandfather had made. She handed her father a hankie she had in her hand. The two of them shared a private joke as he pulled her close to him and grabbed it out of her hand to dab his wet eyes.

"Hey, where's that little sister of mine?" Pearl just noticed Laura and Ira James weren't with her parents. She was so involved with her own excitement she forgot all about Laura, which wasn't at all like her to forget her sister over anything.

"Oh, they have several chores today. They were too busy messing around and knew the risk of missing out on seeing you, but they still didn't get the chickens fed and horses watered in time. They'll learn Mama means business when she tells them to get it done." Electa Caroline sipped her tea while she talked. "Laura cried, but I had to stick with what I said." Electa Caroline suddenly smiled when she said, "You'll soon know what that feels like." Her eyes lit up when she smiled, then added, "I'll say, that Ira James sure does love living in town with us." The two women were enjoying one another's visit while the men started a conversation and shared a chunk of tobacco. "He has just brightened up and loves to be listened to," she said as she stirred some cream into her tea, the spoon making a clinking sound, hitting the sides of the glass. "You should see him thrive, Pearl, as he noticed we all listen to him when he talks." She looked down, smiling more to herself than Pearl.

"Mama!" Pearl cheerfully interrupted her, "You're enjoying Ira James, aren't you?" It was amazing to see her mama so happy. Pearl hadn't noticed it before, but her mother was loving the chance to raise Ira James after he'd lost his mom in the fire. Pearl's poor parents lost their little boys so many years ago, which had devastated them. They were given another chance and cherished it. Laura finally had a brother, and someone close to her age, who she loved sharing her time and life with.

It was the first time Pearl said goodbye to her parents where she didn't feel overcome with sadness. She was genuinely happy, and it felt great.

She still had restrictions and was supposed to be on bedrest most of the day, but was getting restless and had started feeling better mentally. Pearl was also starting to put some weight on and loved keeping food down. Optimism was looking great on her.

"I can't wait to get out and see for myself how Otto is really doing, and help Abbie Jean with whatever she needs. I'm sure she'll want to open the mercantile again, someday." Pearl spread face cream on, rubbing it gently into her face and neck then brushing her hair. She was watching Frank pull back the covers on the bed before taking off his trousers. "What do you think?" her voice full of sincerity and concern. "Hopefully, otherwise someone else will have to purchase the store and supply it for this town." Frank was worried about Abbie Jean. She wasn't right in the head after the fire. Otto was in a lot of pain, and he could see that it was stressful for Abbie Jean dealing with him day after day. Frank didn't want to be a downer, though, and tell Pearl his true thoughts, especially after seeing her so positive now after the weeks of death and despair and a horrible depression she'd tried hiding. Her jovial mood as of late was a treat. He was enjoying it and didn't want to ruin a good thing with bad news.

"Well," he held her hand, pulling her into a loving embrace, "Mmm… this is nice. That's what I think." Frank smelled the lavender in her freshly brushed hair and the clean gown her mother just returned with the rest of the freshly laundered clothes. "I think it's time for my beautiful wife and mother," she looked up into his eyes, seeing a twinkle of excitement as he said 'mother', "To put her feet up and relax and let her husband massage them while she listens to the rest of Thunder Cloud's story."

231

Pearl perked up hearing that. She terribly missed those times together, and hadn't thought much about the stories, so it sounded refreshing. And would be a nice way to end just a pleasant day.

Frank got into a comfortable position on their bed and fluffed up the feathered pillows for his wife. She had just finished up feeding the wood stove and Spot was now snuggled in his doghouse, warm and comfortable right outside their porch. Pearl laid her dainty feet across her husbands' legs and leaned back onto the pillows, finding just the right spot to relax. "Ahhh…this is wonderful Frank."

As Frank started to re-visit Wintoka and Thunder Cloud's story he stopped to examine his wife, still massaging her small but swollen feet. Pearl's eyes were closed, and the lamp was turned down low where he could see the silhouette of her body from the shadow bouncing off her beautiful curves under her long cream-colored gown. Pearl's soft golden-brown hair with natural bright highlights was loosely braided to one side and lay over her right shoulder, her face gently turned the opposite direction so he could see her gentle mellifluous profile, and he felt a tug deep in his heart as his eyes moistened.

He chided himself for getting soft and looked away embarrassed, then was immediately drawn back to watching her and thought to himself, 'She looks like an angel.' He was so incredibly grateful for her. Thankful they still had each other when so many lost so much. Not that he hadn't lost family, he had lost several in his extended family who he was very sad about, but the thought of losing her was too much. 'Oh God, what would I have done if I'd lost her?' A thought he'd never allowed himself to have before tonight. A pain hit Frank's chest that felt like a lightning bolt and his heart was in his throat, tears fell down one by one on the stubble on his cheek. He stopped massaging her feet and lay down next to his now awakened wife and the two of them shared the most intimate love a couple could share, experiencing a gentle tenderness like no other.

There would be another evening to enjoy Thunder Cloud and Wintoka's story because tonight belonged to a new life, celebrating the living, and sharing the passionate love that started it all.

Chapter Thirty-Seven

Frank could hitch the horses up, but not without help from his twelve-year-old neighbor who lived down the lane next to the property he and Pearl purchased. Tim was from a nice family and came to help often, always because he wanted to, not because he was forced into it or asked to. He liked working with his hands and learning new things, and knew his neighbors needed his help after the fire. Besides, Tim always learned a lot from Frank, who was super patient and kind when a teaching moment arose. He never looked at his neighbor lady the same after seeing her that night of the Christmas Eve fire.

The young neighbor boy was just grateful that his mom and little sister were too sick with a bad cold they'd caught the prior week and couldn't go to the Christmas Eve party. His father had been out of town with his uncle helping his grandparents, whose roof had caved in from the heavy snow. Tim wanted to go, knowing he would get a gift and see Santa, who was promised to hand out those candy canes. He hoped he could get one for his little sister too, and asked a neighbor on the other side of Frank and Pearl for a ride so he didn't miss out. His mother had not only allowed him to go but encouraged him to go and enjoy himself, feeling bad she was missing out on taking Trudy, Tim's little sister, who would have liked to see Santa too.

Pearl had no idea that Tim was there when she broke down that night. He'd witnessed the pretty neighbor lady collapse onto the floor behind the counter and was terrified when he watched her stare off into the unknown, mumbling strange words to herself. Tim wondered if she was talking in tongues, but he'd never attended church, so he didn't know what that sounded like other than what he learned when he overheard adults talking about it. He tried to avoid her at all costs when helping her and Frank through the winter with the chores Frank couldn't do because of his injured hip. He was still overcome with a misunderstood emotion of sadness when he thought of Pearl and the mixed emotions he felt when he saw her, but Tim felt very different about Frank. He enjoyed every moment with the cowboy who taught him so much his own father didn't have time to.

Tim hated being treated like a nuisance, and with Frank he wasn't. Frank treated him like a little brother who he wanted around, and seemed like he enjoyed teaching him. He wanted to ask Frank about his beautiful wife, if she was okay after the fire, but was afraid of hurting Frank and thought that it might not be considered neighborly of him, and besides, she looked alright now. It wasn't any of his business either, but he did notice her putting on some weight as of late. Tim may have been slightly shy around Pearl to begin with anyway, as she was the prettiest person he'd ever laid eyes on.

Blowing out a long breath, he wiped heavy sweat from his brow. Frank limped back to the wagon Tim had helped him hitch up after they finished feeding the animals and repairing a broken juniper fence post on the north side of the ranch. "We're all set, little man," Frank told Tim, roughing up his hair after knocking off the newsboy cap he'd rarely been seen without. The roughhousing lasted a bit longer with good natured insults slung at one another, when they heard a noise from the house. The front door had opened, and Pearl eased herself outside, bringing the smell of fresh-baked apple pie drizzled with cinnamon and butter along with her.

"Now boys!" she said in a warm voice and smiled, "If you'll stop this nonsense at once," she shifted her weight, "I may have something to share with you." She put her hand on her hip like she was scolding them. Frank had always admired her ability to catch on and play along with whatever was happening. A scrawny cockerel strutted across the dirt, bossing everyone around.

"Tim," Pearl continued outside with her apron still tied around a thickening midriff. "Can you please carry these pies to the wagon for me?"

The young boy's mouth watered running over and took the pies covered with a deep red heavy cloth tucked into a large tin basket. "Mmm-mmm! smells mighty delicious, Ma'am," Tim put them in the back of the wagon while Pearl went back in the house, smiling. He ran back to escort her when she came out again, shutting up the house, replacing her apron with a shawl and bonnet that matched her outfit. Then he noticed she was carrying a large fresh apple fritter and cold glass of milk.

"This is for all your help! We appreciate everything you do for us, Tim!" Pearl handed him the plate and glass of milk. "Feel free to eat here, instead of taking it home to share." Pearl winked at him and his heart melted almost as much as his mouth watered.

"Wow! Thanks Mrs. Bunyard!" Tim's brown eyes lifted to see her smile. At that very moment he knew he was in love. Pearl's deep brown eyes tore through his soul and captured the twelve-year-old's heart hiding

236

inside. Tim sat down in the warmth the early spring sun provided outside of the ranch house on a post in front of the property the two neighbors shared. He was enjoying every bite of his flaky apple fritter. The happy lad watched Frank help Pearl up into the wagon they'd just hitched before he let out a low whistle and clicked the reins. The horse team took off at an easy trot leaving her favorite horse, Midnight, in her stall to ride another day. Pearl looked back over her shoulder and watched the sweetest little boy she'd ever met lick his fingers.

On their ride to visit Otto and Abbie Jean, Frank and Pearl talked about their plans for the ranch. Hiring more men was undoubtedly needed at this point. They couldn't rely on their neighbor's help forever, and their plan for Otto as the foreman just wasn't possible now. He'd be lucky if he ever felt up to helping at the mercantile, he was in so much pain from all the burns and scar tissue. Even though the scars were healing and thanks to Abbie Jean's constant care and Thunder Cloud's secret poultices he kept him supplied with they were healing incredibly fast, but he would still be in limited on what he could do the rest of his life.

Once Otto could handle going outside and the fresh air didn't sting the scars all over his face, neck, and arms as bad, he and Abbie Jean got married with only a few close friends and family members in attendance. It wasn't anything elaborate or exciting, but Otto wouldn't allow her to take care of him and live at her house if he couldn't make her an honest woman. He knew how people in Silver Lake could be gossipy and he worried over Abbie Jean's reputation, since both of her parents perished in the fire on Christmas Eve. Besides, he was indebted to her for the rest of their lives. If it wasn't for her, he would have been dead or severely disabled a long time ago. No one was beside him more, catering to his every need; not even his mama could have handled all that Abbie Jean selflessly gave.

She was young and hardy. She was also given the gift of being a wonderful nurse who healed not only the physical scars everyone could see but the deeper, more painful ones, his emotional scars from his disfigured face and gruesome, twisted body. It was a lot more than his parents could have taken on at their age. He loved Abbie Jean more now than he ever thought possible. He'd never known love like this, and the two of them grew together as a newly married couple, doting on one another at every moment. She was the best thing in his life, and he was going to make sure she knew it.

Otto knew Pearl's visit was important for Abbie Jean. Pearl was that rock she could lean against when life was too much, even though Abbie Jean was too proud to ever admit it. The first few months had been extremely hard on her. She wouldn't leave Otto's side, not even to bathe or take care of the house or Mercantile. Friends of her parents had to prepare a funeral for Liam and Maeve McFarling. Abbie Jean refused to lose Otto after she'd already lost so much. Guilt, pain, and horrible shame never gave her peace. The once immature young woman was sure that she was being punished for being a spoiled brat all those years to her parents, and would do anything now to take that snotty attitude and bratty behavior back. She would give up pretty much anything to have her loving parents home safe where they belonged.

Anything that is, except Otto. The two of them were all each other had now and she wouldn't leave him alone for even a moment for fear of losing him too. Sometimes when Pearl would come over, she would insist Abbie Jean take a bath while Pearl cared for her brother-in-law. Pearl was the only person Abbie Jean trusted with the love of her life. Her, the doctor, and of course his brother, Frank. The two men had a unique strong bond no one could break. She'd tried that once a long time ago, when she was young and immature, but that was before life spun them around in different directions.

A huge smile sprung to Otto's scarred face when he looked back down the street in time to see Frank and Pearl. Otto slowly stepped down to greet them. "Abb!" Otto yelled to his wife. "Do we have any apples or extra oats we can spare?"

Abbie Jean was walking towards the front door and saw Otto had the biggest grin on his face, which didn't pass by Frank and Pearl. They both looked up at the same time, giving Abbie Jean a nudge and wink towards Otto, then all three shared a quiet laugh behind his back. It was incredible to see him smile these days. Frank helped his pregnant wife with her large belly that got in the way down from the wagon, draping her shawl back over her shoulders. He saw she was struggling, not used to the extra weight this baby was giving her the last few weeks. Frank followed her inside, leaving his brother by the horses. He whispered to his new sister-in-law, "Today's a good day; I can see it in his smile!"

It wasn't a question, Abbie Jean knew. Pearl turned to him once inside the warm cozy room where they lived most of the time, as stairs were still too hard for Otto to climb. "I'm so glad," Pearl said, leaning in to hug the young woman who had grown up almost literally before her eyes in just a matter of months.

"Every day is a new challenge, but he's a fighter." Abbie Jean worried about his thirst for alcohol, but she had been with him every minute of every day since the disaster that changed all their lives forever, and he still seemed as strong as ever to stay sober. It was important to him not to lose her and disappoint her, especially now after everything she'd lost already and had done for him; he owed his life to her but even more than that, he owed her a good life, the best life possible, and he would make sure she got it.

"You're looking great, Otto!" Pearl exclaimed, getting comfortable in the rocker by the wood stove Abbie Jean had kept going all morning.

"You're not looking too shabby yourself there, sis" he teased her. "Except for all the wobbling you do when walking."

They laughed hard. "This is true," she replied.

"How about a slice of Pearl's delicious apple cinnamon butter pies she made us this morning?"

Pearl and Frank told the newlyweds to sit and they'd find their way in the kitchen and get them a slice. Frank was always at her side now, doing what was considered woman's work. He was happy to help, no matter the job, if it meant Pearl was there beside him.

✦

Warm pie, a beautiful day, and loving family who were on the mend was everything the four of them needed this day to be. Talk of the future, making plans, laughing at something funny somebody said and even playing a new game they got in the mercantile that spring, was just what the doctor ordered for the two Bunyard couples that beautiful spring Sunday in 1895.

Chapter Thirty-Eight

As the broodmares and ewes were preparing to birth their young, Frank reached out to Thunder Cloud, Pony, and La'as, asking for their help on the ranch. He would be able to pay them some each month but also provide them with shelter and give them a warm place where they could live peacefully; Frank and his grandfather would make sure of that. He hoped Thunder Cloud would say yes. Frank really needed the help, and in all honesty trusted these hardworking, loyal people who were smart individuals he knew he could learn from.

Pearl was getting close to the end of her pregnancy and Frank knew he wouldn't be able to do much for his wife and new child if he didn't get more help. He obviously didn't plan for the broken hip, much less his brother having long-term health problems. Frank knew it would be years, if ever, that Otto was able to help him on the ranch. But who knew? Otto had made considerable progress everyone thought would take years in only months, but it would still be years before Otto would feel back to himself.

Frank thought of his younger brother while riding his horse, Juniper, to check on the fence posts. Alone, he had time to think about the future of his new ranch and check on his property once more before the night settled in. He had a lot on his plate to worry over, and still hadn't completely recovered himself. He'd also made progress, but not near enough to be pain free yet. Most nights he still had to lie down on the floor next to the fire and stretch his leg out, rubbing his hip where the bones were damaged and scar tissue bothered him. He didn't share all he was going through with his very pregnant wife, but knew she was extremely aware of it. Pearl didn't miss a thing.

With all the fence posts checked, Frank straightened his back and wiped sweat from his eyes with his arm. Squinting up into the bright sunlight above, he watched a hawk circle overhead, its long brown wings unmoving, riding on the currents searching for its next meal. Frank slid his hat back on before he saw some men walking towards him. It looked like they'd already been up to the house and he wondered who they were.

Getting close enough, Frank could see who it was and immediately jumped off his horse and greeted Thunder Cloud with a firm handshake and tipped his hat towards his younger brothers, hoping for good news. Thunder Cloud took the lead, as usual, but first looked around to his brothers who were all staring at him, waiting for him to talk. He was making sure they were agreeable to what he was about to say before he sealed their fate.

Frank took a deep breath, patiently waiting when finally Thunder Cloud said, "We want deal." Frank thought about hugging Thunder Cloud, he was so happy, thrilled they were going to move in and work as ranch hands for him. He was feeling desperate lately, with so many of the injured men whose ranches and farms needed help too, and the busiest time of the year was coming up, starting with the shearing. Without help, he and Pearl would lose everything they'd put their hearts and souls into.

It was Grandfather Duncan's idea. Frank wondered why he'd never thought of it himself, but he didn't know Thunder Cloud as well as his grandfather did. Thunder Cloud looked a little uneasy as they all stood there. Frank caught it and asked if everything was alright.

"We bring Pony's woman?"

Frank could see they were really worried this would be a deal breaker and quickly reassured them it would not be a concern, and she could be a big help with Pearl after the baby came. Little did he know she would become instrumental during his child's birth. It was a great plan, better than he'd even imagined at first. The men shook hands and plans were made for them to fix up the bunkhouse and add another room when they had time. Grandpa Duncan was willing to come do whatever he could to help. It was partially furnished with things Thunder Cloud and his brothers would need to cook, sleep, and store their horse gear and equipment. It wasn't anything fancy, but they could fix it up however they wanted, and it was close to the barn and cow pasture, so they'd be able to keep an eye on the livestock at all times.

Pearl was finishing up with dinner when Frank came home that evening. He walked through the back door, removing his boots in the mudroom before entering the kitchen, and gave Pearl the biggest kiss she'd ever received from him.

"What got into you?" she asked, a little taken back by his enthusiasm, of course loving every bit of it. She stood listening while she reached behind herself and rubbed her lower back. With exuberant confidence and enthusiasm, he shared his conversation with Thunder Cloud and his brothers with his wife.

That evening the two of them had a nice, relaxing dinner, knowing the future was full of happiness, laughter, joy, and a little one running around. They'd be able to keep the ranch. Things were looking up and life was feeling a little more back to normal, and at last the dark days they'd experienced were becoming a part of their past.

Chapter Thirty-Nine

"**P**earl! You have to let go of me so I can fetch Mama." Frank tried to be as gentle as possible, but under the circumstances he was a nervous wreck and didn't want to be anywhere near Pearl when the baby was coming. Not that he hadn't wanted to support his wife, but he'd delivered plenty of lambs, foals, and newborn calves. If anyone knew how scary a birth could be, it was Frank. Besides, there was more to it than Frank could admit to himself.

Pearl, along with their whole community, had been through so much this last year that they were looking to the hope of having a new little one to adore, spoil and comfort when they were missing the loved ones who perished less than a year ago. There was so much excitement and need for this baby to be healthy and live. Frank wasn't so sure his wife could bear it if something bad were to happen to their baby, and he was afraid of losing them both.

It was midafternoon and the sun sat bold and proud among the cloudless bright sky. The birthing pains had started hours earlier after a restless night's sleep. As she cleaned up the breakfast dishes, Pearl noticed the cramping become worse, and she started feeling a burning in her lower back that was a lot stronger than before. As she bent over to pick up the pile of debris on their old dark wood floor she'd just swept up, her water broke, giving her a relief from the pressure she hadn't expected.

"NO!" She screamed at Frank, madder than an old wet hen. She tried sitting up to get Frank's attention and was overcome with another sharp pain down her aching back and fell back, exhausted. Frank could see her stomach tighten when cramping with a contraction and knew it would only get worse before it got better. She still had a long time to go. "Please, Frank. Please..." Begging and breathing as deep as she could, getting a big breath of air she screamed, "Don't let go of me!" while trying to work through the discomfort. Sweat slid down her temples, and her hair was soaked with perspiration already. "Frank!" Pearl pled, giving him a stern look.

He stood there by their bedside trying to comfort her, holding her hand, allowing her to be frustrated, angry, and in agony, and taking it all out on him. He knew, though, that Taw-Kia could handle taking care of Pearl until Electa Caroline came. If he trusted anyone in this world to deliver his child, it was Thunder Cloud's sister-in-law, Pony's wife.

It wasn't all that long ago when they were sitting around a picnic table Thunder Cloud and Frank made for outside afternoon dinners that the once shy and withdrawn Taw-Kia shared her news with everyone that she was expecting a little miracle of their own. The two families from such different backgrounds, cultures, lives, and worlds came together as more than friends that night. Their families were linked before them and now would be connected forever after them. Love and excitement filled that breezy late July evening. Thunder Cloud, Pony, La'as, and Frank sat around the fire pit Pony built outside, thinking and sharing a cut of chew.

247

The pregnant women retired for the night. Taw-Kia and Pearl were becoming good friends, not just women who worked well side-by-side day after day but gave one another the support women needed on a ranch where life could be brutal at times. Pearl enjoyed her comfort and Taw-Kia learned better English working with Pearl and learned that Pearl was an incredibly kind person who genuinely cared, one she could trust. And that meant the world to the woman who had been the only one among three men for most of her adult life.

Pony and Taw-Kia had waited until the baby growing in her stomach was past the stage of common miscarriage to tell their good news. They'd lost many babies over the years since the Modoc war, and Wintoka and the twins' death made them afraid they'd never conceive and keep a baby until full term. That curse from that horrible day all those years ago was finally behind them and they all had a new life to look forward to.

Thunder Cloud, Pony, and La'as took over many of the ranching chores right after moving into the bunkhouse. Along with Tim, the neighbor boy, who still loved hanging out with Frank now and then, but was continually entertained with the Modoc men around, helped catch up on all the back chores and soon they would be ready for branding. Taw-Kia helped Pearl with feeding the chickens, gathering eggs, milking the cows, tending the large garden they all shared, cooking most of the meals, and doing a lot of the household chores that were becoming too overwhelming for a woman who couldn't even bend to lace up her black boots.

Pleading fierce brown eyes burned anger towards Frank, who knew this would pass, but she was scaring him with her anger; it just wasn't like her. Of course, he never had to push something out the size of a watermelon, so he was cutting her a break and really trying to be supportive.

"My poor girl," Frank said holding her hand, sitting on the edge of the bed, wiping her forehead with a cold rag when he heard a knock outside their bedroom door. "Promise." He bent down looking into her large heavy-lidded eyes "I'll be right back," and took that chance to get out from under her gaze to see who was at the door. Thunder Cloud came to tell him he was going to go get her mother so Frank could stay there with Pearl. "Thanks." Frank patted Thunder Cloud on the shoulder. Frank was hoping for the break to retrieve her mother and he knew Electa Caroline wouldn't stand for a man in the room when birthing was going on and would kick him out. "Hurry fast." Frank said, giving Thunder Cloud the look of a frantic animal that was trapped.

Thunder Cloud let out a loud, hearty laugh. "You got it." A

nd out the door he went, on a mission to save his friend from the noose that was getting tighter as the evening's hot air grew thicker.

Chapter Forty

From outside came voices and the sound of a wagon. Finally, Frank felt some relief and willed himself to breathe again. He knew help had arrived. As graceful as ever, Electa Caroline quietly entered the bedroom filled with unspoken tension and a wave of fear bouncing from person to person whenever someone moved. Electa Caroline's presence cut through the thick air, dividing it into pieces when she went to her daughter, who was drenched in a pool of sweat. Pearl lay contorted in a fetal position, wrapped up in horrible pain.

"Oh, my daughter," she whispered ever so quietly, "This too shall pass," not sure if her daughter even heard. Compassion pouring through her soul, she quietly excused an extremely grateful and overwhelmed soon-to-be father out of the room and asked him to keep things quiet. She would let him know as it got close, but he should go enjoy a drink as it was going to be a long night.

Electa Caroline felt, more than saw, her son-in-law's immense gratitude as he slipped out of his bedroom into a dim kitchen lit with a handful of small candles that gave off a relaxing ambiance that Frank needed that very moment. After stepping out of the room and closing the door behind him, he ran his shaky hands through his thick wavy brown hair damp with warm sweat. The kitchen was still tepid, though he could feel the cool night air seeping in to take over. Frank was extremely overwhelmed and so relieved to be out of the room where he felt he had no business being in the first place. He gave a silent prayer to 'the man above' as he grabbed his dark hat and walked out the front door.

Pearl came to after a short period of some relief and saw her mother next to her. "Mama, you're here." Emotion overtook her pain. She was so happy to see her and knew everything would turn out alright with her there now. With a sigh of relief, she relaxed her head back down on the sweat-soaked pillow. Electa Caroline wiped her forehead and neck with a damp rag, which felt heavenly to Pearl who was burning up. It was so stuffy in her room, even with the small window open.

Afternoon had dragged into evening and Taw-kia and Electa Caroline went to work, preparing for the birth by heating water, getting clean cloths and blankets together, sterilizing everything they could, and laying down some old scrap material on the floor at the end of the bed. They also used some of the scrap material to tie it to the base of the bedposts so Pearl would have something to help pull on when it was time to push. A special basket Taw-kia made for the baby, lined with soft deer hide, was sitting in the corner, ready for a healthy boy or girl with a soft baby blanket she made lying over the top. Seeing it for the first time, Electa Caroline picked it up and admired the hard work and thought how lucky these two women were to find one another.

Quietly, out of view, Taw-Kia watched the older woman inspect her artwork, looking at every stitch and design she created and gave her a cautious smile when Electa Caroline turned towards the shy Modoc and smiled brightly. She quietly pointed to the beautiful work showing her approval and admiration and Taw-Kia beamed with pride, forgetting her usual timid self. They continued preparing for the birth and worked soundlessly side by side, agreeably grateful for one another's company while Pearl rested a bit between contractions, when she could.

Meanwhile, the anxious father-to-be smoked his tobacco pipe and paced around the fire pit outside, not sure what to do, hoping to hear news the baby was coming real soon. Thunder Cloud watched his employer and friend, and finally he couldn't stand it any longer. He sprung to his feet, interrupting Frank's concentration, who turned, giving Thunder Cloud a scared look. "You are making me anxious, Frank."

The two men smiled nervously and gave a light chuckle at the way Thunder Cloud had scared Frank. Right then Pony and La'as came out of the sweat lodge they'd built a couple hundred feet from their bunkhouse shortly after moving in. The two half naked Indians were quiet and respectful of the stress Frank was going through, feeling lots of sympathy for him. The last time they'd all attended a birthing, the woman and two precious babies had all died, nearly taking their older brother's sanity with them. He never was the same person he'd been before the Modoc War and after his wife and children's deaths. He'd resented the Klamath and army with a searing hatred he never would let go of.

"I'm heading to bed," Thunder Cloud said with an edge that appeared darker than he'd meant. "I'll meet the little one in morning." He patted Frank's upper right shoulder with manly strength that hid his honest concern for Frank's wife and child.

"I can't even think of sleeping right now, good God! How long do these things take?" Frank tried to keep the shake out of his voice but was agitated and needed to know his wife was alright. He hadn't heard anything for what seemed like hours. "Something must be wrong." Frank turned away from the fire and put his head in his hands. He was ready to go back in to check on his wife. They can try to stop him, but it won't do any good. He needed to know how she was doing. This waiting game was cruel, and he felt his head would explode if he didn't get in to check on her soon, so he said a 'good-night' to Thunder Cloud and turned to go see what was going on.

Stepping cautiously, he entered his house, trying not to alert anyone he was coming. All he could hear, besides the floorboard creaking, were weak moans coming from his and Pearl's darkened bedroom. The oil lamp beside the bed was turned down so low it wasn't hard to adjust to the room once he slowly pushed the door open. The door creaked, announcing him. His mother-in-law knew who it was without looking up and was surprised it took him this long. He'd arrived just in time to see what was going on. Electa Caroline saw the concern in his eyes and the shock that won over every other emotion he was feeling.

She went to put her arm around her son-in-law, knowing this birth would be hard on him. They all had learned just how fragile life was. Frank received the arm around him from his mother-in-law and let her walk him through what was happening. "The baby was trying to come out feet first. Taw-Kia knows what she's doing though—I know she does, Frank," she said with strong reassurance confirming her own trust in the woman. "I can see this. I've been watching her closely, and she is very experienced in delivering babies, Son. She knows what she's doing. Her hands are small, thank the Lord, and she's gentle and is generous in reassuring your wife she'll be alright and is doing a wonderful job getting this little one out."

The two of them watched, arms around each other for support as Pearl lay on her back, arched up high, as instructed by the woman who had half of her sterilized arm inside turning her first-born baby. Frank's eyes were huge at what he was beholding, but was at his wife's side quickly once the initial shock wore off.

He was a rancher. He knew how to do this with his calves, but witnessing your wife experience it, the one person in this world you love and intimately care for more than anyone or anything, go through such excruciating pain like that felt like torture. It was tremendously hard and almost unbearable.

Frank leaned down to kiss Pearl, giving support by holding her hand, and knew she wanted him out of the room. He sensed it before feeling her gentle shove. He completely understood. "You're doing great Pearl. I love you so much!" was all he could get out before he choked up. His mother-in-law tenderly guided him out of the birthing room.

"She'll be alright, Frank." Electa Caroline sympathetically rubbed his arm, hugging and reassuring him that it was all part of birth. Hard as it may be to watch a loved one go through it, it was part of life and part of giving life, no matter the pain it caused. Pure and honest love comes from that pain and he knew this. He just wished he could take that on for her and she didn't have to experience it. He walked out the front door again, hoping it was the last time he did so, praying the next time he walked back in it was to a healthy baby and mother. Wishing Dr. Daly could have been there to assist, but knowing he was called to do some important work in Washington D.C., Frank walked out the front door to a quiet dark night and Spot's wagging tail waiting to support his buddy.

A little before the sun came up a large healthy baby boy finally emerged. An exhausted mom and child were quickly cleaned up by an affectionate and loving mother and new grandmother while Taw-Kia went to get Frank and tell him the news. She found him slumped over on the picnic table, hat next to his folded arms out in front with a quilt laid over his back, probably by one of the guys.

The fire must have died down hours before as there weren't any warm coals smoldering. Before she woke Frank, she checked on her men. Sure enough, they were resting peacefully, so she didn't wake them.

Frank felt a gentle tug on his arm as the sun was just coming up over Hager Mountain. The rooster gave it's usual 'good morning' wake-up call and Frank's eyes opened wide. "We have a babe." Was all Frank heard and before Taw-Kia could explain or say another word he was up and running to the house. She laughed out loud to herself, wearing the biggest smile ever. She knew Thunder Cloud, Pony, and La'as would want to prepare the sweat lodge to celebrate the birth. This was a special day for not just the Bunyard's but also for the town of Silver Lake. Taw-Kia felt her growing belly. Letting excitement fill her veins for the first time, she relaxed and took a deep, calming breath. She'd had icy cold veins for such a long time that she forgot how good it felt to be warm and cared for. Security was a new feeling for her. She would honor it in her own way this day by fixing a breakfast feast then heading to bed to sleep the rest of the day.

Chapter Forty-One

INDIAN SUMMER

Along the line of smoky hills

The crimson forest stands,

And all the day the blue-jay calls

Throughout the autumn lands.

Now by the brook of maple leans

With all his glory spread,

And all the sumaches on the hills

Have turned their green to red.

Now by the great marshes wrapt in mist,

Or past some river's mouth,

Throughout the long, still autumn day

Wild birds are flying south.

-William Wilfred Campbell

Newly cut, soft brown curls gently wrapped around the new mother's glowing face as she held her two-month-old son in the crook of her arm. She'd always loved coming out to the small creek behind her and Frank's property to think or to pick the wild flowers along the bank. Today she was relaxed, her heart filled with gratitude, as she walked around smelling the fresh lavender that was still blooming. Pearl drank in the refreshing autumn air, admiring the Indian summer scenery when she heard Frank coming towards her, crunching the dry yellow and burgundy leaves beneath him. She could tell it was her husband because of the slight limp from his injured hip.

He looked down at their son before asking, "Everything alright?" then putting his arm around her shoulders, pulling her in close to him. Pearl nodded, soaking up her attractive husband's smell. Oh, she loved Frank's smell. He always had a clean fresh scent about him, but it was that combination of the ranch work mixed with pipe tobacco that marked him as hers. It was his smell and she had devoured it since that first day she smelled it when he was trying to talk to her, stumbling all over his words at the McFarling's Mercantile. That was over a year ago. She giggled to herself, thinking back to that day when she met him and wondered who in the world that tall, handsome, gentle looking young man was who was heading her way to introduce himself. He was so pure and so kind, even though she'd just met him, she just knew that if she were to ever marry, she wanted a man that was just like him.

Now look at her life! She had two handsome men that were all hers. Her parents and in-laws were still alive, and her little sister was doing good. Not only doing good but coming out of the shell she was known to hide behind, and Pearl was grateful for that. Life was treating them better than she thought could ever happen again. Pearl thought she would never share another happy day with anyone again after the death of so many and the heartache she thought she'd never be able to put behind her. But she did, and they did; most of the Silver Lake residents, anyway. Even those who lost everyone in their family were trying hard to find a way. They did it together as a community, taking care of one another. No one could have gotten through the deep dark nightmares and anguish thrown at them without the help of their neighbors. They were already a close community, but now, they were more than a community, they were family, and shared a bond no one on the outside could ever break, something others wouldn't understand. Not every town would have been able to lean on one another like this small town did. Silver Lake was a settlement full of special, unique people who truly loved and cared for one another.

It was times like this she thought of Wintoka and how life short changed her and Thunder Cloud's chance at happiness. The greed, intolerance, and ignorance that lead to the Modoc war stole that from them, stripped happiness from many people who wanted nothing more than to be left alone and free to live their lives, hunt and roam the land that had belonged to their people for thousands of years. The Modoc war forced Thunder Cloud, his brothers, Wintoka, and Taw-Kia to walk away from the support they should have had from family and loved ones, from their clan, the ones who knew them best and who wanted to protect them.

But instead, the war divided them, damaging any hope of a happy future. Feeling Wintoka's spirit everywhere around her, it was sad how she should be the one here enjoying Thunder Cloud, their adult twin daughters, and most likely grandchildren. Thunder Cloud's twins would have been a little older than herself, she realized. How unfair life was to them. Shame brought stinging tears and sadness of Frank's stories he'd shared over the last year. She mourned for them. Their story, their past, their pain and the life that should have been their future.

Hearing Frank's concerned voice brought her back to the present. "I couldn't be better Frank," she said with deep sincerity, not wanting to dampen happy spirits today. She leaned her head against him, so grateful for her life and their little bundle of happiness she was looking down at, who they both loved so much. Her husband gave her that heartwarming smile that always made her go weak in the knees and get all giddy. She let him take the baby from her and together they turned and walked back to the picnic table where her mother, Electa Caroline, always the caretaker, a supportive cheer leader, and the glue of the family, was helping her husband into a chair they brought out for him, whereas most everyone else was sitting on quilts they'd laid out. Pearl walked up to see Ira James handing Laura a large spoon so she could put her homemade whipped cream on the apple pie their mother made with her.

It always amazed Pearl how happy and willing to help Ira James was. Pearl and her mother had discussed it once not long ago, how it seemed like he should have been at least sad occasionally that he lost his mom, but it didn't seem to cross his mind, or maybe it was he just wasn't sad about his loss as much as they thought he should be. He was so happy in his current situation that he'd always desired, the young boy soaked up every bit of attention the Hardisty family smothered him with. And when he thought he'd soaked up everything, they always had more to give.

The Hardisty's immediately took the young boy into their home and were raising him as one of their own, which thrilled Charles. Pearl's father finally had a son. It was noticeable that the young boy living with her parents and Laura seemed to make her father mend quicker than anyone had imagined. He loved the young, once fragile boy, and couldn't wait for his leg to be healed so he could take him fishing, teach him how to elk hunt, trap and skin wolves and coyotes, and maybe even be lucky someday to teach him how to trap a silver tail fox and make something special out of the beautiful fur for his new mom. Charles couldn't shake off the fact that the young lad had never been fishing before. "What child hasn't gone fishing?" he'd always say to Pearl's mother—out of Ira's hearing, of course. The boy was as eager to learn as his new father was to ready teach him. They made a fun pair to watch.

Ira seemed to come out of his childish moody fits he sometimes had when his mother was alive. Without her yelling at him all the time it was easy to see he felt, for once in his life, like his own person ,and with the love and positive attention his new family was always giving him he finally had the confidence he once lacked. He was thriving now and would turn out to be a nice young man they could all be proud of.

Frank stood beside his wife, positioning his two-month old up on his chest, and watched all of the interactions taking place with their family and friends who had come out on this Sunday afternoon to celebrate their son's birth, the new harvest, one another, and the gifts life had provided. Baby Elvy yawned with a sweet little baby squeak before closing his eyes, returning to peaceful sleep.

Frank followed Pearl's eyes and silently the two of them watched as Pearl's Uncle Will pretended to listen to La'as and Pony, who had obviously gone out of their way to talk to him, knowing the poor man's plight. Uncle Will's eyes focused on a small brown finch sitting on a low branch in a tree straight ahead, his expression blank, but he would nod at appropriate times until La'as signaled his brother to leave the man alone. It was painfully obvious to the brothers that he wasn't interested in what either of them were saying.

Shrugging it off, Pony headed toward Taw-Kia to see what she was doing, and Pearl shrugged at Frank when he turned his attention back to her. "At least they tried," he said, and Pearl gave a sad nod, agreeing.

Her Uncle was desperately missing his wife of thirty-five years, Aunt Elizabeth, and it showed profoundly in his demeanor. There wasn't a day that went by that she wasn't missed by those who were lucky enough to know her. She was a warm, kind-hearted, loving woman who was always a lot of fun to be around. She wasn't just Electa Caroline's sister-in-law, but her best friend and the one-person Pearl could trust with her secrets, for when no one else seemed to understand her, she knew Aunt Elizabeth would. And now her poor uncle was lost without his other half. He was a good sport and really trying, Pearl knew, for the sake of her, his niece, and her new little family, but the longing in his eyes was too much to bear. Both her and Frank were proud and grateful for their friends, La'as and Pony, for understanding, and gave them a smile that said 'thanks' as La'as walked by them to join his brother, Thunder Cloud, who was visiting with Pearl's mom.

Uncle Will would be moving in with his daughter, son-in-law, and three excited, active and wound-up grandsons. Soon living with them would hopefully help mend his broken heart some and probably keep him busier than he wanted to be. She wished the best for her uncle. Her father, Charles, and her Uncle Will were as close as brothers could be. Uncle Will had moved in with her parent's right after the fire to help. Uncle Will knew living in his house without Elizabeth was something he couldn't do, and besides, his brother and sister-in-law needed his help. He would give them whatever he had to give until he moved on to a new city, a new home, a new life and new role as a new widower.

The guests were finishing up eating while leftovers were getting wrapped up and put away. Laura served her homemade pie and whipped cream when Pearl finally sat down next to her husband and Ira James, who had been saving her a spot in the shade under one of the many large oak trees on their property. She looked over at her new brother with a warm smile and hugged him in to her, just like he'd seen her do several times to Laura. He was thriving on this type of affection.

Ira James returned his big sister's affection before whispering, "Can I hold baby Elvy?" Ira James shifted uneasily on the old blanket they were using. Trying to sound responsible and older than his twelve years, he added, "I promise I'll be extra careful."

Pearl recognized his nervousness, which made her feel guilty when she made up a partially true excuse that it was time to put him down in the cradle for a nap. "Besides," she nudged him, "We wouldn't want Grandfather Duncan and Otto's music to cause little Elvy to go deaf, now would we?" Trying to tease him so he didn't feel bad about it, she tittered. But the truth of it was, she was protective and really wasn't sure if she trusted him yet to hold her precious little gift. "Laura could use some help handing out those pieces of pie Ira. Can you go help her? We'll be sure to save you youngins a spot," she said nodding towards Laura, then added, "Plus, I promise to save some time for later when everyone is gone so you can hold the wee little one." Hearing that, the boy's face beamed with excitement. He was grinning ear-to-ear, uncrossing his legs getting up to go help Laura.

Pearl remembered her mother saying Ira needed lots of positive encouragement with detailed directions. It would take some time to shed away the feeling he always needed to be told what the next step in a direction was and then to get in trouble and yelled at for whatever it was he didn't understand. His mother, Frank's cousin, Eliza, never gave her son a chance for his brain to function and learn on its own or learn from trial and error like kids naturally do.

'Oh mama.' Pearl's heart swelled with emotion at what a wonderful mother she was for young Ira James when her mother shared this with her a few weeks before. She remembered their talk and what her mother had observed about the child. 'You are the best thing that could have ever happened for that boy.' Pearl felt a new respect for her mother she'd never experienced before. She was sure it was because she knew what sacrifices mothers make and the pain and suffering they felt bringing them into this world. Pearl's view on motherhood was all different now that she was one.

Admiring her mother's skills with people, Pearl looked at her loving mother who was listening wholeheartedly to Thunder Cloud. It was plain to Pearl he was in the middle of a story Electa Caroline encouraged him to share after she insisted he sit next to her and Charles. Thunder Cloud's broken English could still get him tongue twisted if he got talking too fast around too many strangers, but he seemed at ease around her mother. Electa Caroline was so kind, so genuine, and knew everything about everyone. She was an old soul who easily figured people out. It was one of her many skills; she treated all people with care and respect. Watching the two of them, Pearl knew her mother would have loved Wintoka and her beautiful free spirit.

Pearl wiped at her eyes and scolded herself for being so emotional today, but she loved her mother and would do anything to follow in her impressive footprints, hoping to be at least half the mom and woman her mother was. Still observing, Pearl saw her father reach over and lovingly lift his wife's shawl up for her, helping her to wrap it around her shoulders as she skillfully thanked her husband without taking her attention away from Thunder Cloud for even a second.

Many of the fire victims knew they owed their lives or loved ones' lives to Thunder Cloud, Pony, La'as, and his sister-in-law, Taw-Kia, for helping so many burned and desperate people with the medicinal herbs they generously prepared. It wasn't hard to tell how many lives would have been lost without their knowledge, which had been handed down from many generations with herbs made into distillations their lands provided year after year. The small clan's concern for a population that had once turned their backs on their people was overwhelming to many who lived in Silver Lake. The residents, neighbors, families and friends owed so much to these people and were grateful for not only their knowledge but their devotion. The white man's medicine never would have taken the sting out of the burn like the poultices the Modoc's medicine did. Thanks to them, there were less addicted to laudanum now, and more were able to get on with their lives after healing. And it was done with one hundred percent compassion. It was an incredible gift and part of why so many did whatever they could to return the help and accept their new friends as part of their community.

Chapter Forty-Two

Pearl laid baby Elvy down in the house where the wind and noise wasn't so disturbing. His mother put him in his hand-crafted cradle made of pine wood that Frank's father, Jesse Bunyard, made for his first grandchild. Pearl heard her sons' tiny complaints, whimpering due to bouts of tummy gas. He was fussy and stirring in his new cradle. She turned and listened for the baby once more before getting shooed outside by Elvy's great grandmother, who was tending her tired aches and pains.

Pearl turned and silently whispered, "Thank you," to Grandma Louisa, who looked relaxed and content in the rocking chair with her feet up, working on a blanket she'd been crocheting. Tiptoeing, Pearl exited the house, shutting the front door behind her just in time to hear Grandfather Duncan and Otto adjust their instruments.

They stood up in front of the small group of family and friends who were sprawled out on blankets, getting comfortable to watch them perform. They were quite the pair. Otto with horrible burn scars covering his face and neck which looked worse than they actually felt. He wasn't about to let a little pain and ugly scars keep him away from a chance to entertain with his grandfather who, judging by his unsteady stance, was already 'three sheets to the wind'.

Otto smiled. He needed this today. His grandfather was so much fun and a great performer when he played his fiddle. Otto never missed a chance to play his harmonica alongside him when asked. The two of them could entertain a crowd for hours. He'd been looking forward to it, no matter how much Abbie Jean tried to persuade him not to play. His wife was worried about his pain and scars, he knew. He tried to explain to her it was something he had to do for himself.

Reluctantly, she gave in. Now, sitting all by herself watching him, she waited to suffocate him with love and attention the minute he was done. This was the longest she'd been apart from him since the night of the fire, and she was starting to panic at the thought of it. Pearl studied her sister-in-law with interest and a huge smile, remembering all those times she'd watched Otto and Abbie Jean, before the accident, before everyone's lives had drastically changed. Most were forced to grow up, and the rest were forced to let go and had to learn to allow others to help. Abbie Jean was still as controlling and as pouty as before, but for all the right reasons this time. She just wanted her husband to be safe and not overdo it. The young wife worried about him every minute of the day. 'They're so happy together, and she does love Otto and does dote on him as any normal wife in love would,' Pearl was thinking.

She was now back to her quilt after greeting everyone along the way, laughter and giggles filling the breezy crisp air. She gave her husband a playful wink and then quietly sat down by both of her younger siblings. Next to them, Frank was lying on his side showing Tim, who showed up to the picnic a little late, how to blow on a tall thick blade of grass to make it whistle. Laura and Ira James watched, fascinated with large eyes.

Frank adjusted himself to get comfortable with the pillow she brought out for his sore hip. Deep aching pain still caught him up once in a while. As soon as he was situated, Pearl leaned up against him, feeling euphorically relaxed. "Where's Grandma?" Frank asked, noticing she was the only one missing in the large crowd of family and friends.

"Grandma's in the house, sitting in the rocker listening for baby Elvy, should he wake." Acting like she was offended to the younger kids who were all ears whenever she and Frank spoke, hanging on to every word, she motioned with her hands. "She shooed me out of there when I tried to protest." With a funny exasperated gasp Pearl continued, pretending to be slighted, "I think she's tired and likes getting a little break to herself, when she can." She gave a little shrug followed by a sigh, then blew strands of fly-away hair out of her eyes. "Besides," leaning in, "I secretly happen to know she's working on a new afghan for baby Elvy." Pearl was so entertaining and playful Frank loved watching her. "Truthfully though," she winked at the kids, "It's the only time alone she gets without that old man up there," and pointed up to Grandfather Duncan, then continued, "Who bugs your poor grandma to death."

Knowing she was teasing, they all laughed out loud.

The three kids started horse playing around and talking amongst themselves, so Frank took a minute to share something with her that he'd just observed. "Did you see this?" He nodded towards Thunder Cloud, who was still in conversation with Pearl's mother. "Thunder Cloud, La'as, and Pony seem really comfortable and at home with everyone here." Frank kept talking to his wife but watched their Modoc friends. "I would have never imagined this in a coon's age."

Pearl nodded in agreement. "Even just a year ago. Look how far they've come." She was happy thinking about it. "They never would have been around so many people, much less white people, at one time. Moving to the bunkhouse has been good for them," She swatted at a fly, shooing it away with her small delicate thin hand. She added, "It's been good for all of us," and smiled at him before adjusting her twisted skirt and got comfortable again, soaking up the warmth her husband provided leaning against him.

He was so passionate about these people. They were his friends and part of his family now. Their family. She watched his large sky blue eyes that always melted her insides. Feeling vulnerable getting caught for falling all over herself in love with her hubby again, Frank made it worse by watching her with a renewed interest when he caught her. Studying her just a moment longer than necessary he saw the sparkle in her eyes that put a huge smile on his lips. Frank couldn't help himself and whispered in her ear as she leaned down enough to hear him, "Are you getting fresh, Mrs. Bunyard?" causing her to snicker. Her cheeks reddened then remembered to be careful because of the young eyes that were always watching them and didn't want to draw attention to their fun, putting a stop to it. But Frank didn't care. He continued with an even quieter whisper she had to get closer to hear. "Two months is up, right?" He waited for her to catch on to his meaning, patient.

Before he could even flinch, she swung her hand down and playfully swatted him. "Francis Bunyard!" she pretended to scold him. The two were so involved in their flirtatious game, neither had heard the music start or saw the large eyes all staring up at them.

Chapter Forty-Three

"Oh heaven's!" Pearl exclaimed when she finished yawning. "I'm plum worn out and ready to hit a nice, warm, cozy bed!" Baby Elvy had been nursed and put to bed while Taw-Kia helped clean up the last of the dishes and the men cut enough wood for a large fire. It was only an hour since the sun started the process of going down around the group sitting by a nice warm fire Thunder Cloud built. As it went down it left a beautiful, bright, star-filled sky behind that created an ambiance to the end of a perfect September day.

There was a chill in the air that made Frank's hip hurt. Out of habit he started massaging it. When his wife saw she leaned in to ask him what she could do to help him, when a loud popping sound consumed the night air, sucking away everyone's breath along with it. They soon enough realized someone must have thrown something flammable in the fire pit earlier in the day.

When Thunder Cloud, La'as, Pony, and Taw-Kia along with Frank and Pearl figured it out and knew they were safe, they laughed at how scared they were over a little noise. "Hey brothers," Thunder Cloud nudged La'as and Pony, who had his arm around his wife with a blanket covering both of them, "We survived the Modoc war and this small noise."

Thunder Cloud spread his hand around in a circular motion showing where the noise came from "Embarrass me." Their giggles turned into laughter. Releasing tension from the fun long day, some in the group bent over in hysterics until their stomachs hurt.

"Oh Mercy," Frank said wiping his eyes. He forgot all about his hip hurting and Pearl forgot just how tired she really was.

It got quiet again as they enjoyed the peace and quiet the cool air provided. Crickets sang to one another as the fire cracked and spit slivers of burning wood, the heat warming them.

The last of their guests headed home a couple of hours before Frank and Thunder Cloud started the fire in the pit which the two families living on the Bunyard's ranch shared as employees, employers, neighbors and friends. They were family now and family takes care of one another, loves unconditionally, forgives and moves on. Family means you never leave anyone out, and on that night in late September in 1895 there was a silent pact made around that fire. Life had led them through some horrible, tragic times of heartache, horror and lots of sorrow, but Providence stepped in and took over bringing the two groups together.

Never again would Thunder Cloud, La'as, Pony, Taw-Kia, or her unborn child feel unwanted, pain, or hatred. They would feel love, comfort, and a sense of ownership in the town they now lived in. The changed Silver Lake community gave them confidence they could walk the streets freely without fear of anger or retaliation, but Frank and Pearl gave them a home, something they hadn't had in a long time. Being displaced most of their lives made it hard to trust white people again. But not here. They were accepted and taken in not as just laborers working the land, but as friends working the land beside one another.

The smell of the fire seemed to quiet life for a moment and time stood still, relaxed and quiet. It had a way of bringing back memories, too. Whether they were from twenty years ago or just nine months, they were still as vivid and as fresh in their minds as ever. Thunder Cloud took a deep breath and held it for what felt like a long time. Frank and Pearl watched. Once he decided to let go, emotion took over.

He'd realized he'd been holding on to it. He'd never felt safe before. He was settled now. He was cared for, and all these feelings were important to him as he got older in life. For once, without fear of being who he was, he started singing a chant that just a year earlier would have made Pearl's skin crawl, but there was something so soothing and tranquil about his tender voice tonight. They understood he was healing himself after years of mourning Wintoka and was finally letting go. The smoke rose around his finely chiseled, dark handsome face. Wintoka's spirit was there with them, not just in Thunder Cloud's memories, and he was sharing her presence with everyone this evening. Pearl snuggled up closer to Frank, large tears swelled as she herself remembered all those they lost during the fire on Christmas Eve in 1894. Smoke circled and danced around the group.

Frank rubbed his wife's arms and shoulders, comforting her. She looked up at Taw-Kia, who had been watching her and, at the same time, the women reached out to one another and held hands. Thunder Cloud watched as Wintoka squeezed in the space between the two women and stared up at him. Beautiful as ever, she gave him that comforting smile he'd missed all those years.

The End

Epilogue

October 3, 1873

It was only 9:30 in the morning and all the children had been let out of school early for the big event. The only bank in town was closed all day to show support. Shops were shut down and picnic lunches made even farmers left their farms so they could someday tell their grandkids about it.

Curious onlookers had been trickling in from towns all over California and Oregon the last few days. They'd heard Captain Jack's trial had ended and wanted to be there for the executions. Those who followed the story close were right when they guessed the verdict for the men involved in General Canby's murder. Newspapers all over the country carried the story of Captain Jack and the Modoc war.

The week of the upcoming executions flew by as coffins were built and the gallows constructed. Fall was settling in, and although the sun was bright that Friday morning, the wind was blowing crisp cool air. Spectators settled down and everything got quiet when the guilty Modocs walked slowly up the stairs, their shackles clanking with every step. They were led to the rope assigned to them while a large rounded soldier with dark receding hair walked behind and calmly slid a noose over each of their heads, making sure to position it just right. The audience watched closely, some were getting their first look at Captain Jack as he took his place on the platform. Wind picked up and swirled colorful autumn leaves around as the last noose was slipped on.

Excitement spread like wildfire as the two thousand people picnicked on their blankets or gathered together in small groups. They seemed to feel a unique kinship gathered together to watch the 'heathens hang'. Men discussed all the rumors they heard while the women gossiped, and their children played.

All except for one man, whose mouth was pinched shut as he watched the noose tighten around his cousin's neck. He gulped back the pain building in his throat, holding back the stuck scream he tried to swallow. No one paid him any mind though. Making sure not to draw attention to himself, he tried to blend in by wearing a red worn-out bandana he'd wrapped around the bottom half of his face, covering his nose and mouth. He tied his shoulder length hair, which had grown out significantly since Wintoka's death, up under a dark brown cowboy hat which he'd slipped in and stole out of someone's stable on his way here, hoping he'd mixed well with the busy crowd. And he was right. No one bothered with him or seemed to acknowledge his presence, thinking he was just another onlooker there to support the army and homesteaders.

Thunder Cloud got as close to Captain Jack and the wagons full of people next to him as possible. He knew the army was still on the look out for any Modocs who ran away during the stronghold, but was pretty sure he was safe enough there today because of the focus on the hangings. Besides, there were a lot of Klamath Indians that showed up, so he was pretty safe.

Next to the large wagon of coffins sat three wagons with skinny, gaunt looking, worn out women, children, and elderly that were rounded up right after Captain Jack surrendered. They were sitting to the right of the large scaffolding where they were purposely positioned so they could see their men hang. Thunder Cloud watched his family and friends, his clan, his people in those cramped wagons, starved half to death, miserable and dying right before his eyes. He scowled, dark brown eyes full of pain and hatred at the scene before him.

He found what he came for and turned to leave, not wanting to see the men die. He was sure he would lose what little bit of control he was hanging on to right now if he stayed. Thunder Cloud's mother and little sister were in the crowded wagon with thin and worn out clothing, while their assigned small and holy blankets handed out to them upon arrival hung on their thin frames.

Large tears rolled down Lizzie's chapped cheeks. She was taking the news the hardest, being Captain Jack's youngest wife. The women wailed while the little ones shook from the cold. They were shocked, confused, and scared. The tribe had been on the run for months, tormented by the government, Klamath, and homesteaders for years, and now they were forced to sit before a huge crowd and watch their loved ones hang. The elderly sat stiff in the cramped wagons that confined them, bodies aching from arthritis and old age.

Thunder Cloud knew what it meant to see his mom and little sister alone without their father there and was instantly grateful that his two brothers were still alive and safe back at the camp they built far out of the way where no one would find them. He would have to share with them the news of their father's death and their mother and sister's condition, which saddened him, but at this very moment he was so grateful he had them and his new sister-in-law, Taw-Kia. He also didn't know what was going to happened to his clan in the three wagons after the hangings were over, but he knew one thing he was sure of he was grateful to George Duncan and his happy plump wife, who fed them and gave them work on their farm. He'd been the most decent white man Thunder Cloud had ever known.

As Thunder Cloud turned to leave, he said a silent good-bye to his leader, cousin, and Chief. Knowing Captain Jack begged to be shot instead of hung like a coward, he couldn't stay to watch his mentor and friend be dishonored this way. Interrupting his thoughts, he heard field music, and turned to watch all three companies of infantrymen march with arms on their right shoulders while the 'Dead Man's March' played. A great cloud of dust rose up around them as they marched past the gallows and then stopped, standing straight as arrows. They, too, watched with interest as history unfolded.

The blacksmith was quickly removing the shackles on the prisoner's feet as the minister read them their last rites Thunder Cloud shuddered, knowing he waited too long. Before he could get out of there, he heard the ax slice through the cold air, cutting the rope in one clean sweep. Trying to walk faster, hoping not to bring attention to himself, he felt a tear drop for each body that fell, and covered his ears before he could hear their last breath.

Index of real-life characters in

the novel

The historical background in these pages is genuine, however, for the sake of the story there are small but necessary changes I made when shifting dates and events to suit my narrative purposes. Nevertheless, I have always tried to stick to the essential facts regarding the Modoc war, the Christmas Eve fire in Silver Lake and the love story between my great grandparents.

Apart from the people listed below, all the characters in the novel are fictional

Frank Bunyard

Jesee Bunyard

Sarah Emmaline Bunyard

Sarilda Duncan

Lucinda Schroder

Eston Schroder

Louisa (Reinhardt) Duncan

George C. Duncan

Pearl Hardisty Bunyard

Electa Caroline (Elliot) Bunyard

Charles Hardisty

Agent Knapp (Captain O.C. Knapp)

Curly-Headed-Doctor, Modoc Shaman

General William T. Sherman

President Ulysses S. Grant

Mr. Chrissman or Chrisman who owned the building that burned.

Authors Notes

A beautiful warm summer afternoon about ten years ago I sat on the porch at my parents' house visiting my mom while we rummaged through old boxes. It was one of my favorite pass times with her. Not just because we were going through family history but because I had my mom's full attention, which didn't happen often. Being the 2ⁿᵈ youngest in a large family and having my own children and grandchildren on top of working full time meant we didn't get this luxury often.

I remember that afternoon like it just happened yesterday. We talked about her childhood and she shared stories about her grandparents and how her grandma Pearl loved to spoil her. Catering to every five-year-old need she had drove her mother, my grandmother, absolutely crazy. She told me the story about how she imitated her sweet old grandpa Frank by walking behind him limping like he did from an old injury. She adored him and wanted to be just like him.

It was these kinds of stories I couldn't get enough of. Growing up we heard about her childhood and grandparents and how much she loved them but on this particular evening she shared with me the love letters they secretly passed back and forth while courting. My mom pulled the old 1890's letters from the shoe box they'd been kept in and handed them over to me. I devoured them, word for word reading the letters two or three times each when I noticed there was some kind of code written at the end after they signed their names. So I asked what they meant and she told me how her mother shared that her grandparents used symbols only they knew, always writing it at the end of every letter. For years, no one could get it out of either of them what the symbols and codes meant. They took that information to the grave with them. I thought that was one of the sweetest and most romantic things I'd ever seen in my life. Tears rolled down my cheeks as I gently folded them and put them back in their box safe and sound. To this day, they are still one my most cherished heirlooms.

That same night, we snacked on cold watermelon and chatted about Frank's grandfather, George Duncan (my 3rd great grandfather), how he was the first Postmaster in Lake County during the 1870's and about the crazy story of his one room cabin that was shot up during the Modoc War. We talked about how neat it would be to go visit the Lone Pine Ranch our Grandpa Duncan built, that I believe is still functioning as a ranch today. We never got around to it, however, life being so busy and all, but it was nice dreaming with her.

Watching her reminisce I thought to myself how nice it would be to do something special for her. And that's when the idea hit me. I was going to write a book for her. We'd always passed our favorite book back and forth and I knew how much she enjoyed a good historical fiction as much as I did and wanted to give her a special gift. A love story about her grandparent's and the horrible tragedy many of my family members experienced during the fire on Christmas Eve in 1894. It was her turn to have tears that night when I shared my dream with her. I remember how touched she was; knowing what kind of work would go into a project like this. For ten years she waited patiently. Always encouraging me, asking when she could read it, telling me she knew it would be great and how excited she was to finally get her hands on it.

As it turned out, I called her this past December and screamed into the phone when she answered "I'm done, mom!" I remember how excited and supportive of my accomplishment she was. Then she asked when she could read it but being the perfectionist I am, I replied, "Well, I still have to have it edited but when it's all done, I promise you'll be the first to get a signed copy," and we laughed. She said she couldn't wait and to hurry because she wouldn't be around forever. Little did I know how much those words would haunt me. Three weeks later I received a phone call from my father at 5:42 on a cold Sunday morning that my beautiful mama had passed away from a massive heart attack.

After almost a decade my journey finally came to an end. Once I got over the shock of losing her and working through the depression of knowing that all my hard work wouldn't be read by the one person, I was doing it for I did some soul searching and realized I can still give her my gift. I can publish it for everyone to see what amazing, loving, beautiful and gracious grandparents she was blessed with.

Please visit my website at www.veladamcelroy.com to learn more about the Silver Lake fire on Christmas Eve in 1894 and Dr. Bernard Daly, who was the Dr. that rode all night from Lakeview to administer the burned and injured. He not only doctored the Silver Lake residents but years later went on to serve in the Oregon Legislature in Salem where he was instrumental in passing legislation and regulating public building safety. Because of him this legislation mandated fire codes requiring that exit doors swing outward and not inward. This would forestall horrible tragedies such as fire entrapment and would also help expedite quick evacuation saving many lives in the future.